BLACK WIDOW

BLACK WIDOW

A NOVEL

E. DUKE VINCENT

BLOOMSBURY

Published by Bloomsbury USA, New York
Distributed to the trade by Macmillan

All papers used by Bloomsbury USA are natural, recyclable products
made from wood grown in well-managed forests. The manufacturing processes
conform to the environmental regulations of the country of origin.

LIBRARY OF CONGRESS CATALOGING-IN-PUBLICATION DATA

Vincent, E. Duke.
Black widow: a novel / E. Duke Vincent.—1st U.S. ed.
p. cm.
Sequel to: *Mafia summer*.
ISBN–10: 1–59691–389–4
ISBN–13: 978–1–59691–389–9
1. Fighter pilots—Fiction. 2. Italian Americans–Fiction. 3. Organized crime—Fiction. 4.
Mafia—Fiction. I. Title.
PS3622.I527B57 2008
813'.6—dc22   2007015633

First U.S. Edition 2008
1 3 5 7 9 10 8 6 4 2

Typeset by Hewer Text UK Ltd, Edinburgh
Printed in the United States of America by Quebecor World Fairfield

As was my first novel, this sequel is also dedicated to those *boyus*—Ed Snider, Herb Simon, Jimmy Argyropoulos, Mike Bonsignore, Jeff Barbakow and Gene Montesano— who continually urged me to fashion a second novel from the many stories they'd heard over the years.

And as always to my incredible, supportive and loving wife, "The Hens" without whom nothing would be possible.

My unqualified appreciation and love to all.

Life is a gamble, at terrible odds—
if it was a bet you wouldn't take it.

Tom Stoppard, *Rosencrantz and*
Guildenstern Are Dead

AUTHOR'S NOTE

Black Widow is the sequel to *Mafia Summer* and picks up the life of Vinny Vesta in 1957, seven years after the first novel's action. The adage "You write what you know" is the genesis of the story and the characters.

I was a naval aviator in a fighter squadron stationed at Jacksonville in the late 1950s, and although the book is written as fiction, it does reflect people, places, and events that took place while I was there and thereafter. As was the case with *Mafia Summer* all the historical background with regard to nonfictional characters, times, and locales is accurate. The descriptions of carrier operations aboard the USS *Saratoga*; the hurricane; the murder of Albert Anastasia; the repercussions; Anthony Accardo and the Chicago Mob; their involvement with Jimmy Hoffa; and the Teamsters pension fund and the Las Vegas casinos, are all based on events that occurred within the time frame.

CHAPTER ONE

AUGUST 30, 1957

THE TRAIN RUMBLED into San Diego's mission-style depot at three in the afternoon. I looked out the window, squinted into a blazing sun, put on my dark glasses, and lit a Lucky. Hopefully it would all be over in a few hours. I'd sign off the body, take a quick shower at the Naval Air Station on North Island, and jet back to Florida. *Finis!* I'd be back in Jacksonville in time for the Saturday-night bash held weekly at my bachelor pad on the St. Johns River—a legendary blowout of booze, belles, and barbecue hosted by the best and the brightest of naval aviation. I took a drag of my cigarette, exhaled, and sighed: I deserved it after a week of pure hell.

The trip had been a seven-day coast-to-coast nightmare on a train that jerked to a halt at every two-bit whistle-stop between Florida and California. Heading west, the temperature rose by ten degrees per state—by the time we hit Arizona 110 was the norm.

And at each and every stop I was required to haul my exhausted six-foot, 185-pound ass out of my seat, walk back to the baggage car, and eyeball the narrow wagon that carried the flag-draped coffin of LTJG David Stanfield. The Navy was meticulous regarding the transport of their dead. It would not do to arrive in San Diego empty-handed because some idiot in East Bumfuck had misread a manifest and mistakenly off-loaded the body. To avoid potential disgrace, the Navy insisted that an officer of equal or greater rank to the deceased's shepherd the body along every step of his final journey—and that the escort be wearing dress blues the entire way. In this case, the escort was me, LT Vincent Vesta, USN, and it meant seven days of sleeping upright in my seat, in my uniform, with no showers—and extremely bad food.

Ten days earlier, Stanfield and I had been practicing formation aerobatics off the coast of Florida. We were both assigned to Fighter Squadron 176 based at Naval Air Station Jacksonville, flying the swept-wing North American FJ-3 "Fury," the Navy's version of the Air Force F-86 "Saber" jet. Stanfield, a Naval Academy graduate who had already been selected for promotion to full LT, had joined our squadron four weeks earlier. We all quickly realized the guy was smart, and an excellent aviator, but he was also unusually quiet and reserved. He just didn't seem to possess the flamboyant exuberance we were used to in a shit-hot fighter jock—and he never took part in the notorious weekend wickedness at my riverside "snake ranch." But we all liked and respected him, and his death was a shock to the squadron.

On the day of the accident, the sky was overcast, visibility restricted by haze, and there was no horizon. I began a loop from two thousand feet with Stanfield tucked in under my right wing. Our two FJ-3s shot skyward, and in seconds we began "going over the top." At the apogee of the maneuver we were inverted at seven thousand feet, and below us the Atlantic was a flat, pearl gray. As we started down the backside of the loop, I noticed that the upper-level winds had caused us to drift fairly close to the beach and that Stanfield was no longer tucked under my wing. He had drifted out a few feet.

I keyed my mike and said, "Keep it in tight, Davey, we're comin' down through the vertical."

"Roger that," he answered, and started edging his plane in closer as we rocketed straight down, then began to pull back out—easing through eighty degrees nose-down—then seventy—then sixty. I led our two jets through the pullout and we continued to accelerate with the g-forces steadily increasing.

It was beautiful.

And then it happened. Pulling four-plus g's at four thousand feet and blowing through four hundred knots, Stanfield suddenly slid off my wing and I lost sight of him.

"Stanfield?" I asked sharply into the mike.

I got no answer, but a few seconds later I spotted the belly of Stanfield's jet less than two thousand feet over the water. Somehow he had become inverted and was hurtling toward the ocean with his nose down over sixty degrees. There was no horizon line—both the water and the sky were that flat, pearl gray, seamlessly blending into one another. I realized he obviously couldn't discriminate between the two and probably thought he was pulling up into the sky when he was actually pulling down into the ocean. This time I actually screamed, "Stanfield!" and then watched in horror as his plane smashed into the surf and disintegrated.

The accident made no sense. Then or now. Stanfield was an outstanding aviator with close to a thousand hours flying jets. The chances that a first-class pilot like that would make that kind of mistake were one in a million. Maybe Stanfield wasn't your typical cocky fighter jock but he was good—damn good. So something had gone wrong. Very wrong. And I was pretty sure it was no goddamn accident.

The next day, what was left of Stanfield's body was recovered from the wreckage, and LT Doug McCaulley and I went to his room in the air station's bachelor officers' quarters to pack up his personal effects. Doug was a solidly built, blond WASP whose heritage combined half the countries in northwestern Europe. A shock of unruly hair draped over his forehead above pale blue eyes, and his ability to ignite the fairer sex with his sunburst smile was legendary—exceeded only by his skill in the cockpit. We shared the bachelor pad on the St. Johns River, and he was both a squadron mate and my closest friend.

We gathered Stanfield's clothes, stereo, tennis rackets, and other belongings, loaded them into boxes, then started going through his personal effects. This was standard procedure but always awkward. Anything considered "embarrassing" would be excised before his belongings were sent to his family. In this case, we knew Stanfield's parents had been notified and wanted to bury him in Morristown, New Jersey, where they lived and he had been born and brought up.

We were going through the last of Stanfield's papers when Doug suddenly cried out, "Jesus Christ! Vinny, look at this!" He was reading a letter—one of a stack bound by a rubber band. He thrust the letter into my hands. "He was married!"

I scanned it while Doug opened a few more. There was no doubt about it. The letter was dated December 28, 1956, and referred to the couple's one-year wedding anniversary. That meant they'd been married a little over nineteen months. Stanfield had apparently never told anyone about the marriage—no documentation appeared in his Navy records, and his parents certainly didn't know, but the clincher was a copy of the marriage license.

Stanfield had married a Caitlin Pennington in Del Mar, California, on December 28, 1955. Twenty letters were in the stack, each growing cooler in tone until the final one, postmarked five days before the accident. In it, his wife asked him for a divorce. Allowing for the molasses-paced U.S. mail, Stanfield had probably received it on the day he died.

Legally, wives take precedence over parents, so Caitlin Pennington was immediately notified of Stanfield's death, and she quickly nixed a burial in New Jersey. His parents were shocked and strenuously

4

objected, but after a short, brutal war of words, the Navy ordered the body shipped to San Diego with me riding shotgun.

The train lurched to a standstill, and the summer-clad crowd surged forward to meet disembarking friends and relatives. I stepped down onto the open platform, ground out my cigarette, and glanced around. The first thing that caught my eye was a hearse and two liveried attendants. The second was a tail-finned 1957 Cadillac convertible. It was new, it was pink, and the girl behind the wheel was dressed in black. All black—complete with hat and veil.

She gently raised her veil and glanced at the wings on my dress blues. A faint smile drifted across her lips and she looked up, giving me a quiet nod. I returned the nod and walked back to the baggage car to oversee the final unloading of the flag-draped coffin.

A few moments later I heard the slow but distinct clicking of a woman's heels behind me. I turned as she approached, caught a whiff of expensive perfume, and tried not to look stunned.

Her black suit was the obvious color for mourning, but it was anything but somber. The designer jacket was formfitting, and her skirt, cut above the knees, revealed legs that could shame Hollywood's best. They were sheathed in seamed nylons that disappeared into four-inch patent-leather spikes. The only touch of "color" she wore was a single strand of white pearls over an open-necked silk blouse.

She stopped a few feet from me and extended her hand. "Caitlin Stanfield," she said. It was a husky contralto voice, etched with a cultured New England accent that virtually echoed Tracy's Hepburn.

"LT Vincent Vesta," I responded, and took her hand.

"It must have been a trying trip. You look tired."

"Seven days crossing the country's underbelly can do that," I answered, trying not to stare but failing completely.

Thankfully one of the liveried attendants walked up and handed me a clipboard. I signed the papers and removed a similar set of documents from my inside uniform pocket. Placing them on the clipboard, I held them out to Caitlin Stanfield. "If you would, Mrs. Stanfield," I said, handing her the pen and indicating, "here and here."

She took the pen saying, "I introduced myself as such for the obvious reasons; however, I've never used *Stanfield*. I prefer my maiden name—Pennington. My friends call me Kat."

I blinked. I couldn't think of a response. I watched and took a moment to study her face as she poised a perfectly manicured hand over the clipboard and signed the transfer. If her voice was pure Hepburn, the physical resemblance, though subtler, was equally pronounced—high cheekbones, emerald green eyes, and a sensuous mouth. Her dark auburn hair had been swept up almost completely under her hat with only a few loose strands curling softly down the back of her neck. LTJG David Stanfield's eyes might have failed him in the air, but he definitely had no problem on the ground.

She handed back the paperwork. "You look like you could use a drink."

I nodded. "And a shower."

"Staying at the air station?"

"Tonight. I'll try to catch a flight back to Jax tomorrow."

She tilted her head toward the Cadillac. "Well, unless you've arranged for another ride, hop in. I'll drive you over."

I accepted her offer, grabbed my hanging bag from a porter, and followed her to the car. As I opened the driver's door for her, I noticed a matchbook-size monogram just below the window. Two letters in flowing script—*VM*. They certainly didn't stand for either Pennington or Stanfield, so who the hell was VM?

We pulled out of the station, picked up speed, and caught a refreshing breeze as we accelerated. "Nice car," I commented.

"Two weeks old," she responded, removing her hat and veil. She shook out a shoulder-length mane of auburn hair and let it trail in the breeze. "Vic picked it up just before he left."

"Vic?"

"Victor Marino."

"The actor?"

"The same."

So Kat didn't just look like Hollywood. She was. Victor Marino was a star. "You have nice friends."

"Don't I?" she quipped. "Vic's on location in Mexico doing a horseshit-and-sandal movie for Fox." She threw me a fleeting, flirtatious look. "Gone until next week."

I stared at her—the attitude, the dialogue, her clothes, the monogrammed convertible—nothing about this woman even came close to my idea of a mourning widow. I knew she'd written and asked Stanfield for a divorce, but, Christ, there wasn't even a *hint* of sadness about her. What the hell was flowing in this broad's veins?

As I pondered her and Stanfield's relationship, I watched as she broke most of the speeding and a few of the stop-sign laws en route to the Coronado ferry. "What's the hurry?" I decided to ask.

"Nothing, I just get a buzz out of speed—but I would think you'd be familiar with that, Lieutenant." There was no doubt about it—she was definitely flirting.

We drove onto the ferry, crossed the bay and sped down First Street to the Naval Air Station. As we drove through the gate, the guard managed to salute me—just barely. I watched with amusement as his mouth opened, his jaw dropped, and his eyes glazed over. A gorgeous redhead in funereal black in a pink Cadillac with a lieutenant in dress blues? Not your normal drive-on.

Kat took us straight to bachelor officers' quarters without asking for directions and I stated the obvious: "Been here before."

"Many times. Dave was staying here when I met him. How long do you need?"

"For?"

7

"A shower and a change. I'm taking you to the O club. You deserve a drink. I'm buying."

"Twenty minutes?" I suggested before I had the good sense to change my mind.

"I'll be back," she said, the pink Cadillac's tires squealing as she drove off.

CHAPTER TWO

I CHECKED IN and the duty yeoman handed me a message. I noticed that it had originally been sent to the squadron in Jacksonville a day earlier and then forwarded to North Island. It read:

Call me. You know the number.
Angelo.

My heart dropped. Instinct told me my week from hell was just about to get worse. Angelo was Angelo Maserelli, a member of the New York Mafia and my father's underboss for ten years until my father was killed in 1950. He'd then succeeded him as a caporegime in the Mangano family and had taken over my father's crew—running a stretch of New York's West Side docks for Albert Anastasia.

I loved Angelo like a second father, and Angelo's son, Attillio, whom we called Stuff. We had grown up together and Stuff had run with my street gang until the gang broke up in the summer of 1950. I'd gone off to college, graduated in three years, and entered Navy flight training in Pensacola. Stuff had remained in New York, and after a brief stint as a professional musician he'd quit and become a member of his father's crew. Fortunately most of the phone calls I received from Angelo and Stuff weren't about the family business—a life I had happily given up. Unfortunately, they were about my mother.

My mother and I had been estranged from the time my father was murdered and I'd refused to drop out of college and follow in his footsteps. She wanted me to avenge his murder and had never forgiven me for not doing it.

It was four o'clock—seven New York time—and Angelo was probably sitting down to dinner. He never missed a meal. His five-foot-six, 260-pound frame required a lot of fuel. I went to a phone booth in the lobby and dialed a number I'd known since I was thirteen.

A woman with a heavy accent answered with "Itsa me. Who's this?"

It was Lena, Angelo's wife. I chuckled. "Vinny . . . Vinny Vesta. How are you, Lena?"

"Fine! But no you! How come you doan call?"

"Been a bit busy, Lena. But I'm calling now—"

"Shue *now*! Be-causs Angelo call *you*!"

"I'll do better . . . promise."

"Atsa good . . . Angelo!" she called out. "V-cenzo!"

A moment later Angelo got on the phone and without a hello said, "How soon can ya be here?"

That stopped me a second. "There? New York?"

"No, Tibet! Where the hell d'ya think? Of course New York, fer Christ's sake!"

"Angelo, I'm in California . . ."

"I thought you was stationed in Florida, what the hell are you doin' in California?"

"I had to escort a . . . forget it. Don't ask."

"I won't . . . So—how soon?"

"Angelo, I've already been away from the squadron a week. I'm not sure I can get there. What's goin' on?"

"Yer mother. I love her but she's a pain in the ass and she's causin' trouble."

"Christ . . . what kind?"

"Costello made his decision. He's steppin' down before he's carried out."

Damn! I thought.

Three months earlier Frank Costello had been the target of a failed hit outside his apartment in the Majestic Towers on Central Park West. Costello had been the head of the Lucky Luciano crime family since Luciano had been deported in 1946. There was little question that the hit had been ordered by Vito Genovese, who was a caporegime in the same family and his bitter enemy. The bullet had missed but not the message. Obviously, at age sixty-six Costello had decided retirement was better than entombment.

"Yesterday," Angelo continued, "the Commission announced Genovese is takin' over the family and yer mother's goin' apeshit."

I immediately knew the reason. My mother held Genovese responsible for my father's death. He'd been killed protecting Albert Anastasia during a failed assassination attempt by Genovese in 1950. Anastasia was capo of the Mangano family and my late father's mentor. He had become the head of the Mangano family in 1951 when Vincent Mangano, the head of one of the original five families, had disappeared and his brother Philip Mangano was found floating in Sheepshead Bay. Vincent was never found.

The killer was undoubtedly Albert Anastasia—Mangano's underboss. With the sudden disappearance of Mangano, Anastasia took control of the family—three hundred deepwater New York berths, and forty thousand longshoremen.

Anastasia and Genovese hated each other, and it was only a matter of time before one or the other wound up in the marble orchard. Anastasia had considered my father his protégé and had never gotten over his murder. And partly because he felt responsible for it and considered me and my mother family, it wouldn't take much for him to do something foolish.

Angelo continued, "She's been tellin' me, Albert, and anyone who'll listen that Genovese is an outta control bastard who's gotta be hit! She's makin' so much goddamn noise that some crazy fuck is liable ta listen and start a fuckin' war! Worse—Anastasia's worried that Genovese's people might hear what she's promotin' and whack her just ta shut her up!"

"Christ!" I repeated exasperated. "What am I supposed to do?"

"Talk some sense into yer mother."

"Me?" I said, confused. "Are you nuts?"

"Ya gotta try."

"Angelo . . . ," I insisted, "she's still pissed at me for staying in college and not going after Genovese seven *years* ago! Joining the Navy was the last straw! Why the hell would she listen to me now?"

"You're her son. Make her listen. If ya can't get here—call. This thing could get outta control."

"Okay," I said, resigned to what I thought impossible. "I'll try."

"Good. Attillio says hello."

"Tell Stuff hello back."

"Right," he said, and hung up.

I'd call, but at the moment I had another problem to deal with—an enigmatic widow who was too attractive to ignore.

CHAPTER THREE

FTER AN INVIGORATING shower and a quick
shave I headed out wearing slacks, loafers, and a sport shirt.
Caitlin was already at the curb, and she'd also changed—a white,
sleeveless blouse, tan slacks with heels to match, no stockings, and loop
earrings. The pearls were gone but in their place was a brooch the size of
a silver dollar. It was shaped like a spider and its body was a grape-size
emerald that matched her eyes.

Christ! I thought. A spider? Again, I couldn't decide if I was
attracted to or appalled by this woman.

I climbed into the Caddie and commented, "Quick change."

"I always carry spares. Plus, I still have friends on the base. I am—or
was—a Navy wife, remember?"

"That's why I'm here," I couldn't help but answer back. "Remember?"

It was after five, "the sun was over the yardarm," and the smoke-
filled officers' club bar was packed. Friday's happy hour was roaring.

Local beauties were always willing guests and thronged to the club with a gleam in their eyes and hope in their hearts. Fighter pilots treated the weekly event with the fervor of a revival meeting. The uniform of the day for officers was short-sleeved summer whites—for the ladies their most alluring combinations of heels, skirts, and low-cut blouses. Pilots could be seen using their hands to demonstrate dog-fights for impressionable young lovelies while music and laughter all but drowned out their accompanying braggadocio. Potent drinks, poured with three-finger shots, went for fifty cents a pop. For five bucks you could go blind.

I got us a pair of king-size martinis and we nudged into a comparatively quiet corner booth and sat. She raised her glass and in a sultry contralto voice that could have mesmerized a cobra said, "To better times."

"And departed friends," I answered.

We touched glasses and drank. I let half the contents slide down my throat, and my body relaxed for the first time in a week.

She appraised me for a few moments. "Vesta . . . dark skin, swarthy build, curly hair, and arrow-straight nose. Italian, obviously."

"Looks deceive. Sicilian."

"Ah . . . is there a difference?"

"A big one."

She smiled and sipped her drink. "Married?" Once again her delivery made a simple one-word question have carnal implications.

"Single."

"Girlfriend?"

"Several."

She cocked an eyebrow. "I'm impressed."

I waved off the comment with a flip of my hand. Right now I just wanted to know the truth. "I'm flattered, but what about you?"

"What about me?"

I shook out a Lucky and offered it to her. She declined, shaking her head—I took it and lit up. After a slow exhale I got to the point. "Well, Caitlin, I—"

"Kat."

"Kat, I read the letters you wrote to Dave . . . part of the job."

"Ahh." She nodded.

"You said you wanted a divorce."

"True. Are you asking why?"

"If you don't mind."

"Idle curiosity or 'part of the job'?"

"Maybe both."

"Long version or short story?"

I shrugged. "Whatever."

She gave me a quick nod indicating a resigned *Okay* and I got the sense we were through fencing and I might be about to get some straight answers. "We were married for nineteen months, together in person for seven weeks."

"It happens. Navy types go down to the sea in ships."

"So I found out. I wasn't warned."

"Enter Vic?"

I saw her jaw tighten. "A girl can get lonely, Lieutenant. Vic was there for me."

"Did Dave know about Vic?"

She looked away, took a deep breath, and turned back. "Maybe. He could have—Vic's pretty high profile. We've occasionally been seen together."

It was the first real touch of sorrow I'd heard in her voice. It was slight, but it was there. I took another long pull on my drink. "He probably got your letter the day he augered into the surf."

"There was more than one letter. Dave knew it wasn't going to work for a long time."

"But the letter he figured ended your marriage came the day he made the stupid mistake that killed him."

"What are you suggesting?"

"It shouldn't have happened. I'm looking for a reason."

She stared at me a few moments absorbing the implication, then asked incredulously, "You think the accident was my fault?"

"The accident was his fault—you might have been the cause."

She took a deep breath and her whole body tensed. "Look," she said, slowly drawing out my rank as derisively as she could, "Lieu-*ten*-ant, I don't know where the hell you're going with this. Whether it's standard Navy procedure or 'just part of the job,' but I don't like it and I don't have to listen to it!"

She snatched her purse, shot up out of her chair, and sent it flying into the next table. I watched briefly as the tipsy foursome next to us failed to react, then I jumped up and gently grabbed her wrist. What was I thinking?

"Hold it," I soothed. "I'm sorry. Really, please sit down."

"I can't think of a single reason why," she seethed.

"Sit and I'll give you several."

She glared at me a few seconds before sitting. Her eyes didn't leave mine as I mashed out my cigarette and ticked off the points.

"Look, I didn't know Dave well—I didn't even know he was married—but I liked him. He was a fellow fighter pilot and squadronmate. And then I suddenly find out not only is he married, he's about to be divorced. I certainly didn't understand why his soon-to-be-ex-wife wanted his body shipped out here instead of to his family. And finally when I meet his widow—who acts like anything *but* a widow—I find out she has a movie star for a boyfriend!"

Kat sat very still, her eyes glistening. She finally glanced away, then looked back. "I'll take that cigarette now."

I handed her a Lucky and she put it between her lips and leaned in while I lit it. I caught another whiff of her perfume before she leaned back again, inhaling deeply. She pinched a fleck of tobacco from the tip of her tongue, exhaled a languorous flood of smoke, and began.

"Dave and I met here at the club in December '55. Dashing naval aviator, beautiful young starlet. He was home for the holidays from Japan—I was here on location doing a B part in a B movie." She smiled genuinely at the recollection. "You've heard the term *whirlwind romance*? The next two weeks were the reason for the cliché. Of course Daddy found out about it and went crazy. And of course because Daddy forbade it and I wanted to assert some independence, we got married right after Christmas. We celebrated New Year's Eve in Mexico. On our one-week anniversary he shipped back to Yokosuka. My career was just starting up here so I wasn't prepared to move to Japan. When Dave finished his tour in Yokosuka and came home last September, I hadn't seen him in eight months."

A raucous roar of laughter from the next table interrupted her, and she finished her cigarette—and then her drink. "We spent another month together when Israel invaded Egypt—the Suez crisis. Dave was ordered to Norfolk and sailed to the Med on the USS *Forrestal*. When his squadron got back, he stayed with the ship until last month, when he joined you guys in Jacksonville."

"Late last July," I said.

"The fourth week," she said, and then to be sure I knew how well she'd kept track of time added, "the twenty-seventh to be exact." She pointed her index finger at me—"Twenty months"—then pointed back at herself—"seven weeks." She ground out her cigarette and in a monotone asked, "Any more questions?"

"Only one. If you didn't give a damn about him, why'd you insist the body be shipped to you?"

She sighed. "So it wouldn't go back to his parents. They're a socially prominent family in New Jersey who'd pushed him all his life. As a kid he said he'd been a shy loner, but they kept pushing him and he hated it. They demanded he be the best in everything from grammar school through high school to the Naval Academy. Honor student—team captain—top of the class. Whenever he came home on leave, they would make sure the local papers ran a story trumpeting his accomplishments. They'd throw lavish parties so they could bask in his glory. He finally stopped going home and hadn't seen or communicated with them for a long time. I knew Dave would hate letting his parents bury him with all of the hoopla they were certain to arrange, so I stopped it. It was my right and the least I could do."

"So at the end of the day you did feel something."

She sipped her drink and nodded. "Of course. At one point we were in love. The romance ended practically right after it started, but what little time we had together was good. When he came back from Yokosuka, I knew it wasn't going to work and I told him. But Dave thought we should at least try. Then he was shipped out again. We wrote less and less until I finally decided to end it. When he was killed, I did what I would have done for a close friend. For a long time, that's all he'd been . . . I'm sorry."

She suddenly seemed vulnerable. My initial impression was slowly changing. I found myself actually liking her.

"Yeah, so am I," I said. "I really had no right to accuse you—"

"Apology accepted."

"Is there anything I can do for you before I go back to Jax?"

She nodded. "Yes, you can take me to dinner. I hate eating alone."

"Done. I'll take you to your favorite restaurant."

"You sure?"

"Why not?" I answered.

She flashed me a brilliant smile.

CHAPTER FOUR

A N HOUR LATER we crossed the Mexican border. Her favorite restaurant turned out to be Caesar's in Tijuana, home of the famous Caesar salad, and although the bistro was crowded with Friday-night customers waiting to be seated, the owner greeted Kat with a warm abrazo and immediately led us to a prime table. She laughed and flirted with him in fluent Spanish, giving him our order as we sat.

A waiter bound for another table passed by with a tray of frosted margaritas and our host unceremoniously plucked off a pair of the globe-size drinks and placed them in front of us. We toasted him while a guitar trio strolled the candlelit room singing three-part harmony in a spice-scented atmosphere designed to anesthetize your senses.

A few minutes later the headwaiter rolled up a serving cart and we watched him break romaine leaves into a huge wooden bowl, then add oil, vinegar, spices, anchovies, grated Parmesan, and squeezed lemon. As we downed our second frosted margarita, he cracked an egg, expertly drizzled the yoke into the bowl, and exuberantly tossed the salad.

His creation was as much a floor show as a taste sensation. Between the martinis, the music, and the margaritas I was finally beginning to feel mellow. The mood practically demanded a third round—so I ordered one.

Over the carne asada—a heaping portion of steak, chili, and beans— Kat told me that her mother had died while she was in grammar school and her father had brought her up. He'd never remarried, and she'd grown up in Beverly Hills, enjoying a privileged youth of country clubs, European vacations, and a Vassar education.

The probable reason for the Hepburn-like accent, I thought. She talked, I listened, and the more I heard of her husky, honeyed voice the more intrigued I became. It was hard to fathom, but even when her words were cutting, the delivery was so charming it lulled you into thinking she was being kind.

She blithely admitted she was the spoiled apple of her father's eye. An overprotective but extremely influential theatrical lawyer, he had used his power to start her career.

"I'm good and getting better," she said, smiling, "but I still haven't nailed the part that's going to make me a star." It came out as a simple statement of fact. "It's driving Daddy up the wall."

"How'd Daddy feel about Dave after you were married?" I asked.

She laughed. "He remained furious. He even refused to meet him and threatened to use his influence to send Dave to the ends of the earth. In the end, Israel did it for him."

"Does he know about Vic?"

"Oh, he engineered Vic. He introduced us at a dinner party he threw for Darryl Zanuck and was elated when we started seeing each other. He would be even more ecstatic if I married him."

"That the plan?"

She cocked an eyebrow and flatly stated, "Not a chance."

"Why not?"

"I don't love him," she said simply. "But he's convenient."

"A good career move?"

"Exactly. Being seen on the arm of a major star starts the rumor mill, which starts the gossip columns and magazine stories, which whips up the shutterbugs. And once your picture begins showing up everywhere, that's when your agent's phone starts ringing."

"That simple."

She smiled and smoothly said, "Only if you have the key to the lock."

"Vic," I observed.

She nodded. "But in spite of what you think of me, I really did want to avoid becoming an item with Vic until after Dave and I were divorced. I didn't want to do that to him."

"So your career officially starts now."

"I've already hired a flack, a publicist."

She'd done it again. Delivered a calculating, emotionless statement of fact completely without remorse. "Kat"—even her name was fitting. I shook my head, looked away, and lit another Lucky.

"What?" she asked.

I blew a twin stream of smoke from my nostrils. "For Christ's sake, you've only been a widow a week. Couldn't you at least have waited until he was in the ground before you launched into your career? I've heard Hollywood's a tough town, but that's downright frigid."

"Then you're going to think my next suggestion is even colder."

"Nothing would surprise me."

"Good. I want you to take me home and spend the night with me."

I was wrong. I was surprised, but by now not quite stunned. My eyes drifted to the emerald body of the spider and back to her matching eyes. "Just like that?" I asked incredulously.

"Just like that." I sensed my own alcoholic glow, but noticed she wasn't even close to slurring her words.

I shook my head. "Six hours ago I delivered your husband's body to you. I don't think I can live with that kind of parlay."

"You don't find me attractive enough?"

"I find you stunning. That has nothing to do with it."

"Conscience?"

"Decency. It's flat-out twisted."

She smiled and made a pair of quotation marks with her fingers. "For an 'officer and a gentleman' . . ."

"Even for a bum and a bastard." Then I added incredulously, "What drives you?"

"At the moment, the libido of an intelligent, unattached twenty-four-year-old woman who was in the middle of divorcing a man she hadn't considered her husband for a very long time—then suddenly found out he was dead and became a widow. As I told you, Vic is a convenience, so I use him, but my taste lies in other areas. I have an obvious attraction to gold wings, Lieutenant, and I find you a very handsome, unattached representative of the breed." She paused and smiled. "So. . . ?"

"I accept the compliment, but . . ."

"Not the offer."

Her auburn hair was glowing in the candlelight and her cheeks were slightly flushed from the alcohol. Her eyes became an even deeper green. "No," I said—and could have killed myself for the answer. What the hell was I thinking?

She shook her head as if she were looking at a monumental fool. "The rebuff is accepted, Lieutenant. I'll take you back."

CHAPTER FIVE

W E LEFT THE RESTAURANT, recrossed the border before midnight, and beelined for San Diego—Kat's taste for speed obviously now fueled by alcohol and anger. Once or twice I tried to open a conversation but got a terse one- or two-word answer in response. I should have been flattered that she wanted me enough to be so pissed, but the truth was, I was as pissed as she was—at myself.

The longer we were in the car, the more I found myself becoming infatuated with this woman. She had tried to get a divorce for a long time and hadn't considered herself married even longer than that. By the time of Dave's accident, he was just a good friend. And he was even less than that to me. Christ—I'd only known the guy for four weeks! When I looked at it from her perspective, everything she'd said and done made a warped kind of sense. I began to feel like a goddamn idiot.

Kat pulled into the line of cars waiting for the Coronado ferry and I turned on the radio. Sinatra's *Songs for Young Lovers* was playing as if on cue. I caught a scent of salt coming off the bay and watched her rest her head on the seatback. A tiny sliver of moon was allowing stars to light up the blackened night, and I sensed her soften. I found myself spilling out words.

"Look—for what it's worth, I feel like an ass. You have every right to feel like you do, and to do whatever you want. No one's got a right to judge you—especially me, so if the offer's still open, there's nothing I'd like better than to take you home and spend the night with you."

Her head slowly swiveled toward me. "Just like that?"

I nodded. "Just like that."

She thought about it for a few seconds, and cocked her eyebrow. "I can't think of one good reason why I should accept."

"Neither can I."

A thin smile played on her lips. "But then again, I don't need one."

Kat lived on Point Loma, a narrow, exquisitely beautiful peninsula that stretched south like a four-and-a-half-mile finger separating San Diego Bay from the Pacific Ocean. The ridgeline was a few hundred feet above the water, and the flickering lights of the city and Coronado Island were dazzling. We drove into an area called Sunset Cliffs and pulled into the driveway of a low-slung Spanish villa that overlooked the Pacific. A pair of emperor palms framed a spacious yard, and the front of the house was awash in bougainvillea. The scent of jasmine came from beds on either side of the entryway, and the entire area was softly lit with hidden yellow floodlights. It looked like a movie set.

"Yours?" I asked.

"One of Daddy's college graduation presents. There's another in Beverly Hills and a third in Sun Valley. Daddy loves real estate."

"Nice Daddy."

She reminded me of our earlier dinner conversation: "Controlling Daddy."

We got out of the car and entered the house through an unlocked front door.

"Very trusting lady," I commented.

"All the honest folk don't need to be locked out, and all the criminal types know who Daddy is. They wouldn't dare rip off Marion Pennington's darlin' daughter."

"Marion?"

"Don't let the name fool you. John Wayne's real name was Marion Morrison."

"Should I be intimidated?"

She sized me up playfully. "You don't look the type. Daddy only hates naval aviators if they want to marry his daughter."

She led me across a spacious living room, richly decorated in lush Spanish-colonial style, and pointed to an arched alcove. "The bar's over there. Think you can manage two more margaritas?" She smiled.

"I've been known to excel." I smiled back.

"I can't wait." She pointed to a pair of floor-to-ceiling doors leading to the back patio. "I'll meet you by the pool."

I watched her disappear before crossing to the alcove, where I noticed a silver-framed, eight-by-ten headshot of Victor Marino on the back bar. There was no denying it—he was one handsome son of a bitch. The inscription read:

To the loveliest woman in my world . . . Vic

Was I jealous? I couldn't tell yet.

As expected, the bar was well stocked and contained everything needed to blend a virtuoso margarita: tequila, triple sec, fresh limes, ice, a cocktail shaker, stemmed margarita glasses, and even a plate of salt in which to spin their wetted mouths.

I concentrated on creating the perfect cocktail, added a slice of lime on the rims for a finishing touch, and carried them toward the patio.

Stepping out, I heard a splash and saw a beautifully lit free-form pool. It was indigo-colored and looked like a small lagoon. Kat was swimming a slow breaststroke, her auburn hair floating behind her head. She was completely and dazzlingly nude.

I put the glasses on a patio table and watched her reach the end of the pool, do a racing turn, roll over on her back, and begin a backstroke. Her long auburn hair drifted over perfect breasts and floated toward her pelvis. The collars and cuffs matched.

She saw me. "As the saying goes, 'Come on in—the water's fine.'"

It took me all of a nanosecond to strip and join her. Fortunately we came together toward the shallow end or we might've drowned. She wrapped her legs around me and I backpedaled until I slammed into the wall. The frustration of the past few hours vaporized, and the frenzy generated a series of small tsunamis sweeping across the pool. Suddenly she gasped, let out a muted scream, and went limp in my arms. It was over almost as quickly as it began.

Only slightly out of breath, she murmured into my ear, "If the margaritas are as delicious as the sex, you're a real find, Lieutenant."

I chuckled. "Lieutenant? A little formal considering the last few minutes, no?"

"Vincent?"

"Vinny."

She cocked her head. "I like it. Buy a girl a drink, Vinny?"

"Nothing I'd like better."

"I think there will be."

"Such as?"

"Round two." She broke away from my arms and pulled herself out of the pool.

She picked up a towel and threw me one as I climbed out after her.

"This way, Vinny."

CHAPTER SIX

S ATURDAY MORNING announced itself in a blaze of
vicious California sunshine that makes opening your eyes painful.
After several tries, I managed to squint at my watch, realizing it
was closer to Saturday noon. So much for an early start and that flight
back to Jacksonville in time for the "weekend follies." And whom was I
kidding? Was I really in a hurry to leave?

I was alone on a canopy bed in a room overlooking the pool. A
lawn spread from the swimming pool to a low sandstone wall that ran
along the top of the cliff. The wall was awash in roses, and coconut
palms on either end framed a cloudless sky. Below it, the Pacific
stretched out to the horizon. The pool teased back memories of the
night before—three more margaritas and rounds two, three, and four.
My head throbbed. It felt as if Gene Krupa were using my skull for a
drum.

Somehow I made it into the bathroom and planted myself under a
large multinozzled shower. Cold, then hot, then cold again. It almost

worked. I finally gave up, got out, and reached for a towel. I sensed a presence and looked toward the door. Kat was leaning against the doorjamb holding a covered tray.

She ran her eyes over me from head to toe and smiled approvingly. "Good morning."

I wrapped the towel around my waist, massaged my temples. "Not so good."

She lifted the lid off the tray, revealing a Bloody Mary. "Hair of the dog?"

"Praise the Lord." I took it and gulped down half the contents. It was liquid blowtorch. "Whoa!"

"Half-vodka, half-juice—and a shot glass of Tabasco."

"Your recipe?"

"Vic's."

"More than I needed to know."

She laughed. "Don't get snippy. Just another convenience that works. Get dressed, and we'll have some brunch."

"Can I ask you a question?"

"Sure."

"Don't you feel even a *little* under the weather?"

"Why should I? I've had a delightfully memorable evening with a charming man I've just met and I'm feeling *excep*tional!"

She was wearing white shorts and deck shoes with a white cotton shirt tied at her midriff—an outfit that complemented her perfectly tanned body to perfection. She chuckled, spun around, and left me gaping.

We had brunch in Coronado at the San Diego Yacht Club. Daddy, naturally, was a member. It was becoming apparent that Daddy did really get around.

We picked our way down a four-star buffet, selected a table overlooking the harbor, and ordered Ramos gin fizzes. Beautiful—both the view and the drink—and I was beginning to feel better. We watched sailboats swoop across the bay while I managed to nibble at some shrimp and a salad.

We finished eating, sipped the fizzes, and after a long pause she asked, "Any guilty feelings about last night?"

"Yeah. About not having any."

"Life goes on, Vinny."

I nodded. "For what it's worth, I won't be forgetting it anytime soon."

She held up her glass in a toast, finished her gin fizz, and looked out over the water. "Still going to try catching a flight back to Jacksonville today?"

There it was. The unavoidable.

"They'll be expecting me. I'll at least have to call the air station to check if there's anything going east."

She looked back at me. "And if there is?"

"I'm hoping there's not."

"Is it really that important for you to get back?"

"Before Monday? Not really. But we've started workups for a Mediterranean cruise next January, and the skipper knows my mission was accomplished the moment I arrived and signed off the body. He'd expect me to catch the first plane available and head back home."

"You know, I hadn't thought to ask. Where is home?"

"New York."

"Manhattan?"

I nodded. "Hell's Kitchen."

"Tough place."

I shrugged. "I can take care of myself."

"You made that very clear last night."

"I pass the test?"

"Uh-huh. But another exam would be nice."

29

"Let's call the air station and see if we get lucky."

There was nothing going to Jacksonville out of North Island or NAS Miramar until Monday morning.

I bought a bathing suit, T-shirt, and boat shoes in the Hotel del Coronado gift shop, paid with my credit card, and we spent the afternoon on Daddy's forty-two-foot sloop.

Why would I have thought he wouldn't have one?

She was an excellent sailor, but by now nothing she said or did would have surprised me. The girl was magic in motion. She handled the sloop with the cocky ease of a lifelong sailor and enjoyed every moment of my awe as I watched her.

That evening we drove to La Jolla and checked into La Valencia Hotel, the fabled hideaway of stars from Garbo to Gable. Walking along its classic colonnade and palm-shaded patio, we entered a lobby with a hand-painted ceiling and two-story windows overlooking the Pacific.

We had twilight cocktails at the Whaling Bar, a moonlit swim in the Pacific, and returned to the bridal suite, where I gaily ordered two magnums of Dom Pérignon and damn near everything on the room-service menu.

We never even touched the banquet on the serving cart, but we put a good-size dent in the champagne. The sex was passionate, if somewhat less violent than the prior night, but we matched the output and I felt a subtle change from lust to something more. For a fleeting moment it crossed my mind that we were probably having the same kind of whirlwind romance Kat had had with Dave Stanfield, but I let it go, hoping ours would be a happier story.

I lit a Lucky, sighing as Kat slid next to me and rested her head on my chest. Within moments her breathing eased into the steady rhythm of sleep. If body language was an indicator, she was experiencing the same feelings that were flowing through me. An ocean-scented breeze billowed the curtains; I heard gulls shrieking and looked out the window at the first glint of dawn. I was in the afterglow of an unforgettable two days with one of the most beautiful and exciting women I'd ever met, and I was beginning to think I could never get enough of her.

Sunday was an attempt to match our glorious Saturday. We woke up—made love, had brunch, and swam—made love, rented a sailboat—made love, had dinner, went to bed—and made love.

Then at six thirty on Monday morning, Kat drove me through the gate of the Miramar Naval Air Station in Victor Marino's pink Cadillac. The response we got from the sentry was identical to the one we'd gotten sixty hours earlier at North Island.

It felt as if it had been sixty days.

She pulled up in front of Flight Ops, cut the engine, and turned to me. "Bon voyage?"

I nodded. "Or something." I didn't know what else to say, so I finally asked, "What are the chances of you shooting a picture in Jacksonville anytime soon?"

She shrugged. "Less than slim—more like none." She smiled hopefully. "What are the chances of you popping back here anytime soon?"

"Better, but as I said, we're in the middle of workups for a Med cruise."

She sighed. " 'Down to the sea in ships'?"

"It's what we boys in blue do."

"I don't want it to end, Vinny."

"Neither do I." I realized how much I meant it.

She leaned forward and brushed me with a feathery kiss. Her eyes were moist when she leaned back. "See you around, sailor."

"Right." I tried to put something more into words. I couldn't and settled for "I'll call you when I get back."

Grabbing my carry bag from the backseat, I threw it over my

shoulder and headed into Flight Operations. A moment later the sound of screeching tires forced me to turn around. The pink Cadillac careened away, a stream of auburn hair whipping out behind it.

CHAPTER SEVEN

THE FLIGHT BACK east in a Lockheed Constellation was uneventful but exhausting. The Navy's "Connies" were early-warning aircraft fitted with huge radar domes and powered by decades-old reciprocating engines. Compared with jets, they were lumbering beasts, and even with the wind on our tail, the trip took almost six hours. Admittedly it was a helluva lot better than the seven-day schlep it had taken to go West.

We landed at the Jacksonville Naval Air Station in steam-room humidity, and I caught a ride down the flight line to the VF-176 hangar. A dozen swept-wing North American FJ-3 Furies were parked next to it looking like feral cats waiting to pounce. The squadron insignia was emblazoned on the hangar as well as the aircraft: a grinning mask of comedy imposed over a black death's head with crossed machine guns behind it—the Harlequins.

The VF-176 duty officer informed me the skipper wanted to see me as soon as I returned, so I took the stairway to the balcony on the upper deck. The balcony ran the entire length of the building—the squadron's offices were off it, and below them on the floor level were the shops—maintenance, parachute riggers, armorers, etc. The opposite side of the hangar mirrored the arrangement with offices above and shops below, and the cavernous center floor cradled sick aircraft needing attention. Both ends featured deck-to-roof doors that opened their yawning mouths onto the flight line.

The entire area reeked of jet fuel.

CDR Kelly Concannon had his Wellington boots propped up on his desk and was reading dispatches when I entered his office. An unlit cigar stub jutted out under a flaring mustache, and his coal black eyes matched his hair. The skipper was from Brockton, Massachusetts, as Black Irish as they came, and was affectionately known as the Black Thing.

The battle of Midway had earned him a Navy Cross and the Korean War a DFC and a pair of Air Medals. He was a brilliant fighter pilot and an outstanding leader whom every pilot in the squadron would have followed to hell. The last thing he wanted from his men was formality. Respect—but not formality—so I wearily leaned against the door and reported.

"Lieutenant Vesta. Home from the wars, Skipper."

He looked up, his eyes squinting. "I kahn see that," he said in his pronounced Boston accent, sounding like the junior senator from his home state. "You look like a shipwreck."

He was right. I did. Seven days on a train, followed by three nights of debauchery and a six-hour return flight had ripped a few pounds off my frame and given my cheeks a sunken look.

"That's what I was told when I got off the train in San Diego."

"What happened?"

I shrugged and kept it short and simple. "The train was a bitch, the trip long, the widow grieving."

Two truths and a lie.

"Go see the doc. You look like a poster boy for 'ridden hard and put away wet.'"

"Right."

"Our two young nuggets checked in this morning. They're yours and McCaulley's."

"They should've been here a month ago," I said.

"Call the Pentagon and complain."

He flipped his thumb toward a white plastic calendar on the side wall, a five-foot square with black grease-pencil markings slashed over various dates. The week of October 14 was circled with the legend *CQ*.

"In the meantime," he said, "we've got a ready deck on the fourteenth. Get 'em primed."

Our final workups for the January Mediterranean cruise would occur just before we deployed on the USS *Forrestal*. But now it looked as if the USS *Saratoga* had a break in her schedule and would be available to us the week of the fourteenth for some unscheduled carrier-landing practice, otherwise known as CQ. She was in nearby Mayport, and the Navy never let a ready flight deck go to waste when it had an opportunity to jam in some extra training. Every pilot in the air group would get an early refresher, and our two late-arriving nuggets would get an early jump. Six weeks wasn't a helluva lot of time to get the new kids checked out in the FJ-3s and ready to hit the carrier, but it was doable if we pressed it.

I said, "We'll get it done, Skipper."

"Goddamn right you will. I wouldn't have it any other way." He grinned, revealing the set of snow-white teeth that clenched his cigar, and waved me away with a flick of his hand.

Walking back down the balcony, I passed several of our enlisted men, who greeted me with jaunty waves. "Good to see you back, Mr. Vesta." "Welcome back, sir."

The squadron was composed of eighty enlisted men and eighteen pilots. Most of us had been together almost three years, and the casual but respectful camaraderie reflected the outstanding leadership of Concannon.

The squadron ready room was a fifty-by-twenty-foot combination briefing room and assembly area furnished with tables, chairs, and a couple of sofas. The walls featured bulletin boards and posters, and at the far end were two dozen desk chairs in front of a podium. It was the gathering place and heart of all squadron activity, and when I entered the smoke-filled room, a half dozen pilots in flight gear were preparing for a late flight, while several others in short-sleeved khaki uniforms played acey-deucey, our version of backgammon.

Doug spotted me as soon as I entered and jumped up, calling out, "Vinny! How'd it go?"

I shrugged, knowing the full story would have to wait. "It went."

"You look like shit."

"So I've heard."

He checked his watch. It was 1650. "Happy hour in ten. You can tell me why over a drink. You up for it?"

I smiled wryly. "No, but what the hell could it hurt."

I spent a few minutes greeting the guys and introduced myself to our new pilots. The first of the twenty-three-year-old nuggets was ENS Edward "Whitey" Ford—his call sign obvious because of the New York Yankees' star pitcher. He was a redheaded, six-foot Nebraska farm boy and had an endearing aw-shucks look about him that I would soon learn made women want to mother him.

The second pilot was ENS Pedro Zazueta, a third-generation Mexican-American. "Zaz" was a tanned Ricardo Montalban look-alike with a winning smile and affable demeanor that the women not trying to mother Whitey found irresistible. Cruising the watering holes together, the two nuggets were as effective as Seabiscuit on a stud farm.

They'd been told of my long train ride with Stanfield's body and peppered me with questions.

"At every stop?" Whitey asked incredulously. "You had to get out at *every* stop?"

I nodded. "At every stop. Up, out, and back to the baggage car."

"When'd you sleep?"

"Mostly, I didn't."

"Wow," he said, his admiration obvious.

Zaz shook his head and asked, "And you were wearing dress blues?"

"All the way."

"Were there at least any good-looking women on the train?"

"On? No."

Doug, finally fed up with the delays, made our apologies and pulled me away.

Happy hour at the Jax O club was a dead-on duplicate of the one on the opposite coast—which could be said of every happy hour, in every O club, at every base around the world. The only difference would be the décor and the faces. Cigarettes were in every hand and booze was measured in the standard three-finger shots that could buy you alcoholic poisoning if you didn't pass out from smoke inhalation.

The bar was three to four deep with naval aviators in whites vying for a chance to take home a flock of Southern belles sporting their flimsiest summer best. Jimmy Dorsey's "So Rare" was blaring out of the audio system, while a 150 or so of the hopeful belles and eager studs fought to be heard over the din.

Doug and I elbowed up to the bar, shouted out our usual order, and a pair of double martinis materialized. We scooped them up, weaved our way out to the patio, and grabbed a relatively quiet umbrella table.

We toasted, took sizable slugs of our martinis, and Doug began our routine opener to any conversation: "So?"

"Promise you won't laugh?" I asked, not missing a beat.

He deadpanned the usual reply: "No fucking way."

I laughed, but said, "This time it's serious."

"Okay, so what's the big news?"

Doug and I had gone through flight training together and had been assigned to VF-176 as soon as we got our wings. In the following three years he'd become my closest friend and housemate. I could tell him anything.

"I met a girl."

His eyebrows shot up and he nearly guffawed. "That's news?"

"Not *that* . . . who."

"So? Who?"

"The widow."

I'd never seen Doug look stunned. Not when one of his girlfriends drove his car into the St. Johns River because he pissed her off—not when the admiral's daughter told him she was pregnant and was going to rat him out—not even when he returned from Guantánamo, Cuba, and was caught smuggling thirty-two quarts of rum in the ammo cans of his jet.

But this time he looked genuinely surprised. "Stanfield's?"

I nodded. "Stanfield's."

He shook his head in disbelief. "Jesus Christ, Vinny, what happened out there?"

I went through the pink Caddy pickup, the happy hour, Tijuana, Point Loma, and La Jolla. I finished the story over our second set of doubles and admitted I might be hooked.

He whistled quietly. "What now?"

"I have no fuckin' idea . . . except I've gotta see her again."

"She gonna give up her career and move here?"

"No way."

"You gonna desert and move there?"

"No way."

"So . . ."

"I have no fuckin' idea."

"You already said that."

"It's still a fact."

38

Doug was aghast. "That's it? Just you have 'no fuckin' idea'? That's all?"

I nodded.

"Un-fucking-believable!"

"Ain't it?"

CHAPTER EIGHT

IT WAS ALMOST six when we headed down Route 17 toward Holly Point, a small suburb south of the air station. Ten minutes later Doug whipped his Austin-Healey convertible into the long drive that led to our bachelor pad. We drove into a turnaround circle with a gushing fountain in the middle of it and parked in front of the house—a fourteen-room, antebellum mansion built in Greek Revival style that featured a two-story colonnaded façade with wide balconies on the first and second floors. The four-acre property also boasted cypress, ash, magnolia, and live oaks and sat directly beside a mile-wide stretch of the St. Johns River.

It was magnificent.

The house had been erected in 1850 by a lumber baron, fallen into disrepair, and became a white elephant that had been on the selling block for years. Doug and I rented it for a song—basically just covering the owner's utilities. Our squadron mates saw its potential as one of the great snake ranches in bachelor history and helped us clean it up.

The sprawling backyard featured a large patio and pool, shaded by cypresses dripping with Spanish moss and ending at the river, where a sixty-foot dock reached out over the water. A classic wooden Chris-Craft was moored to its far end—when it wasn't flying over the water towing four skiers at twenty-five knots.

Our final coup was Jess and Jessie—a feisty black couple looking for work as a handyman and cook. Their compensation included room, board, and use of our ski boat for stalking catfish. Born and brought up at the turn of the century, their customs and attitudes were pure Old South. We were as in love with them as they were with us.

Jess was washing down the lower balcony with a garden hose as we pulled up to the house. He flashed a warm smile, waved, and shouted, "Welcome back, Mistah Vinny!"

Jess was cocoa-skinned, in his early sixties, and had a full head of chalk-white hair that topped a solid, six-foot frame. His wife, Jessie, was also cocoa-skinned, in her early sixties, and had a solid, six-foot frame topped by a full head of chalk-white hair.

On drunken weekend nights when uninitiated revelers thought they saw the same person in two places at the same time, the drama was as confusing as it was hilarious. But in the two and a half years we'd all been together, Jessie had grown fond of the VF-176 pilots and became known as the Squadron Mother.

I said, "It feels like I've been gone a month, Jess. All good?"

He nodded and cackled. "Uh-huh, but you missed a real knockdown whup-up las' night."

I turned to Doug. "Oh?"

"Some new talent showed up."

Jess cut his eyes toward the house and back to us. He flashed a sly grin. "Still some 'xamples drapin' the dock. Jessie spied me spyin' them and told me, 'Git out front and wash down the porch!'" He chuckled and waved the garden hose.

"And you're too smart to argue," I said, knowing it was true.

"With Jessie? Lord no! Only a fool tangle with my Jessie." He chuckled again and I clapped him on the shoulder.

Doug led us into the entrance—a rotunda with an inlaid walnut floor and a massive circular staircase. We walked down a long central hallway past two parlors—music and dining rooms on the left and right—to the end where a sunroom sat opposite a large country kitchen. The final two rooms overlooked the rear porch, sprawling backyard, and river.

Doug said, "I should warn you, Jessie's ridin' the warpath."

"Why?"

"The weekend party didn't break up until three this morning and she threatened to quit again."

"Wonderful."

"And she said we're turning Jess into a voyeur."

"She said that?"

"Yep—claimed she learned the word from reading one of your *New Yorkers*."

The tang of cinnamon and simmering apples laced the air, and we stopped to look into the kitchen. Jessie was at the large central island rolling dough for a piecrust that would soon cradle the apples. She was wearing a bib apron and flecks of flour were on her arms and face—but not a hint of perspiration even in the oppressive heat.

She glanced up, cocked an eyebrow, and stopped her work. Taking in my appearance with a practiced eye, she drawled out, "My, my. You sure look poorly, Mistah Vinny."

"That seems to be the consensus," I said.

"Whatchu been up to? I thought you was deliverin' a body, not tryin' to be one."

"It's a long story, Jessie."

"With you boys it always is. Git you anythin'?"

"No thanks, Jessie. I'm beat—just want to log some z's."

"Then you'd best not be tempted by a look out back." She

harrumphed, sprinkling a handful of flour on the dough, and resumed her rolling.

I threw a questioning look at Doug, and he led me out onto the rear porch. Sprawled out on the end of the dock, bathing in the late-afternoon sun, were three gorgeous nymphs in all their topless glory.

Doug shrugged and quipped, "Stragglers from last night's Shakespeare seminar."

"Impressive."

"Interested?"

"Only in the thought. I'm goin' to go thwart the mattress thief."

"Anything you need?"

"Just a hot tub and a good night's sleep."

We walked back into the house, and the phone in the sunroom rang.

"McCaulley . . . Well, hello there, how's the Big Apple?" He chuckled. "Good, same here. He just walked in." Doug handed me the phone, saying, "Angelo," then went to a rolling bar caddie to make himself a drink.

"Hi, Angelo, I—"

As usual, without preamble he asked, "What'd she say?"

There could only be one "she" based on our last conversation. "Mom?"

"No—Grandma Moses! Of course her! What'd she say?"

"Christ, Angelo, I haven't had a chance to—"

"I called ya three days ago!"

"I know, Angelo, but I got tied up on the coast and just got back."

"Look—Vinny. This thing is gettin' serious. She called Anastasia again and he called me. She's beggin' him to whack Genovese before he's got a chance ta settle in. Now you know Anastasia would love to whack the prick, but not now! He's in the middle of a pissin' contest with Lansky and Costello because he wants a piece of their casino action in Cuba."

I was aghast. The Cuban hotels and casinos had been set up ten years earlier by Lucky Luciano, Frank Costello, and Meyer Lansky, with the Cuban dictator Fulgencio Batista as their partner. It was a gushing cash cow and they guarded it like the mint that it was. I couldn't imagine them letting anyone muscle in on their golden baby—even someone as feared and powerful as Anastasia.

"It'll never happen, Angelo," I said. "Even with Costello on the way out and Luciano in Italy, they're still a force—not to mention Lansky. What the hell is Anastasia thinking?"

"He's thinkin' he can make it happen because he knows ninety-nine percent of the world is scared shitless of him. What he ain't gettin' is that the one percent that ain't includes Luciano, Costello, and Lansky—not ta mention Batista who's got the whole fuckin' Cuban army behind 'im."

I lowered my head. "Christ."

"He loves yer mother and he don't wanna say no to her. But this is stupid! Crazy as it sounds, I'm worried he might take a shot at Genovese just to prevent Genovese from takin' a shot at yer mother."

"Okay, Angelo, I'll talk to her. I don't think it'll do any good, but I'll try."

"Good. Lemme know what she says. Stuff says hello."

"Tell Stuff—"

But he'd already hung up.

Doug had heard the conversation and asked, "Trouble?"

He'd met Angelo on several occasions when he'd visited New York with me. The sanitized version of Mafia events was always in the papers, but the real facts he got from me.

"Always," I said. "This time it's Anastasia against his former friends Costello and Lansky. And of course it's always about Genovese."

"Anything I can do?

"Yeah—pour me a Scotch. I've gotta call my mother."

He handed me a drink while I dialed. It was my habit to call every week, but with the trip to the coast and my weekend with Kat, I'd skipped a week. Not good. After six rings my mother finally picked up.

She answered with a testy "Yes?"

Since my father was killed, she never sounded happy. His death had torn her heart out and her spirits went with him.

"Hi, Mom, it's me."

There was a moment of silence before she acknowledged my greeting in her light Sicilian accent. "So, Mr. Me, you remembered the number?"

"I'm sorry, Mom, I've been busy."

"There's a war I didn't hear about?"

"No, Mom, but Angelo called and he's worried you're about to start one."

"So—he calls my son because he thinks you can shut up me saying what he knows is right!"

"Mom, he's worried. Angelo loves us. We're like family to him. But Albert is his boss and he's trying to protect him. Going to war over Genovese someday might be the right thing to do, but not now. The Commission voted. Genovese is in."

"The Commission! What did the Commission do when that animal killed your father? What did Angelo do? What did *you* do? Nothing!"

"Mom—"

"Scusi! You did do something. You ran off to college and joined the Navy!"

"Mom, I beg you—"

"Good! Beg! Beg Angelo and Albert to understand that the man who killed your father will someday kill them! And then beg God to forgive you for doing nothing!"

She slammed down the phone and I drained my glass.

It was hopeless. She was whom she had to be. The hate she felt for Genovese was as powerful as the love she felt for my father. In spite of what she said, I knew Angelo and I were in her heart somewhere, but I also knew there was no stopping her. Angelo would have to withstand the barrage and try to hold back Anastasia.

I picked up the phone again and redialed. Angelo answered and I said, "Vinny—I talked to her. She hung up on me."

"Figures," Angelo answered, sounding resigned. "I just figured it was worth a shot."

"Yeah. What now?"

"Doris Day."

"What?"

"*Che sarà, sarà*. Thanks, kid. Talk ta you soon."

He hung up and I headed up to my bedroom and dialed Kat. The line was busy so I lay down for a minute and was out as soon as I hit the pillow. The phone rang again at nine, but I ignored it until Doug knocked and popped his head in.

"It's the widow," he said. "She sounds like Hepburn."

I picked up the phone on the bedside table. "Kat?"

"Hello, sailor. Miss me?" Her voice over the phone was even more honeyed and her accent more pronounced than I remembered. I could feel myself falling for her all over again.

"Yeah," I said, smiling. "How about me?"

"I'm the one who called."

"You get a film in Jacksonville?"

"Not a chance. You get a trip to the coast?"

"Same answer."

"Did you tell your skipper there was a grieving widow out here who needs consolation?"

"No, but if I did and told him whose it was, he'd probably have me confined to quarters."

There were a few seconds of silence and she finally said, "I really miss you, Vinny."

"I know the feeling."

"We have to figure something out, you know."

"I know."

"Okay, but in the meantime let's see how far we can run up our phone bills—deal?"

"Deal," I said.

I heard the sound of a kiss. "Night, sailor. I'll be thinking of you."

"Hold the thought," I replied, and we hung up. I went back to sleep in the afterglow of the call, determined to ignore as long as possible the indisputable facts:

This was a geographically impossible love affair. Kat was a devastatingly beautiful widow with a superstar for a lover. Her father was a powerful and possessive lawyer driven by his desire to see *her* become a superstar. And he hated naval aviators.

The warning signs were dazzling.

CHAPTER NINE

DOUG AND I spent the next three days checking out **Whitey** and Zaz in the FJ-3s, and I talked to Kat every night, still determined to ignore our impossible situation. On Friday, Concannon called a squadron meeting and we all gathered in the ready room. We sat in the desk chairs and took notes while the skipper briefed us from the podium on the events leading up to October 14 and beyond.

We were already in the middle of our predeployment workups for the January Med cruise—six months of strike planning exercises, a host of refresher drills, weapons training, and carrier qualifications—prior to an operational-readiness exercise. Finally there would be a concluding month of prep at a more relaxed tempo to prepare personnel and families for a six-month deployment.

But now, added to the above, we'd have to prepare for the previously unscheduled CQ on *Saratoga*. We'd be working Saturdays when necessary and starting field carrier landing practice, or FCLPs as we called them, immediately. FCLPs simulated landing on an aircraft carrier—without the carrier. They were conducted on a normal runway, but all the procedures presumed you were headed down to a carrier deck. The LSO—landing signal officer—the mirror system, patterns, speeds, and verbiage were all as they would be at sea on *Saratoga*.

Doug and I took Whitey and Zaz aside for a final briefing of the hop before we took off. Doug had already checked the weather at Whitehouse, an outlying field about eighteen miles southwest of Jacksonville, and he rattled it off.

"Sky clear, winds ten to twelve out of the west. A bit of blowing dust and reports of beaucoup birds in the area, so keep your heads on a swivel."

I pointed at Whitey. "Whitey, you're with me. Doug's got Zaz. We'll fly out in two two-plane sections and join up in echelon en route. We hit the break at eight hundred feet, four hundred knots, and wrap into a four-g pull to downwind. Establish your intervals, reduce your speed, and ease down to six hundred feet. Abeam the runway, drop your gear and flaps and call, 'One eighty—gear and flaps down.'" I looked at Doug and he picked up where I left off.

"Roll into a twenty-five-to-thirty-degree turn, adjust your power, and begin a three-hundred-to-four-hundred-foot rate of descent. When you hit the ninety you should be at five hundred feet—at the forty-five at three fifty to three seventy-five feet. When you roll out in the groove, pick up the mirror, and call, 'Ball.' You should be about fifteen to eighteen seconds from touchdown. Glue the ball dead center—check your speed and rate of descent—make any final adjustments and *plant* that baby."

"The second you hit the deck," I continued, "firewall it—take off, pull the gear and flaps, and climb to six hundred feet. About a mile out, start your downwind turn and do it all over again. Any questions?"

"Eight bounces?" asked Whitey.

A *bounce* was what we called a touch-and-go landing after an FCLP.

49

"At least eight. Ten—fuel permitting. After the sixth bounce start calling your fuel states at the one eighty."

Zaz confirmed the number. "Bingo at twelve hundred pounds."

Bingo was the minimum fuel left in the tanks before mandatory return to base.

"Right," I answered. "Anything else?"

Whitey and Zaz shook their heads.

I smiled. "Then let's do it!"

Our two young tigers whooped enthusiastically, and we all headed for the flight line where we climbed into our assigned Furies and cranked up the engines. With Whitey on my wing and Zaz on Doug's, we taxied out to the end of the runway.

"Jax tower—Harlequin 105, flight of two ready for takeoff."

"Harlequin 105, cleared for takeoff. Winds two-six-zero at ten."

I advanced the throttle and we roared down the runway. Breaking ground, we pulled up the landing gear, and a few seconds later I nodded my head, indicating to Whitey that I was retracting my flaps. We headed southwest, were joined a minute later by Doug and Zaz, and proceeded to Whitehouse in a four-plane echelon. Five miles out I called the field.

"Whitehouse—Harlequin 105 five miles out for the break."

"Harlequin 105, cleared to break. Winds two-six-zero at ten to twelve, pattern clear."

Directly over the field we broke and set up our intervals. At the one eighty I called gear and flaps down and started my approach. LCDR Kenny Willis, our squadron LSO, was in position next to the mirror on the right side of the runway, and I saw both as I came into the groove and called, "Ball." I made a damn fine pass, landed, and immediately took off again. Seconds later I heard Whitey call, "Ball."

The interval between my takeoff and his call was perfect. Not so Whitey's first approach. Kenny called for several corrections as Whitey came down the groove and finally was given a wave-off.

I could almost hear him swearing at himself in the cockpit.

Doug came in next and made his usual fine approach and landing. Zaz followed and also got several corrections from Kenny as he came down the groove. But he was given a *cut*, not a wave-off. He landed, accelerated, and took off for his first successful FCLP in a Fury.

I chuckled. There was going to be one helluva ration of shit shoveled from a puffed-up Zaz to a humbled Whitey before the day was out.

We continued "bouncing," and after Whitey's initial wave-off, the kids did well for their first FCLP hop. We managed to rack up ten landings before we bingoed and returned to Jax.

Because we were on a tight training schedule, we had a quick dinner at the O club, then took off again after dark to get Whitey and Zaz some night-flying time. Doug returned first with Zaz, who had an intermittent oil-pressure warning light winking at him, and I came back with Whitey a half hour later.

Since we were flying the following day, we'd canceled the weekend follies. When I got back to the house, I noticed Doug's Austin-Healey and Jess's car to the left in front of the garages, then I saw a third car I didn't recognize on the other side of them. I walked up the front steps into the rotunda and found Doug standing at the bottom of the staircase.

"Waiting for someone?" I asked.

"Uh-huh. You."

"May I ask why?"

"Sure. Check the sunroom." He started up the stairs two at a time.

"Huh?"

"The sunroom. Check it."

Before I could ask why again, he disappeared on the second-floor landing. I walked down the hall to the sunroom, which was dimly lit with just enough light for me to make out the figure sitting in the window seat.

She smiled. "Hi, sailor. Buy a girl a drink?"

Barely recovering from shock, I stupidly asked, "Kat?"

She noted the look on my face. "You don't look happy to see me."

"I'm still not sure I *am* seeing you."

She got up and crossed to me. "Let me help you." She put her arms around my neck and brought me down to her lips.

I recovered enough to wrap my arms around her and lifted her off the floor. Our lips parted just short of asphyxiation and I put her down. "How? When did you . . .?"

"Two hours ago." She smiled. Cocking an eyebrow, she added, "Jess answered the door and told me there was no party tonight. I explained I wasn't here for the party. He called Jessie. I told her who I was and she believed me. She said I was too classy to be here for the party. And then Doug showed up and *he* thought I was here for the party. I must confess I can't wait to hear about the party that I wasn't here for."

"We always have a—"

"I know," she said, laughing. "Doug told me about the monastic life you've been leading."

"I can't believe you came."

"I missed you, Vinny. And when we talked on the phone it got worse."

"And worser."

"Not a word."

"But a fact." I kissed her again. "Right now I think we both need a drink."

"Margaritas?"

Now we were both smiling.

I led her into the kitchen and pulled together the ingredients while she perched on a stool beside the center island and watched me.

"Anything new on the West Coast?"

"There was a little excitement last week when you were the object of a rather intense manhunt at the yacht club."

"Huh?"

"One of Daddy's cronies told him I had brunch with a very handsome young man last Sunday and then went sailing on his sloop. So naturally he had to know who it was."

"Curious Daddy," I said, knowing she wouldn't tell him and there was no way he could find out.

"Persistent Daddy," she corrected. "The dockmaster saw us board the boat carrying a shopping bag from the Hotel Del where we bought your outfit."

"So?" I said, nonchalantly pouring the margaritas.

Kat took hers, sipped it. "So he sent one of his minions to ask around about the handsome man and beautiful woman who were in the gift shop around noon last Sunday."

That stopped me. "You gotta be kidding!" I said in complete disbelief.

"Daddy doesn't kid," she said, straight-faced. "Some money exchanged hands, a credit card receipt appeared, and voilà! Lieutenant Vincent Vesta, USN."

"Un-fucking-believable," I said, shaking my head. "How do you know all this?"

"Vic told me," she said calmly.

"Victor Marino?"

"Uh-huh. Daddy told him, and he told me. Vic of course threw a tantrum." She smiled and took another sip of her drink. "I'd put over two hundred and fifty miles on his brand-new car and he found a valet receipt from La Valencia under the seat and saw me light a cigarette with a matchbook from Caesar's. He and Daddy had a little chat and pretty much pieced together our weekend."

I was speechless.

"Oh, it's typical for Daddy. He's protecting his baby girl. Vic, on the other hand, was miffed for different reasons. He's a star and I'm one of his baubles. He's a big baby who hates losing a toy. It was more about his bruised ego than anything else."

"You don't seem too upset about it all."

"Why should I be? Vic ranted and Daddy raved, but they don't own me. I'll do what I want, when I want, where I want. Right now I want you, Lieutenant."

She slipped off the stool, came around the island, and put her hands around my neck. I lifted her off the floor, cradled her in my arms, and took her back into the sunroom. The journey down the hall, up the stairs, and into the bedroom would have seemed endless.

We savaged each other in the window seat for an hour, slept for an hour, and did a repeat. At two in the morning I took her up to my bedroom. Jessie had enough reasons to rail at me without finding us in the window seat in the morning, in the altogether.

CHAPTER TEN

THE NEXT MORNING Doug woke me up at seven. We had to get out to the squadron by eight for early briefings and our first hop of the day. I managed to slip out without waking Kat and left her a note saying I would meet her at noon for lunch at the naval air station. There would be a drive-on waiting for her with directions to the officer's club.

I added a PS, warning her that the Florida Highway Patrol was very intolerant of speeding redheads. If she didn't want a taste of jailhouse food on Alligator Alley, she should keep it under a hundred.

Kelly Concannon was in the ready room with the rest of the pilots when we arrived. His greeting was slightly frosty, "You're late."

It was three minutes after eight.

We both muttered, "Yessir—sorry, sir," and took our seats.

"All right," he called out, "listen up."

He briefed us on the day's schedule, assigned us to our aircraft, and we all headed out. We repeated Friday's drill, but this time Whitey and Zaz went without any wave-offs. They were eight for eight.

We returned to the air station, debriefed the hop, and after we set up the afternoon flight schedule, I called the house from the ready room.

I got Jessie. "You sure kin pick 'em," she said.

"What?"

"Little gal's a keeper. First one ever been around here with a brain."

"Thanks, Jessie. Where is she?"

"Had breakfast, asked a lotta questions about you, and left a couple hours ago. Said she was meetin' you."

I checked my watch. Almost noon. I'd told her she was only ten minutes away so even if she had decided to go sightseeing—and obey the speed-limit signs—she should have come through the gate by now.

"Thanks again, Jessie, we'll see you later." I hung up and called the main gate. No joy. She hadn't yet arrived and I began to worry.

Doug noticed the look on my face. "Something wrong?"

"I'm not sure—Kat left the house two hours ago to meet me at the club. She's not the type to be late and she's not here yet."

"Maybe she got lost."

"Her? Never, and we're a straight shot down the highway for crissakes."

"Then maybe she wanted to check out Jax Beach."

"She'd have waited to do that with me."

"Okay, then maybe she had an accident."

"The way she drives, that's possible," I admitted. "Let's check the Highway Patrol and the hospitals."

"Christ, Vinny, it's only a couple of minutes till twelve, maybe she had a flat, or—"

"You start on the hospitals," I said, cutting him off. "I'll check the Highway Patrol."

We made several calls for the next ten minutes, but got nowhere. There were no reported accidents, and the emergency rooms hadn't admitted a Caitlin Pennington.

I was about to recheck the main gate when a hand touched me on the shoulder. "Lieutenant . . ."

It was Benson, the duty yeoman. "There's a call for you on our line, sir. It's Jessie, from your house."

Doug followed me as I shot down the stairs to the lower deck and into the duty office. LT Bill Raney was the duty officer and held out the phone to me as I entered.

I was breathing hard when I took it. "Jessie?"

She sounded panicked. "Mistah Vinny, Jess found the car."

"What car? Whose?"

"Your lady friend's. That rental."

"Where? I thought you said she left in it."

"She did, but when Jess went down to git the mail, he found it at the very end of the driveway, facin' the road. It was jest sittin' there, empty."

"Was there an accident?"

"Nosir. Nothin' wrong wit it—it jest sittin' there."

I absorbed what she was saying and dropped my head in angry frustration.

"What?" asked Doug.

I didn't answer him, but said to Jessie, "Don't do anything. I'll be right there." I handed the phone back to Raney and headed for the parking lot.

Doug chased after me, yelling, "What? What'd she say?"

"Jess found Kat's car at the end of the driveway. Empty. He only saw it because he went to get the mail."

You couldn't see the end of the driveway from the house because the damn thing was almost a hundred yards long and it curved.

Doug said, "So whatever happened, happened over two hours ago when she left."

I stopped at my car and turned back toward Doug. "The only thing that figures is when she got to the end of our driveway, it was blocked by another car. She stopped and whoever was in the other car grabbed her."

"Who for chrissakes? She doesn't know anybody here. Just us!"

"Right. So it had to be someone from the West Coast, and the only person who could have possibly tracked her down and ordered it is her father."

"You're shittin' me!"

"No. He knows who I am, knows we were together last weekend, and hates Navy pilots. Starting with Stanfield and now me."

"You really think he'd snatch his own daughter?"

"From the little I know so far," I said, getting into my car, "I'd bet on it."

"What the hell are you doing? You're on the flight schedule this afternoon!"

"Take me off," I said, starting my car.

"What do I tell the skipper?"

"Tell him I'm sick." I jammed the car in gear. "You won't be far wrong."

As I pulled away, Doug yelled, "You're still in your fucking flight suit!"

When I got back to the house, everything was just as Jess and Jessie had described it. The rental car was parked at the very end of the driveway facing the street. Abandoned.

I called the police and filed a missing person report. A joke. Kat had only been missing for a few hours. They sent a pair of detectives because I told them I was convinced she was abducted.

They weren't.

The car wasn't damaged and there was no evidence of a struggle. They said they couldn't waste time on my suspicions and it would be ridiculous to dust the car for prints since it was a rental. They'd probably come up with latents from half the Eastern seaboard. If any new information or evidence turned up, I should let them know. There was nothing they could do.

I tried calling her house a dozen times during the rest of the afternoon, but no one answered. I couldn't think of a single thing to do but sit in my flight suit and drink margaritas.

At six o'clock, eight hours after she disappeared, I got the call. It was from a man who identified himself as a friend of the Pennington family's. His voice was unthreatening and cultured, and he spoke slowly and deliberately as if he wanted me to weigh his words carefully.

"Lieutenant Vesta. Miss Pennington didn't want to cause you any undue concern, so she asked me to call and let you know that she is safe and sound back here in California."

"That's bullshit!" I yelled. "Let me talk to her."

"Unfortunately, that's not possible."

"Why? Because her father had her kidnapped?"

"I've been instructed to tell you she came of her own free will. As you know, her father is very concerned about her welfare and has convinced her that returning home was in her best interests."

"More bullshit!"

"He also wishes you to cease and desist trying to contact her."

"And how exactly does he think he can do that?"

"Lieutenant Vesta, Mr. Pennington is a powerful man with friends in very high places. He can make life very difficult for you."

"Really? Well, you can tell your employer I don't like threats and I'm used to doing whatever I damn well please."

"Perhaps, Lieutenant, but if you have any feelings for Miss Pennington, consider the fact that she has a career here, and you have a career there. The match would be impossible even if you weren't two thousand miles apart. Take my advice. Consider your escapade a delightful fling and relegate it to history." He hung up and the line went dead.

I stared at the phone for a long time thinking about a father who was so driven that he'd had his daughter chased across the country, abducted, then flown back to California rather than let her get involved with anyone other than Victor Marino.

Who the hell *was* this guy?

It was six thirty. Dinnertime in New York. I picked up the phone and dialed Angelo.

His wife, Lena, answered, "Itsa me, who's you?"

"Vinny. Is Angelo there?"

"Vincenzo, *sì* . . . Ee just come in. Angelo," she called out, "Vincenzo for you."

Angelo answered, "Hey, kid! How's the flyboy?"

"Good, Angelo, good. But I'd like to ask a favor."

"Sure. What?"

"I need a rundown on a guy named Marion Pennington. He's a lawyer in L.A. Works for Twentieth Century–Fox."

"He? He's got a girl's name?"

"Don't let it con you. John Wayne's real name was Marion Morrison."

"No shit?"

"No shit."

"What's your connection?"

"I'm seeing his daughter."

"And he don't like it?"

"He hates it. She came to visit me in Jax and he had her kidnapped and flown back to California."

"Ya gotta be kiddin'."

"Not even close."

"How d'ya know what happened?"

"One of her old man's flunkies called. Said they picked her up and then warned me to stay away from her."

"Whaddaya lookin' for?"

"Anything you can get me. The guy's an asshole."

"I'm on it. Anythin' else?"

I thought for a second. "Yeah. See if you can get me a couple of phone numbers. San Diego and Sun Valley for a Caitlin Pennington. Probably unlisted."

"The daughter?"

"Yes."

"Anythin' else?"

"That's it. Thanks, Angelo."

"No problem. Ciao."

I hung up and, on an impossible shot, dialed Kat one more time. No machine—no answer. I leaned over my knees and put my head in my hands, trying to think of something—anything—I could do.

Jess came in. "You goin' out again, Mistah Vinny?"

"No, Jess."

"Put up the Pontiac? Top's down and looks like rain."

"Sure, Jess, put it away."

"Anythin' else I kin do, boss?"

"No. Thanks, Jess."

"I sure am sorry about today."

"I know, Jess. Thanks."

He said, "Yessir," and walked out just as Jessie walked in.

She said, "He feels bad he didn't notice the car before he went to fetch the mail."

"Not his fault, Jessie."

"I know that. Git you some supper?"

"Not hungry, Jessie, but I could use another drink."

She knew me well, so she said, "I 'spect you could use more than one. I'll bring the bottle."

I decided to put myself out of my misery and dispensed four fingers of Scotch into a tumbler. I tossed it down, but it didn't help so I did it again—and kept doing it until I staggered up the stairs and passed out on my bed.

CHAPTER ELEVEN

ON MONDAY MORNING I was greeted with the hottest ass-chewing I'd ever gotten from CDR Kelly Concannon—or anyone else for that matter. The second I arrived at the VF-176 hangar, the duty officer informed me the skipper wanted to see me. Immediately.

I wasn't confused about why.

Concannon was sitting behind his desk staring down at his tightly clenched hands. His back was straight as a board. When I entered, his eyes shot up and he bellowed, "Stand at attention, Lieutenant!"

I instantly snapped to and glued my eyes to a spot directly over his head like a wet-eared cadet.

"Just what the hell did you think you were doing, Vesta?"

"I'm sorry about Saturday, sir, I—"

"Sorry? You ran off without telling a bloody soul, fucked up the entire afternoon training schedule, and sped though the main gate in your goddamn flight suit!"

"Yessir. I got a call—"

"The next words out of your mouth had better be 'from the president of the United States' or I'm gonna *have* your sorry ass!"

"Sir, it was an emergency—"

"So I heard from your friend McCaulley. A missing chippie! That's an emergency?"

"Yessir, I know what it looks like—"

"This is not a fucking kindergarten, Vesta! You don't waddle out of here like some goddamn dumb-ass toddler! This is a United States Navy fighter squadron, and you are an officer in this squadron—not an irresponsible dipshit!"

"Yessir. It won't happen again, sir."

"You're goddamn right it won't happen again. Because if it does, I'm gonna strap your sorry ass across the tailpipe of an FJ-3 and light off the engine!"

"I understand, sir."

"I certainly hope so. Now get the fuck out of my sight!"

I executed a quick about-face and marched out. If I had had a tail, it would have been tightly jammed between my legs. Having your ass chewed out was bad enough, but knowing you deserved it was damn near intolerable.

Doug was waiting for me in the ready room. He took one look at me and asked, "Bad?"

"The worst."

"Next to the worst."

"Why?"

He pointed at the flight schedule—a chalkboard with pilots' names, their plane assignments, launch times, and missions. There were originally eight names slated for the early launch, but the one at the top of the list had been erased—mine. You could still make out the name *Vesta* where it had been wiped out, but was legible in blurred white chalk on the black slate. A new name had been added to the bottom of the list bringing the schedule back up to the original eight pilots.

Doug said, "You're grounded."

"Shit, my whole life is in the toilet." I told Doug about Pennington's latest gambit to keep me away from Kat.

"Lemme ask you a question."

"Promise I won't laugh?" I deadpanned.

"Usual answer."

"Figures."

"You fall in love with the widow of a squadron mate you've just met who has a father wacky enough to kidnap her just to keep you away from her, which makes you wacky enough to storm off base in your flight suit while you're on the flight schedule—which winds up getting you goddamn grounded!" Doug paused and took a breath. "Don't you think this girl is making you act just a little bit crazy?"

"Maybe, but—"

"Is there any *more* shit headed your way?"

"I have no fuckin' idea."

We got the news before sundown. Doug and I were about to sit down for dinner on the patio when Jessie came out and announced, "A Mr. Angelo on the phone."

"Thanks, Jessie." I headed into the kitchen.

"Don't you be talkin' too long, Mr. Vinny. My pork roast likes to be et hot."

"Be just a couple of minutes." I picked up the phone. "Hello, Angelo?"

"You sure as shit got a talent for trouble, kid."

"Pennington?"

"Pennington. Preliminary report is he's a big-time player. But he doesn't actually work fer Fox. He's a consultant and has an office there. His real office is in Beverly Hills. Mainly he represents show-biz unions in studio relations. Big contributions to both political parties and high on the social ladder. So far nothin' on the phone numbers in San Diego and Sun Valley, but I'm still workin' on it."

"Thanks, Angelo, I appreciate it."

"No problem, I'll call ya when I get more."

I went back to the patio and told Doug about Angelo's report.

He said, "Your track record for stepping in shit remains uncontested."

I said, "Thanks, I needed that."

He nodded in agreement. "I know."

Concannon kept me grounded for the rest of the week. It was pure hell. Fighter pilots live to fly. Ask any one of them, at any time, under any conditions since the Rickenbackers and von Richthofens first soared over France during World War One, and I guarantee they'd repeat the oft-heard mantra "We'd pay *them* to let us fly these machines."

Every day I had to watch our planes roar down the runway and into the blue while I sat and ate my heart out like a goddamn land-locked Gooney bird. I couldn't fly and I couldn't reach Kat.

Doug suggested being grounded might take my mind off her.

I suggested he was full of shit.

I kept racking my brain for new ways to reach her. The problem was I knew so little about her. We'd been together less than seventy-two hours in San Diego and less than twelve hours in Jacksonville. I had a phone that wouldn't answer in L.A. and two unlisted numbers in San Diego and Sun Valley. Even if Angelo ferreted them out, they'd probably be dead as a eunuch's dick.

She wasn't doing a film so I figured calling all the studios wouldn't help. I tried it anyway. It didn't work. I didn't know the name of her agent or publicity manager, and there were so damn many of them in L.A. it would be an impossible search.

In a totally ridiculous move I even tried calling her father's office at

Fox. I told his secretary I was a friend of his daughter's and it was important that I to speak to Mr. Pennington. She was polite and said she'd give him the message. No return call—but what the hell did I expect after the message I'd gotten from his minion?

For a split second I even thought of appealing to the skipper for a few days leave so that I could fly out to the West Coast. But only for a split second. One, Concannon would have locked me in a rubber room for even asking, and two, even if he didn't and I *could* get out to the coast, where the hell would I start looking?

By the end of the week the squadron was ahead of Concannon's timetable, but the jets were taking a beating because of the intense schedule, so the skipper gave us the following Saturday afternoon off.

Doug was elated, and the time-honored weekend follies began at one P.M. with a buffet lunch on the patio. Jessie laid out salads, cold cuts, shrimp, and crayfish along with rolls, and a variety of breads and condiments. Jess manned a roaring barbecue for anyone interested in hot dogs or hamburgers, and Doug popped a keg of Jax beer.

He handed out foaming schooners to all comers while I stacked Sinatra, Bennett, Goodman, Dorsey, James, and Basie on the record changer. By 1957, rock and roll had stormed the country, and Elvis was a major star, but we'd all grown up in the late forties and early fifties when the big bands were king, and that's what blared out of a pair of oversize stereo speakers facing the river.

Fifteen young lovelies had been invited for the weekend and were frolicking with our squadron pilots at a horseshoe pit, in the pool, and on water skies behind the Chris-Craft. I noticed the three beauties that were nude sunbathing when I got back from San Diego and returned their wave. For the first time in years I wasn't tempted. Doug, however, rounded up the trio and brought them over.

"Vinny, say hello to Priscilla, Willou, and Joy."

You couldn't help loving the names—direct descendants of Scarlett, Melanie, and Miss Pittypat.

Joy stuck out her hand and obviously referring to her name said, "And Ah assure you Ah am."

Cute. Sexy—but cute.

"And I assure you I believe it," I answered graciously, but by now my sexual appetite resided solely across the country. I just couldn't get with the program. Bowing slightly, I took my leave, saying, "Ladies."

As I walked away, I heard Joy ask Doug, "I declare, is he a fahgot?"

Doug laughed. "Why don't you ask half the ladies present."

Joy must have liked that answer because the last thing I heard her say was a thoroughly intrigued, *"Reeally . . ."*

The rest of Saturday and Sunday were typical of our weekend shenanigans—couples eventually pairing off and either leaving for the night or commandeering one of the five spare bedrooms on the second floor. That of course drove Jessie up the wall because she had to wash extra bedding, make up extra beds, and clean extra rooms.

I could never figure out if she was opposed to the casual coupling on moral grounds or because extra work was against her general principles.

Doug and I instructed the hot-sheets guests to always leave a little something under the pillow for Jessie. They did—usually a ten—but Jessie never acknowledged the largess and continued to grumble. Now *that*, I knew, she definitely did as a matter of principle.

For the first time in as far back as I could remember, I ended a week without the Three F's that were the lifeblood of any fighter pilot worth the powder to blow him to hell. Fun—flying—and fornication.

CHAPTER TWELVE

ONCANNON TOOK ME off his shit list the following
Monday morning, and I was back in the air that afternoon. It
helped. The next days were a blaze of flying, flying, and more
flying. We were doing so well we even got another Saturday afternoon
off. Once again the weekend follies burst forth on short notice and in
full flower. This time, however, I couldn't pretend I was even vaguely
into it, so I grabbed a flight to Key West for some billfishing that
turned out to be as scoreless as my love life.

I returned cursing Poseidon *and* Aphrodite.

Predeployment workups continued apace, and the nuggets continued to ace the program with three weeks remaining before we "hit the
boat." Morale was soaring.

Everyone's but mine.

I continued to call Kat's L.A. number every day with the same
result—no answer. Out of desperation I even tried her father's office
three more times—"I'll give him the message, Lieutenant."

Finally, on Monday night I tried taking a shot at *Finnegans Wake*, but by eleven o'clock I was ready to pack it in. The phone rang and I picked it up wearily. "Vesta."

"Hi, sailor."

My breath caught. "Kat?"

"The same."

"Christ! Where are you?"

"At the moment having dinner at my girlfriend's house in L.A. I got back this afternoon."

"Are you all right—where were you?"

"Yes—and in Mexico."

"Mexico!"

"Daddy's idea of a cooling-off period. When his stooges got me back here, they put me on the Fox DC-4 and whisked me off to Baja. Quiet, isolated, and no phones."

"How'd you get away?"

"I didn't. They let me go when I finally said I'd make up with Vic and be a good girl—I lied of course."

"Christ—I was worried sick!"

"I'm sorry, Vinny, but there was no way I could reach you. We were in the middle of nowhere. I even tried to bribe the staff to get a message out, but they were all securely under Daddy's thumb."

"Are you going to stay there?"

"With Sally? No. At my Beverly Hills house. But I'm sure he's had the phones tapped to see if I call you, so our best bet is to use this one. Sally Richards, 434–6757."

I jotted down the name and number next to Joyce's picture. "Any particular time?"

"No—I'll call you, but she's got a machine. Sally's an actress and we have the same agent. We're always checking for calls."

"How the hell are we ever going to see each other?"

"We'll find a way, Vinny—I promise."

"I'll hold you to it."

"I'll call you tomorrow. Soon as I get back here. Same time."

"I'll be next to the phone."

I heard her blow me a kiss and say, "Night. Love you."

I stared at the phone a few seconds. She'd uttered the *love* word, but hung up before I could respond. I put down the phone, realizing if she'd wanted me to respond, she wouldn't have hung up so quickly. Now I was torn between two emotions. I was ecstatic over hearing from her, and miserable over having no way to see her.

I sighed. Back to *Finnegans Wake*.

The following day moved like molasses in Siberia. For the first time since I'd gotten my wings, even flying didn't help.

My attitude around the squadron ready room reflected my misery, and even Concannon noticed it. "Are you sick, Vesta?"

"Nosir."

"Well, you looked better when you got back from the coast—and then you were really lookin' like shit."

"I'm fine, sir. Maybe something I ate."

"Looks more like something ate you, mister." He stalked off not realizing how close to the truth he was.

After the first launch of the day and the debriefing, Doug and I went to the O club for lunch. It was a beautiful October day—billowing clouds, azure sky, and a magnolia-scented breeze drifting across the patio. Doug commented on the idyllic scene, and I grunted an indifferent assent as I picked up a menu.

Never one to mince words, he said, "How long are you going to let that torch keep scorchin' your ass?"

"I wasn't aware of a torch."

"Any bigger and it'd be a bonfire."

"What's your point?"

"You're behaving like a lovesick schmuck!"

"Where the hell'd you get *that* word?"

"Don't dodge the question."

I threw up my hands in frustration. "What do you want me to do? Admit I'm in love and can't figure out a way to handle it? Fine. I admit it. Are you happy now?"

"I'm not looking to be happy. I'm looking for a way to make *you* happy."

"Fine. Figure out a way for me to go West or for her to come East."

"There is no way."

"Exactly. So let's order."

I signaled a waiter, we gave him our order, and we spent the next hour discussing the relative merits of guns versus missiles in a dogfight.

That night Doug had a date and I stayed home waiting for Kat's call. Jessie grilled steaks and I asked her and Jess to join me for dinner on the patio. Jess and Jessie were products of the Old South, and even though Martin Luther King had begun his assault on bigotry, Jim Crow was still alive in their hearts.

Jess said, "It don't seem fittin'."

I said, "I don't give a shit."

I won. We ate.

After dinner I paced, took a walk, took a swim, took the Chris-Craft out for a spin, and finally took another shot at Joyce. He hadn't gotten any simpler. The hours crawled by with every one seeming to be twice as long as the last. Finally, at eleven the phone rang.

I snatched it out of the cradle before the first ring ended. "Hello," I gushed.

"Are you all right?" she asked.

I smiled. "Fine now."

"Well, you're about to be better than fine—"

"Wait, there's something I need to say first: I love you." I waited several seconds for a response—got none, and finally said, "Kat?"

"I'm here . . . I just choked up . . . terribly unlike me, huh?"

It certainly was but I loved it. "You hung up before I got a chance to tell you last night."

"Premeditated girl stuff. The hoped-for response was 'I love you, too,' but I didn't want to put you on the spot before you had a chance to think about it."

"I have—since our second night together."

"La Jolla."

"Christ! What the hell are we going to do?"

I felt her mood brighten as she said, "We're going to see each other."

"How? We're stuck on opposite coasts!"

"Not for long, my love! My agent got me a perfume commercial for Chanel—huge! It's for Christmas and it's shooting in New York. It'll get me back to the East Coast!"

"Great, but I'm not sure I can get to New York."

"How about Sea Island?"

Sea Island was just north of the Florida/Georgia border, about an hour north of Jacksonville, and famous for its world-class resort, The Cloister. I'd visited it a couple of times, but at the moment I didn't see what the island had to do with Kat and me.

"Huh?" I responded stupidly.

"I'll meet you there next weekend."

That made no sense at all. "Your father's letting you go to New York and Sea Island after kidnapping you and keeping you in Mexico for over three weeks?"

"Daddy has two problems. One—he can't get me bounced out of the commercial in New York because the director and the company are French, so he has no political pull. And two—he wants his daughter to be a star. He's dedicated his whole damn life to it. I told him if that's what he really wants, he'd damn well better not make me pass up this kind of exposure."

"When do you leave?"

"Tomorrow. We rehearse Thursday and shoot Friday. We're off Saturday and Sunday, and then shoot again Monday and Tuesday. We'll be staying at The Madison."

"I still can't believe he's letting you go off alone like that."

"Oh, he's not. He's sending a minder with me. But Daddy's had me followed before, and it doesn't take me long to spot who it is. I'm taking Sally with me and we'll figure out a way to duck him on Saturday morning. She looks enough like me to pull a switch. While he's watching her, I'll be on my way to you."

"This sounds like something out of a spy novel."

"Doesn't it though? But I'm an actress and I love it, especially since it gets me to you."

"What am I going to do, say no?" I laughed. "But your tail won't be fooled for long. As soon as he realizes there's suddenly only one of you, he'll confront Sally, and you'll be busted. You disappear again and Daddy's gonna have a conniption."

"Let him. By then we'll be at The Cloister on Sea Island. I'll lease a plane and fly in by noon Saturday. The reservation's under Sally Richards. Don't be late, darling."

"Not a chance." I laughed again. "I'll pick you up at the airport."

Kat sighed. "Two whole days together. I'll think of nothing else until Saturday."

CHAPTER THIRTEEN

DOUG NOTICED the change in my demeanor over breakfast the next day. The whole household was delighted with the
reason. Doug said that he just couldn't get enough of my smiling
face and asked if he could come along for the weekend.

I asked him if he'd like a broken jaw.

That afternoon, we flew two training missions with Whitey and Zaz
and at five o'clock stopped by the club for happy hour to buy them a
drink. The place was jammed with the usual suspects, and before long
Doug was zeroed in on a University of Florida coed who was probably
lying about her age.

The Jacksonville Naval Air Station was conveniently located about
an hour north of Gainesville, and the coeds were more than familiar
with the route. They were equally familiar with who and what was
waiting for them at happy hour. It made for a rather nice arrangement
on both sides. I, however, was thinking about what would be waiting
for me at The Cloister, so I bade the revelers farewell and left.

When I got home, however, I was hit with another surprise. This one in the form of Angelo and Stuff. Neither father nor son ever seemed to change. Stuff was a squat five foot five—his father an inch taller. Angelo, at fifty-seven, was thirty-one years older than his twenty-six-year-old son but could easily be taken for an older brother. Both were a pair of 250-pound fireplugs with heads.

They'd rented a car at the airport and were sitting on the patio drinking gin and tonics. They were both dressed in suits, and both had loosened their ties and removed their jackets.

After I got over my initial surprise and we exchanged hugs, Angelo ran a handkerchief around the inside of his shirt collar and said, "Christ, kid—is it always this hot?"

"No. Sometimes it snows in winter."

That amazed him. "No shit?"

"No shit."

Angelo shook his head and pointed to a tray of chips and dip. There was also a liquor trolley with glasses, mixers, and ice that Jess had rolled out to the patio.

"That Jessie lady and 'er husband are real sweethearts," he said. "I called and said we were flyin' down and she remembered me from callin' before."

"They're our secret weapons," I said, still wondering what had brought them.

Angelo indicated the liquor trolley, "You want a drink?"

They obviously hadn't flown down for the waters, so I asked, "Do I need one?"

"Probably."

I glanced at Stuff. He nodded in agreement. "Scotch," I said, and sat down while he poured me a hefty one. He handed me the drink and I looked at Angelo. "What's up?"

"That guy you wanted checked out—Pennington? I got the rest of the rundown."

"And?"

"Like I said, he's big-time. Big lawyer. Big money. Big political connections."

"You didn't come all the way down here to repeat that."

Angelo shook his head. "No. I said he had connections. He does. What I didn't say is he's also connected."

That could only mean one thing and I raised a questioning eyebrow.

Angelo nodded. "Jack Dragna."

I knew the name. "The L.A. capo."

"The same. Pennington's his lawyer."

That came as another surprise but I wasn't too concerned. "So what? From everything I've heard all my life, L.A.'s a Mickey Mouse Mob."

"It is," said Angelo. "And it's in a Mickey Mouse town. But Dragna's in tight with Chicago. Tony Accardo and Johnny Roselli. And they *ain't* Mickey Mouse."

Ten years prior, when Bugsy Siegel got whacked, Chicago took over the unions and the studio shakedowns, and Tony Accardo had put Johnny Roselli in charge.

"Christ," I said. "But, Jesus, Angelo, isn't that what lawyers do—represent clients?"

"This client is Jack Dragna—a shakedown artist controlled by Accardo and Roselli, and my information is that your girl's old man's involved."

"He's bent?"

"Like a corkscrew. But that ain't all. He not only represents Dragna. He also represents the Desert Inn."

"Vegas?"

Angelo nodded. "As in Moe Dalitz."

I'd read that early in his life, Dalitz was a bootlegger and racketeer mentioned in the same breath as Meyer Lansky and Benjamin "Bugsy" Siegel. In Cleveland, one longtime member of law enforcement would tell the Senate's Kefauver Crime Commission, "Ruthless beatings, unsolved murders and shakedowns, threats and bribery, came to this community as a result of this gangster's rise to power." Dalitz was considered part of that rise, and back in 1950 he had purchased the still unfinished Desert Inn.

Angelo continued, "The word is that Dalitz is puttin' together a syndicate ta buy The Stardust from Jake 'the Barber' Factor. And he's usin' Teamsters' pension-fund money. That means Jimmy Hoffa."

Angelo paused and I took a slug out of my drink.

"Four months ago," Angelo continued, "Pennington applied for a license from the Nevada Gamin' Commission. There's no doubt he's gonna be the president of the syndicate, which means he'll be the front man in The Stardust for the Chicago Mob."

"Christ!" I said again, and finished my drink.

Stuff said, ticking off each player's name with his fingers, "Your girlfriend's old man is in tight with Accardo, Roselli, Dalitz, Factor, and Hoffa."

"You're talkin' a world a hurt," Angelo said, "if you're thinkin' of crossin' assholes with that bunch."

Stuff picked up a chip, scooped it through the dip, and said, "You latched onto a time bomb in a skirt, ol' buddy."

"How?" I exploded. "She's a first-class act! College. Country clubs. Beverly Hills. I can't believe this!"

Angelo said, "This ain't about her, it's about her old man."

"I know, but it still doesn't make sense. She never mentioned it—and she had to know."

Stuff said, "Maybe she didn't wanna scare you away."

Dismissing the thought, I waved him off.

Angelo said, "So how deep are ya with this chick?"

"Up to my neck. I love her."

"Wonderful," said Angelo. "So what we got is, you two in love—her old man in hate—and the Chicago Mob in the wings."

"That about says it."

Angelo shook his head. "You're not up to yer neck, Vincenzo, you're over your head. These guys can be serious heat, and my arm's gonna have a rough time stretchin' all the way out to the West Coast to cover your ass."

I threw up my hands in frustration, went over to the trolley, and poured myself another hefty Scotch. I threw it down with my back to them, then turned. "I'm seeing her next weekend."

I saw Angelo's eyes narrow in confusion. "How? I thought she was in L.A."

I shook my head. "She's in New York. And Saturday she'll be on Sea Island, about an hour north of here. I'm meeting her there."

"I'm not even gonna ask if her old man knows."

"Don't. He doesn't."

Angelo glanced at Stuff and again shook his head. "I want ya to think about this thing real good, Vincenzo. It's the reason I flew down here in person. Her old man's got big-time connections—political and Mob. He was wacky enough to snatch his own daughter. And then he's cocky enough to follow it up with a threat if ya try to see her. He's a serious asshole who's got a hard-on fer you and the juice to back it up. Drop it."

"I've got to see her, Angelo."

"Think, Vincenzo, this is a girl you just met. Like I said, I don't know if I can have yer back all the way out there on the coast. With Anastasia tryin' to muscle in on Cuba, and Genovese takin' over from Costello, I'm up to my ass in alligators in New York and this girl could be paintin' a bull's-eye between yer tits. Is she worth it?"

I paused. He was right about the facts. We'd only just met and I already knew it was a geographically impossible relationship that included her past and a controlling father. And now I'd been told there was far more to Marion Pennington than just a controlling father. He could be a serious threat. But there was only one answer and I gave it as simply as possible:

"I love her, Angelo."

Angelo lowered his head and shook it, then looked back up and put up his hands in surrender. "You asked fer my help and advice. I gave it. It's all I can do. I wish I could do more."

"Maybe you can."

"How?"

I'd been thinking about it since the call from Kat. "See if you can keep an eye on her while she's in New York. She'll be staying at The Madison with a Sally Richards."

"You want I should put a tail on her?"

"Yeah, but she'll already have one from her father, so make sure our guy isn't spotted by him."

"I'll put Gus Chello on it. He's a walkin' ghost. You want her to know?"

I nodded. I knew Gus. He'd also worked for my father and was as reliable as sunrise. "I'll tell her she'll get a call from Gus, and if she needs any help to let him know."

"Ya got it."

"Great. When do you head back?" I asked.

"Now."

"You can't even stay for dinner?" I asked.

"We'll grab sangwiches on the way to the airport. There's a seven-o'clock plane. We done all we could here and we gotta get back." Angelo put out his hand. "See ya, kid."

Stuff gave me a hug. "Watch your ass, Vinny. I don't like you out there alone."

"I'm not exactly alone, Stuff. I'm in a Navy fighter squadron."

"Yeah, and those guys may be great in the air, but how are they on the street? Because that's where the action's gonna be."

CHAPTER FOURTEEN

KAT'S FIRST CALL from New York was proof that Stuff had reason to be concerned.

Her father had sent *two* minders, and neither was part of the threesome that had abducted her in Jacksonville. One worked days, the other worked nights. She described them as a pair of shadows right out of central casting. The day guy was in his thirties, medium height, buff, and well dressed in suit and tie, whom she'd named Frick. The night guy was older but bigger and looked tougher—over six feet, two-hundred-plus pounds. A sport-coat-and-open-collar guy. She'd named him Frack.

The humor escaped me. I told her if they were working for her father, I was sure they were competent.

She told me not to worry—she and Sally had a plan. Plus, she'd already heard from Gus and had a phone number if she wanted to reach him. She admitted, though, that as hard as she'd tried, she couldn't spot him. I told her not to waste her energy. Gus would be invisible sitting at a table for one.

As it turned out, Kat said the minders didn't really bother them at all. One or the other always remained in the background—about twenty or thirty yards behind on the street, always a few tables away at a restaurant, and just off the fringe of the set while they were shooting. The duo had had little trouble bribing the French production manager for permission to observe the shoot, and less trouble bribing hotel security to let one of them watch from a room across the hall at night. But they'd taken no real pains to hide that they were tails. Kat said it seemed as if they wanted Sally and her to know they were there.

Probably Daddy's idea of intimidation, I told her.

Their escape plan was simple: establish a rigid routine and then change it on the last day. For three days Kat and Sally got up at seven and dashed off to an early breakfast at a small restaurant a block from the hotel. When they left their room, Frack would exit his and follow them to the elevator. He never spoke. And neither did the girls. Then, once they left the hotel and entered the restaurant, Frack was relieved by Frick, who would enter and sit at a table across the room.

When they ordered breakfast, Kat would get up and go to the ladies' room. Two minutes later, Sally would do the same. A few minutes after that Kat would return to the table, followed by Sally shortly thereafter. For three days they followed the same pattern before heading off to a day of filming at the studio.

On Saturday they sprang the trap.

That morning, since they weren't working, they dressed like tourists out for a day of sightseeing. In spite of feeling ridiculous, Kat wore a bright yellow skirt and blouse combo, and Sally wore one in bright blue. Both slung matching sweaters over their backs, with the arms tied in front. They both tucked their hair under baseball caps. New York Yankees for Kat, Boston Red Sox for Sally. And finally, Kat wore Converse sneakers and Sally wore Keds.

Before leaving the hotel, they paused at the concierge desk and asked for flyers to city landmarks. As she exited through the revolving door, Kat glanced over her shoulder and saw Frick talking to the concierge.

Perfect.

The girls entered the restaurant and ordered breakfast. A minute later Frick came in—he sat across the room, ordered coffee and a Danish, and opened the New York *Daily News*.

While they waited for their order, Kat got up and left for the ladies' room. Sally slowly counted to thirty and followed her.

Kat was already in her bra and panties when Sally entered—she tore off her clothes and within minutes the girls had completed the switch.

Sally left the ladies' room wearing Kat's bright yellow ensemble and Converse sneakers with her hair tucked under a Yankees baseball cap. She was a dead ringer for Kat as she crossed back to their table, sat down, and began studying the Circle Line flyer.

Frick glanced up, then went back to reading the sports page.

Meanwhile Kat ducked out of the ladies' room and into the kitchen, where she gave the Puerto Rican chef the second half of a fifty-dollar bill she'd torn in half the prior morning. The bribe was payment for his promise to let her exit through the back door and into the alley. She gave him a quick peck on the cheek, reminded him that he never saw her, and flew out the door.

Sally watched as Frick slowly realized that only one girl had returned to the table, and when he tore off into the ladies' room, she exited the front door.

Stuff picked Sally up the second she left the restaurant and drove her to Grand Central Station, where she paid cash for a ticket to Chicago before changing trains to L.A.

Kat was picked up in the alley by Gus Chello, who drove her across the river to Teterboro Airport in New Jersey. She chartered a Cessna 310—a six-seat, light twin—paid for it in cash, then settled down for the four-hour flight to Sea Island.

I was sure Frick and Frack would try tracking them down by canvassing cabs, airlines, trains, and bus stations and trying to trace credit-card payments. But their efforts would all be in vain.

It was nice to have friends.

It helped to be rich.

Sleep on Friday night had avoided me like a long shot at Belmont. I finally rose before the roosters, went down to the kitchen, and started preparing a pepper-and-eggs breakfast.

Jessie, whose room with Jess was off the kitchen, had the nose of a bloodhound. She got a whiff of cherry peppers frying in olive oil and came to see who had invaded her domain. She entered wearing a robe and a scowl.

"Whatchu doin', Mistah Vinny?" she asked testily.

I twirled the spatula around, gave her a wink, and stated the obvious. "Making breakfast."

She harrumphed. "You figurin' on firin' ol' Jessie without notice?"

"No. But it's so early, I—"

She snatched the spatula out of my hand. "Tell you what. Ah won't try flyin' if you don't try fryin'. Fair enough?"

I held up my hands in surrender. "Won't happen again."

Jessie stirred the peppers with one hand while she expertly cracked eggs into a bowl with the other. "You been happy, then mis'able, then sleepless, then *cookin'*! That gal's got you spinnin' circles. Thank the Lord y'all be together soon."

Jess came in wearing an old terry-cloth robe and floppy slippers—obviously awakened by the predawn activity. The paisley hair cap he slept in was still covering his head, and he was wiping the sleep out of his eyes with the back of his fist. He squinted blearily. "Anythin' wrong?"

I burst out laughing. "Not a thing, Jess. God's in his heaven, Jessie's in her kitchen, and I'm on my way to paradise. Let's all have breakfast!"

*   *   *

An hour later I tossed an overnight bag and shaving kit into the back of my Pontiac and lowered the top. I donned my aviator glasses, lit a Lucky, and checked my image in the rearview mirror. I was going to be several hours early, but I wanted to scope out the town before Kat arrived. She'd be arriving sans luggage, which meant we were going to have to buy her a weekend wardrobe before checking into the hotel.

Sea Island was snuggled up close to St. Simons Island, which was adjacent to Brunswick, Georgia, on I-95. I took the exit onto a causeway that connected all three and headed across the salt marshes. The airport where Kat would be landing was on St. Simons, so I headed there first to check out the town. After a quick survey of the shops I drove over to Sea Island.

The entire area was a natural resort with moss-draped oaks, shady lanes, and creek-fed pockets of marshland teeming with life. The early-October day answered a chamber-of-commerce prayer, featuring cloudless skies, temperatures in the midseventies, and not a hint of humidity. Surrounded by beauty, with the wind in my face and the smell of the sea in the air, I was in paradise.

At eleven thirty I drove back to St. Simons and parked at the airport's admin/tower building, where I checked out every light aircraft that taxied in. At 12:05—damn near dead on time—a Cessna 310 landed.

I walked out to the ramp and spotted Kat in the copilot's seat, waving ecstatically before the airplane came to a stop. When it did, she threw open the door, climbed out on the wing, and literally leapt down into my arms.

I twirled her around a few times, her auburn hair catching the sun. "God, I've missed you."

"We're about to change that, darling."

"You look fabulous."

"Of course! I'm the new Chanel girl!"

I put my arm around her and led her to the car. "How did the 'superspy' bit go?"

She laughed. "I may have a whole new career."

"Sally okay?"

"Should be halfway to Chicago by now."

I opened the passenger door. "Cute outfit."

"Frick is probably still trying to explain to Frack exactly how cute!"

Rounding the rear of the car to get to the driver's side, I asked, "So exactly how much time do we have together?"

"I told the pilot I'd meet him at six P.M. tomorrow. It's about four hours back to Teterboro. That way I'll be back at the hotel before midnight for my beauty sleep so I can be fresh as a daisy for my eight-o'clock call on Monday morning."

I got behind the wheel and she tucked herself under my right arm, resting her hand on my upper thigh. "Mmmmm . . .," she said.

"Keep it up and you'll get us busted for indecent exposure—either that or for a vicious rear-ender."

"It might be worth it."

"Only if you want to forfeit a shopping spree on the local Fifth Avenue."

"Bloomingdale's?"

"Molly's Smock Shop."

She chuckled. "Somehow I don't foresee the need for a lot of inner—or outer—wear."

We parked near the lighthouse in Pier Village and strolled down the island's historic center past shops, boutiques, and restaurants. Many were typical tourist traps, but we easily found slacks, blouses, bathing suits, and toiletries before driving to The Cloister.

Kat checked us in under Sally and Vincent Richards and got a cocked eyebrow from the clerk when I paid cash and handed the bellhop a couple of shopping bags but no luggage. He hung my overnight bag on his cart and we followed him to an oceanfront suite with a patio leading to the beach.

The bellhop attempted the standard spiel about the suite's amenities, but I quickly slapped a ten-dollar bill into his hand—his mouth was still moving when I eased him out the door and closed it.

Kat met me as I crossed back into the room and we toppled onto the king-size bed, stripping each other on the way down. I felt myself straddled and immediately slid into her, clasping her hands and helping her rock ever faster until she cried out. I exploded, and she collapsed on my chest.

She caught her breath several seconds later and chortled, "Timing is everything."

"Ain't it the truth?"

We lay there panting in silence for a while until she said, "Stop time, Vinny. Right now. Stop it."

I caressed the back of her head. "Consider it stopped. It doesn't start again until tomorrow at six."

She lifted up until we were nose to nose. "Are you up for a swim?"

"Poor choice of words, but absolutely."

"Point taken. I don't suppose we could go nude?"

"We could, but then we'd probably be asked to go."

She bit my ear. "Let's not give them the option. Suits on!"

A minute later we ran across the beach hand in hand and plunged into the ocean. In midsummer the water temperature could get as high as eighty-two, but in early October it was hovering around seventy-four.

We swam out a hundred yards but were still only up to our shoulders. I thought a saltwater repeat of our original pool scenario might be exciting, but enough guests were on the beach to thwart the plan, so we swam back.

Toweling off, we settled on to a padded double chaise on the patio. The strains of Patti Page warbling "Old Cape Cod" came from a radio in the adjacent suite and I shook out a Lucky. I offered it to her, she declined, and I lit up, watching dolphins cavort not far from where we'd been swimming. It was almost two o'clock.

"Hungry?" I asked.

"I've already feasted." She curled up next to me and nuzzled my neck.

"Dare I ask if you're thirsty?"

"Only at the risk of having your bodily fluids drained."

"Cheeky little tart, aren't you?"

"You bring out the worst in me—which turns out to be the best."

She got up, taking my hand, and I followed her back into the bedroom, where we spent the rest of the afternoon until too little food and too much passion left us famished.

At six we were getting up to shower and dress for dinner when the phone rang. Kat went into the bathroom and I picked it up. It was Doug.

"Hi, sport, how goes the action?"

"First and goal in a high-scoring game."

"Happy days are here again?"

"In spades."

"Congratulations. But I thought you ought to know that two out-of-towners just came looking for you. They weren't fans."

I could hear the telltale sounds of the weekend follies in the background—a raucous mixture of music and laughter. Doug spoke over the din, saying, "Jess held them at bay outside the door and sent Jessie to get me."

Uh-oh, I thought. "Describe them."

"One was in his midthirties—a weight lifter in a suit. The other was bigger. I'd say midforties—boxer's nose, in a sport coat."

"Frick and Frack."

"Who?"

"The guys who tailed Kat to New York. She named them Frick and Frack."

"Cute. They introduced themselves as Smith and Jones."

"Masters of disguise. What'd they want?"

"They wanted you. When I told them you weren't here, they wanted to know where you were. I told them for all I knew you could be in Bangkok. That pissed them off and they got belligerent. So I invited them in. They got a sobering look at fifteen fighter pilots who didn't want their party crashed and readjusted their attitude. Then I told them to get the fuck out of my face."

"Nice," I said. "Always a foolproof way to make new friends."

"My feelings exactly—but they left anyway."

"Thanks for the heads-up."

"Don't mention it, but I have a feeling they'll probably hang around until you get back."

"I have a hunch you're right—I'll be checking my six. Go back to the party. It sounds like you're missing a helluva good time."

"Anything for a friend."

"Later." I hung up.

I decided not to tell Kat about the phone call. There wasn't anything either of us could do anyway. I'd just tell her the call was Doug saying he missed us.

After my turn in the shower, we dressed and had a seafood banquet in the dining room, followed by a moonlit walk on the beach. Completely exhausted, we fell asleep in each other's arms and didn't wake up until a red fireball slid over the horizon and lit up the bedroom.

CHAPTER FIFTEEN

SUNDAY BEGAN WITH a swim and Ramos gin fizzes for old times' sake—all of five weeks of it. After breakfast we took a walk under a green canopy of stately trees dripping with Spanish moss and made love under a massive live oak that was already ancient when Sherman marched through Georgia.

Lunch and the afternoon arrived much too soon. We took a final swim, showered, and settled onto the patio chaise, drinking up the sun and ignoring the clock. By four o'clock, an empty bottle of sauvignon blanc was nestled upside down in an ice bucket, so I ordered another. We lay there with our eyes closed listening to the surf and the wheeling seagulls until I finally brought up some of the things that had been bothering me.

"I have to ask you a question, Kat."

"Mmm-huum," she said dreamily.

"How much do you know about your father's clients?"

"The usual I suppose. I grew up around a lot of them after Mom died and before I went off to boarding school and college."

"Did you learn anything more when you got back and your father got you into acting?"

"A lot. As I told you, he's an influential show-business lawyer who hobnobs with stars, politicians, movers and shakers. Daddy seems to know everybody, and everybody knows him. Why do you ask?"

"Because he also has some clients who are known criminals."

"Isn't that what lawyers are for?"

"It is, unless you become part of their business."

She rose up on her elbow and turned to me. "What are you saying?"

"Kat, I got suspicious when your father somehow had us traced in Coronado and La Jolla—and then had the balls to have you kidnapped in Jacksonville and sequestered in Mexico. When one of his minions warned me not to try and contact you, I had some friends of mine check him out. He's got very long tentacles, and all of them aren't very kosher."

"And you think *he's* not." It wasn't a question.

"From what I've been told? No."

She slowly shook her head, pulled her knees up to her chest, and stared out across the water.

She was about to respond when there was a knock at the door. I answered it, admitting a waiter carrying our second bottle of wine.

Kat had meanwhile got up and was sitting at the umbrella table combing out her hair. The wind had come up and her hair fanned out behind her like silk.

I poured two glasses of wine, sat, and stared at her. "Did you know?" I asked.

She put down her brush, sipped her wine. "No, but I suppose I've suspected something ever since I got back from college—more by innuendo than anything else. Often I would see shady-looking types coming out of his den. If they were clients, I thought, why weren't they seeing him in his office? Several times I noticed the reaction of people working for him when his temper flared—fear. You could almost smell it. Once while we were having dinner, three men arrived unannounced. One was in his sixties and had a gruff Italian accent. The other two were young toughs—obviously bodyguards."

Probably Jack Dragna and some muscle, I thought, but didn't mention it.

"When they left, I asked Daddy about them, but he was unusually evasive and seemed upset. I didn't pursue it."

"Did you ever hear the names Accardo or Roselli?"

She thought about it a few seconds, then slowly shook her head. "No, I don't think so. Who are they?"

"The Chicago Mob. Heavy into studio shakedowns and union control."

"And you think my father's part of it?"

"I do. The same men are the power and the money behind a syndicate that's buying a Las Vegas casino. Your father's negotiating the deal and he's applied for a gaming license. The rumor is that he'll be the syndicate's president, which means that he'll be the Mob's front man at The Stardust."

She studied me a few moments, then narrowed her eyes. "Because 'your friends' who 'checked him out' said so."

"Yes."

"That couldn't have been easy, Vinny. Who are they? These 'friends'? FBI? CIA?" She paused. "Or perhaps an organization equally powerful? I'm a smart girl, Vinny, and you're a Sicilian who was born and brought up in Hell's Kitchen. Not exactly the Bel Air of New York. Before I left your house the morning I was kidnapped, Jessie told me that your father had been killed seven years ago—shot. And now you tell me that you're able to uncover the shady affairs of one of the most prominent lawyers in Los Angeles." An ironic half-smile crossed her face, and she cocked her head to one side as if to ask, *Any questions?*

I shook out a Lucky and lit it. "You're right, Kat. The information came from friends in the New York Mob. My father was part of it, and seven years ago, so was I. But I left, went to college, and joined the Navy. I haven't been a part of it since. That's it. I'm sorry. I should have told you. Eventually I would have, but honestly we've had so little time together there never really seemed to be an opportunity."

She shook her head and reached over to touch my hand. The late-afternoon sun made the beach glow, and it lit her face more beautifully than the best of Hollywood's cinematographers.

"It doesn't matter," she whispered.

I hadn't expected that. "What?"

"It doesn't matter. I love you, Vinny. And I don't care about *anything* in the past. Not about you, not about me, and not about my father. I suppose I should be shocked or mortified about what he's into, but right now I really don't care—about his connections or about his aspirations for me."

"I hear you, but why?"

"You. Before I met you, I really thought I wanted everything Daddy was trying to set up. I even put up with Vic Marino because of what it could do for my career. But now I'm not even sure I want to go back."

I was shocked. "To New York?"

She shook her head. "To L.A."

Now I was incredulous. "You're kidding."

She shook her head. "All during the shoot in New York I should have been ecstatic. I wasn't. I saw the rushes, I was fabulous and I knew it. This really could be the big break I've been waiting for. But somehow I wasn't into it—all I kept thinking about was you."

"Christ, Kat, you'd give all that up?"

"As of now I could care less about the business, L.A., and my father's craziness. I just want to be with you."

I realized that I wanted that as much as she did and was really trying to be happy, but I couldn't ignore the truth—especially after Doug's phone call.

"He won't let you go," I said.

"He'll have to when he realizes it's hopeless."

"I'm not sure, Kat—he's a very determined man with big-time connections."

"All of which he used to further my career. And I went along with it because I wanted to be a star. But now I don't care. I don't want it. He can't hold his power over my head to keep me in line anymore. Don't you see? I'm free."

"Kat, face it. He'll come after you."

"Do you love me?"

"Of course! And I want to marry you!" I shouted before I could stop myself. "I just don't see how the hell it can work."

Kat suddenly laughed and smiled ear to ear. "Should I take that as a proposal?"

I laughed, too. "Yes! You want me on one knee?"

"No, but are you sure?"

"As sure as I'll ever be." Then I added, "But I'm still in the Navy, and you've already been through that once."

Her face lost a bit of its glow. "I know, and it didn't work out very well," she said sadly, but then she smiled again. "But I can't picture you as a civilian."

"Neither can I. It's never entered my mind as even a remote possibility. But if it ever came to a choice between you and the Navy, the Navy's in trouble."

"Do you mean that?"

"I can't let you go, Kat."

Her eyes welled up. "I'd never ask—besides, I'm an experienced Navy wife. I know what to expect."

"You really think you can be a Navy wife again? In three months I'll be on a Mediterranean cruise."

She shrugged weakly. "Whatever it takes."

I got up, lifted her out of her chair, spun her around, and laughed. "I adore you, you know that?"

She teared up and buried her face in my neck. "Oh, Vinny, I can't believe this is really happening to us."

"I don't think anyone else will either." I put her down. "But let's get married over the holidays before I deploy. We can honeymoon in Europe. The ship will have ports of call all over the Mediterranean—Villefranche, Naples, Taormina. You can fly in and meet me at every stop. We'll tour Europe on liberty weekends!"

"They'll be very short tours."

"Not really—because there won't be any travel time involved. We'll already be in the city we're touring."

"Let's do it, darling!" Her words came tumbling out in a rush. "I've got a bunch of things to clean up in L.A., and I'm teaching an acting class at Cal State until the Christmas break. But I'll fly into Jacksonville for the weekends."

"Done." I was soaring. I picked up my glass and held it out. "And now I'd like to toast to the future Mrs. Vesta."

We touched glasses, drank, and she said, "And I'd like to celebrate by taking my future husband to bed one more time before the six-o'clock plane."

She did, and just as we were about to rush back to the airport, the phone rang. It was Doug again.

"You headed back this way anytime soon?"

"Yeah. I should be back by seven thirty. Why?"

"Because when Whitey and Zaz were whisked off by a pair of horny coeds, they spotted the two clowns who tried to crash our party. They're in a car parked down the road. I'm amazed those two overheated nuggets could've noticed anything the way they were being pawed, but they called me when they got back to the BOQ. It's gotta be the same two guys."

"Okay—get everyone out of there. When I show up, I'll let them think I haven't spotted them and I'm sure they'll follow me in."

"And then what?"

"First we'll see what they have to say—and then I'll give them a message to bring back to their boss."

Dusk was rapidly approaching as we drove to the airport, the hum of crickets replacing the sound of seabirds. A warm breeze swayed the cascades of Spanish moss as I drove under a tunnel of oaks with one arm around Kat. Neither of us said anything.

It had all been said.

Her pilot was waiting on the airport ramp next to the 310 as we pulled up and got out. I took her hand and she put her head on my shoulder as I led her toward the airplane. The acrid smell of oil and fuel was wafting up from the concrete, mixing with the subtle perfume of her skin.

I gave her one last hug and she whispered, "I love you. I'll call when I get to the hotel."

"Jax—next week?"

"Cecil B. DeMille couldn't keep me away."

The roar of the 310's engines starting up kept me from answering, and she blew a final kiss as they taxied out. I watched the plane take off into the setting sun and walked back to my car humming quietly to myself. I saw them turn north for New York, and I headed back across the salt marshes and south to Jacksonville.

CHAPTER SIXTEEN

WHEN I GOT BACK to Jax it was dark and the night air had turned chilly, but I left the convertible top down. I wanted Daddy's hired help to see me clearly when I passed their car. They did. They were parked a hundred yards from the driveway, and after I pulled in, I hurried into the house, knowing they wouldn't be far behind. I told Jess to let them in as soon as they arrived and to bring them back to the sunroom.

Doug was already waiting there when I entered. "The fearless lover returns," he said. "You're glowing."

"We got a lot of sun."

"Sure you did," he smirked. "We gonna have company?"

"On the way."

A few seconds later we heard the bells chime. The sound of Jess answering the door was followed by the clicking of footsteps in the hall.

I sat back in the window seat and tried my best to look like the relaxed master of the manor awaiting supplicants.

Doug settled into a wicker chair facing the door and perched his right ankle atop his left knee. He blew a perennial shock of unruly hair out of his eye and began strumming his fingers on his shoe.

Frick entered first, followed by Frack, who leaned against the door-jamb, "guarding the entry." Both were pretty much as Kat and Doug had described them—Frick was wide in the shoulders, slim in the waist, and wore a suit. His hair, a brown brush cut, topped a face that might have been handsome if it weren't for what looked like a permanent sneer. Frack was a fortyish Rocky Marciano double with a fleshy face, flattened nose, deep chest, and wearing a sport coat. Formidable.

Frick cast his eyes around the room dismissively, then let his gaze settle on me. "Pretty fancy digs for a swabbie."

"You should see the main house."

"Cute." He glanced over at Doug and back to me. "You know why we're here." It was a statement, not a question.

"And who might *we* be?" I asked.

"That's not important. Who we're from is."

"So far I'm not impressed."

He scornfully raked me with his eyes. "Then you're makin' another mistake, swabbie. So far you've made two. There won't be a shot at three."

I kept up my smart-ass routine, thinking if I got him to lose it, he might say something he shouldn't. "Lemme ask you a question," I said. "How much do they pay inept assholes like you?"

His face reddened. "Don't piss me off, swabbie. It's unhealthy."

"I'm quaking in my shorts."

"You should be, but you're too stupid to realize the shit you're in."

"Very observant." I turned to Doug, pointed at Frick. "He's very observant."

"Okay, wiseass, here's how it is—straight and simple. Mr. Pennington don't want you talking to, seeing, or being anywhere near his daughter. Period. You don't get another warning."

"Or what?" I asked.

"Or you may get shipped to an iceberg to clean up penguin shit."

"The Navy doesn't own any icebergs."

"We'll buy them one."

"Who will? You? The guys who are so fucking incompetent they can't even tail two twenty-four-year-old girls?"

He tensed and his hands became fists. I kept going. "Now that's embarrassing. How are you going to explain that one to Pennington—asshole?"

That did it. His face turned red and he exploded. "Asshole? I'll show you who's an asshole!" He whipped out a .38, cocked it, and pointed it straight at the center of my forehead.

Doug sprang out of his chair, but Frack quickly stepped into the room and trained an automatic on him. Frack blurted out, "Easy, Spig, he wants 'em warned, not whacked!"

Spig's eyes were blazing furiously, and his hand was trembling. For a moment I thought I might have gone too far.

Then I heard Jess's voice. It was as calm and soothing as a lullaby. "You'd best be puttin' up that gun, mistah, or I 'spect I might have to blow the top of yo haid off."

Jess stood behind Frack and rested the barrel of a shotgun against the back of his neck. It was angled up toward the ceiling and would actually have blown off the top of the man's head if Jess had pulled the trigger.

Spig spun around and screamed, "Godammit, Paulie, I told you to watch the door!"

Doug laughed. "You boys are having one *helluva* bad day!"

Jess cooed, "Now you jes' go ahead and put up those shootin' irons, boys." He winked. "The hee-ro says that in all the westerns."

Both men bristled, but lowered their guns and put them away. Spig was struggling to control himself. He stared at me and hissed, "You know what, swabbie? I sincerely hope you don't take the warning. 'Cause then I promise, no—I *guarantee*—we'll meet again."

"Looking forward to it, *Spig*," I said, wanting him to know I'd registered both their names. "And it was a pleasure meeting you, too, *Paulie*. Now please do me a favor and take a message back to Daddy Pennington. Tell him I don't scare easily and I don't give a shit what he wants. As long as his daughter wants to see me, I'll be more than happy to oblige. Clear?"

I waited and got no answer. "You want me to repeat it?" He still didn't answer. "Stop by anytime."

Doug crossed the room and got nose to nose with Spig. "But for now—like I said yesterday—'Get the fuck out of my face.'"

I watched Spig take a frustrated breath, then spin around and stomp out. Paulie followed him, and Jess followed them both with a leveled shotgun. He practically purred, "I do declare, y'all should drop around more often! Gits downright *tiresome* boring round here sometimes."

We heard him cackle and the door slammed.

After dinner I poured myself a snifter of Hennessy and loaded a random stack of 33s on the changer. The first up turned out to be Ella Fitzgerald. I went out to the patio, stretched out on the chaise, and listened to "Stars Fell on Alabama" and stared at the stars over Florida. I lit a Lucky and tried blowing a few smoke rings, but a light breeze broke them up, and I finally put the cigarette out.

Doug had come out on the patio and joked, "You can't blow smoke into the wind, and you can't piss into it. The former gets you frustrated and the latter gets you wet."

"Thanks for the heads-up," I said without laughing or turning his way.

He put a hand on my shoulder. "I'm outta here. You need anything?"

"I'm good. Hot date?"

"Plural—dates. I'm meeting Priscilla and Willou at Joy's house."

"A foursome?"

"Hopefully."

"A bit extreme, even for you, no?"

"What? You fall in love and become a religious fanatic?"

I chuckled. "Hardly—good luck, stud."

Doug left laughing. "I'll give them your regards—you know they still think you're a faggot."

Now I was laughing, too. There was no doubt that seven weeks ago I would have been going with him. I sipped my cognac, stared out across the river, and thought about how much my life had changed in that time.

Nice going, Vinny, I thought. You really know how to keep things simple.

Jess came out. "You needin' anything else, Mistah Vinny? I'm takin' Jessie to spend the night with her sister in town."

"No thanks, Jess. Have a nice night."

"Thank you, suh. See you in the mornin'."

I checked my watch—it was almost nine. Kat would be landing back at Teterboro in about an hour. I closed my eyes, started to rewind the weekend, and promptly fell asleep.

I was shaken awake by the roar of a speedboat at full throttle shattering the night. I looked out at the river and saw its running lights literally skimming over the water.

"Crazy bastard," I thought. "If he hits any solid debris at that speed, he'll flip into next week." I glanced at my watch—almost eleven. I'd been dozing for over an hour.

The phone rang and I picked it up.

"Hello, darling." Kat's voice washed over me like a soothing wave and I smiled.

"What happened to 'Hi, sailor'?"

She laughed. "Hi, sailor . . . Better?"

"Love 'em both. How was the flight?"

"Long, but I'm back in the hotel thinking of you."

"Doing the same from the patio."

"How was your night?" she asked.

I had no intention of telling her about Spig and Paulie, so I said, "Quiet evening—cognac and music after dinner." Three truths and one lie—not bad. I'd upped my average to .750.

"I miss you already, and it's only been five hours."

"I know, and I don't think it's going to get easier."

I heard her sigh and she said, "Friday, my love . . . five days. Say it fast and it seems shorter."

"Are you going to tell your father where you're going?"

"Why not? It'll save him the trouble of sending Frick and Frack after me when I disappear again."

"Maybe, but he doesn't sound like the type that takes a slap in the face lying down."

"He's not, but he'll get over it. I'm not giving him a choice."

"Call me after you talk to him, okay?"

"Absolutely. But don't worry. I can handle Daddy. I've been doing it for years."

I didn't share her confidence, but decided to lighten up. "Is that what I can look forward to?"

I heard a rich chuckle. "If I thought you could be handled, I wouldn't want to handle you."

"Not even physically?"

"Every rule has exceptions."

"I like your thinking, baby."

I heard her blow a kiss and she said, "I'll call you tomorrow."

"Tomorrow."

We hung up and a few minutes later Doug came out onto the patio and plopped into a chair. "You're home early," I said.

"If I stayed any longer, I'd be on a respirator."

"Spare me the details."

"Well, since you asked, they should be working for Ringling Brothers."

"Is that a criticism?"

"A critique. Scarlett, Melanie, and Miss Pittypat give a whole new meaning to 'The South shall rise again.' "

I got up. "You'd best hope you've got a rise left. We've got the dawn patrol at five A.M."

"That's more than I needed to know," he groaned.

We both pushed ourselves off our chairs, wearily climbed the stairs to our bedrooms, and hit the sack.

CHAPTER SEVENTEEN

MONDAY WAS EXACTLY one week from our date with *Saratoga*, and all squadron activities picked up in anticipation and intensity. Doug and I and the rest of the veterans were flying three sorties a day while firmly but gently building Whitey and Zaz's confidence until they thought they were indestructible and invincible.

It wasn't easy. Air Force pilots routinely land their airplanes on ten thousand feet of concrete that is spread over level earth that's immobile. Navy pilots, on the other hand, land their jets on short aircraft-carrier decks that are steaming away from them at twenty to thirty knots—sometimes pitching in a wild sea, sometimes hiding in a black night, and sometimes shrouded in weather so thick that it makes them wonder what the hell they're doing there in the first place.

In spite of the above, Whitey and Zaz were responding like the young pros they were. Even the supercritical Concannon managed a smile and a good word when Kenny Willis, our landing signal officer, brought their grades into the ready room where we all awaited the debriefing.

LCDR Ken Willis was a sharp-witted Nashville boy who grew up within sight of the Grand Ole Opry. His hero was Hank Williams because he loved his music and with his slightly dimpled smile and protruding ears he looked enough like him to be his son. As the squadron LSO he graded and critiqued every carrier landing by every pilot in the squadron, including the skipper's.

"Boys'll be ready by next week, Skipper," reported Willis in his Tennessee drawl. "Be willin' to bet the farm on it."

Everyone knew the admiral would be aboard *Saratoga* watching the exercise, and Concannon wanted to be damn sure that if anybody fucked up, it wouldn't be one of his boys.

"Glad to hear it, Kenny." Concannon was grinning and clenched his unlit cigar stub between eighteen pounds of teeth. "It's your sour-mash-sippin' ass if they're not."

"I got that, Skipper. Not a problem."

Just then, LCDR Jake Raymond walked into the room with a scowl on his face and blood in his eyes. A wiry, six-foot Texan with a handlebar mustache and high cheekbones, he had the look of a rodeo cowboy—which he once was.

"Godammit, Skipper," he fumed, "you're burning up my fucking airplanes! We keep going like this and we'll be flying spare parts bound up with ordinance tape!"

The ten-year-veteran fighter pilot was the squadron maintenance officer, and he was hard-pressed to keep our jets in the air. It was difficult under normal conditions, but when the flight schedule doubled, it became damn near impossible. And when his department couldn't get a jet ready to go on schedule, the meticulous and dedicated Raymond took it personally. Concannon loved it—and him.

"Okay, Jake," Concannon said calmly. "We'll ground all the planes so you can put 'em in top-notch condition. That make you happy?

Good." And then his voice began a steady rise. "Because then what we'll do is watch our boys fly those wonderfully perfect machines of yours *into the goddamn ocean* because we haven't trained 'em to execute the fucking mission!"

"There's gotta be a middle ground!" yelled Jake.

"Where? There is none!" Concannon yelled back. "There never is. You just keep on being the best goddamn maintenance officer in the fleet because you *can* put those machines in the air with spare parts and tape, and we'll keep flying 'em because we *have* to!"

Raymond threw up his hands in frustration, spun around, and stormed out of the ready room shaking his head. The one consolation he'd gotten was being called the best.

The debrief lasted until seven, and Kat called later that night to say she'd finished the Chanel shoot and would be on a morning flight to L.A. She'd call me the minute she finished talking to Daddy. I was more anxious than she knew.

Tuesday at the base was a duplicate of Monday, and after Doug and I got home, I fashioned a shakerful of perfect martinis to blunt the edge of another fourteen-hour day. We took them out to the patio, where Jess was grilling sausages and Jessie was heating up roasted peppers in tomato sauce. The combination, folded into a half loaf of Italian bread, was legendary.

We finished our martinis, Jess cracked open ice-cold cans of beer, and the feast began as the sun set and the crickets went wild.

The phone rang at eight. I took a deep breath, went into the sunroom, and picked it up. "Hello."

Kat immediately chirped, "Hi, sailor!"

The chipper greeting was the last thing I had expected. I flopped into the window seat slightly stunned. "Kat?"

"Who else calls you that?"

"No one . . . I mean it surprised me. You sound great."

"I am great!"

"Why? I mean, your father . . . Did you—"

She cut me off, laughing. "Talk to Daddy? Of course I did. I just left him. That's why I feel great."

I was completely confused. "He wasn't angry?"

"No! He was perfectly calm. Even apologetic. He actually said he was sorry he had me followed. He said he loved me and insisted it was only because he was a concerned father who was worried about his daughter's safety in the big, bad city."

"Bullshit."

"Of course. But who cares? The point is that he's agreed to let me see you if that's what I want to do . . . and I told him I do."

"And that was it?" I asked, amazed.

"That was it. He's not happy about it, and he made me promise not to elope again, so I told him that when we got married, he would walk me down the aisle."

Somehow, I couldn't quite picture that particular walk down the aisle. I was quiet for a moment.

"Darling . . . Are you there?"

"Huh?" I said.

"Are you all right?"

"Yes . . . fine . . . just shocked that he'd react like that after all that's happened."

"Truth be told, I was a bit shocked myself. I expected a blowup, but I didn't even get a very strong argument. He actually made me feel a little guilty."

"It's just too screwy. I should be dancing, but I'm waiting for the other shoe to drop."

"Isn't there a cliché about mouths and gift horses? I didn't expect Daddy to back off either, but I know he wants the best for me, even if it's usually what *he* thinks is best."

I shook my head and relented. "Okay. Let's see where it takes us."

"It's taking me to you in three days, Lieutenant—and as of now I'm counting the minutes."

"Should we revisit The Cloister?"

"A 'no tell motel' would be fine with me. I'm yours for the weekend, sailor."

I laughed. "I can do better than that. I want to see the clerk's reaction at The Cloister when he sees 'Sally and Vincent Richards' checking in as Caitlin and Vincent Vesta."

"That's the first time I've heard that name out loud."

"Well, get used to it. It's gonna be around a long time. Call me when you've booked your flight."

"Take care, sailor, I love you."

"Ditto," I said.

She laughed and blew a kiss and we hung up.

I walked back out to the patio and watched Jess as he finished shutting down the grill. "Kin we git y'all anythin' else?" he asked.

"Not for me, thanks, Jess," I said.

"I'm good, too, Jess," said Doug.

Jessie carried the dishes into the kitchen, saying, "Buzz if y'all need us," and they disappeared through the porch door.

"So?" asked Doug as soon as they left.

I sat opposite him, shook my head, and told him what Kat had said in one flat, rambling statement: "Her father wasn't pissed and says it's okay for me to see her."

Doug's head jerked back in shock, and his wayward forelock came down over his eye. "You gotta be shittin' me!"

I shook my head again. "She'll be here Friday."

He brushed away the hair from his forehead. "After everything that's gone down he's calling off the war?"

I looked off across the river, not believing a word of it. "So it seems."

"It makes no sense! What changed his mind?"

"According to her, she did. She said he loves her and he saw the light."

Doug said, "I may be one cynical son of a bitch, but from what I've seen and heard, I wouldn't trust that bastard for an eyeblink!"

I nodded. "I agree. But what can I do except go along?"

"Christ, Vinny, to quote you, 'I have no fuckin' idea'!"

CHAPTER EIGHTEEN

T HE FOLLOWING MORNING I flew an instrument refresher hop with Whitey. We both had some extra fuel at the end of the drill so we decided to mix it up with some simulated air-to-air combat. We began the drill at twenty thousand feet, our two FJ-3s about one mile apart off Jax Beach—near the spot where Stanfield had crashed.

The contest began with each of us hurtling toward the other in a head-on pass at max speed. When our two airplanes crossed, the drill called for us to pull straight up into the vertical at maximum g's. Too timid a pull meant not gaining the highest possible altitude at the top of the maneuver. Two harsh a pull would cause a high-speed stall at the bottom, and the airplane wouldn't gain the highest possible altitude. Maximum altitude was critical. And to get it, the initial high-g pull-up had to be executed perfectly—at the edge of the airplane's performance envelope.

Whoever wound up on top would be able to reverse his position and come down on his opponent's tail, scoring a "shoot down" recorded by the camera gun.

Whitey and I passed each other in our head-on pass and pulled straight up into the vertical as planned. We were several hundred yards apart and canopy to canopy as we shot straight up. At the top of the maneuver I was less than a hundred feet above him—not enough of an advantage. We performed a wingover split seconds before our airplanes ran out of airspeed, stalled, and spun out. Both of us were flying perfectly and shot back toward the ground— straight down, wide open. As we hit the FJ-3's redline speed, we scissored across each other and again pulled straight up. This time I was over seven hundred feet above him when he ran out of airspeed and was forced to do a wingover rather than spin out. I'd obviously pushed my airplane to its limit, and he hadn't done the same with his. I performed a wingover and dropped down onto his tail in perfect firing position.

I keyed my mike. "You're torched m'man!"

"Roger that," he returned a bit despondently.

I'd nailed him again. But the kid was coming along. It had taken me two passes to "shoot him down" when it had only taken one the prior week. I complimented him on his extended survivability, and we headed back to NAS Jax.

After we debriefed in the ready room, Jake Raymond popped his scowling face through the doorway and called out, "Vesta! Skipper wants to see you."

I called back, "Thanks, Jake," and headed for Concannon's office.

He was standing behind his desk reading dispatches on a clipboard when I entered. He looked up, frowned, and pinned me with his coal black eyes.

Uh-oh, I thought, he isn't happy.

He wasn't. With a look of complete disgust he slammed the clipboard on his desk. The impact sounded like a rifle shot. He didn't say anything for a few long seconds. Finally, he calmly asked, "I would be obliged if you would do me one small favor, Mr. Vesta."

I nodded unnecessarily.

He continued, "Do you actually go out *looking* for trouble or does it find its way up your ass on its own?"

"Sir?"

"I just got a phone call from Washington. The Pentagon. It came from a very disturbed undersecretary of the Navy." He paused. "Would you like to know what it was about?"

"I have no idea, sir," I said in a controlled voice.

"No?" He took a step toward me. "Then let me enlighten you. It was about a certain young lady. The one you went storming off the base in your flight suit to rescue last month. The one you said was kidnapped."

"She was, she—"

"Not according to the undersecretary of the Navy! He was told by a very upset senator from California that her very livid father from Los Angeles said that *she* ran away from *you* because you were abusing her!"

"Abusing!" I shouted. "That's bullshit! She was—"

He shouted over me, "And while she was in New York shooting a commercial, you had her picked up by a pair of Mafia goons and delivered to Sea Island, Georgia! He said she was terrified!"

I couldn't control myself. "That's insane! She came of her own free will! We love each other! We're engaged! It's her father who's trying to keep us apart!"

"Well, he goddamn sure has a foolproof way of doing it! He's got a California senator and the United States Navy behind him!"

"Sir, I—"

"And *they* want what he wants! Quote, 'All contact with her should cease and desist immediately!' unquote!"

I was so frustrated I threw up my hands and yelled, "Or what, God damn it? Or what?"

"Or they'll ship your ass to the most remote rathole on this fucking planet!"

"Christ." I hung my head.

My obvious distress seemed to break the tension and he visibly softened. He emitted a long sigh, held out his hands, and sat. "Okay," he said quietly, "grab a chair."

I did, and he studied me for a few moments. "Just so you know . . . I don't believe a goddamn word of it, and I told the secretary that. I've known you too long."

"Thank you, sir."

"You're welcome—but the secretary doesn't give a rat's ass about my opinion. He's being pounded from above and shit rolls downhill."

I smiled thinly. "Thanks anyway, Skipper. I appreciate it."

"Thanks noted, Lieutenant. Now the good news is that it was a back-door call. No official channels—yet. If you behave, you're off the hook. But there's got to be a reason for this guy to have a fucking U.S. senator threaten to flush you down the toilet."

"How about because he's a controlling asshole who hates the Navy."

"But why for Christ's sake?"

"Because his daughter ran off and married a Navy pilot against his wishes. The pilot had a fatal accident two months ago."

We weren't at war and Navy pilots don't get killed very often outside of combat. When they do, it's news.

I saw Concannon's eyes narrow as he put the situation together. "Stanfield."

I nodded. "His widow."

"Un-fucking-believable."

"Yessir."

Concannon slowly got to his feet and went to the window overlooking the flight line. Without turning he asked, "May I ask your intentions, Lieutenant?"

"I don't know, Skipper. I need some time to think about all of this."

"I'd hate to lose you, Vesta. You're a damn fine pilot." Then he turned and added with genuine regret, "But I don't see how I can do anything to stop it if you make the wrong decision."

"Yessir. I understand. Thanks, Skipper."

I left his office in a daze and walked out of the hangar. A pair of FJ-3s roared down the runway in a formation takeoff and left the ground tighter than Siamese twins. I'd seen the flight schedule and knew it was Whitey and Zaz. I found myself smiling appreciatively—our too young nuggets were kicking ass.

On the flight line, ground crews were scurrying about the rest of the sleek jets, refueling them for the next hop and checking everything from tire pressure to canopy seals. I watched their quick, cool efficiency and welled up with pride, certain that I was in the best goddamn squadron in the fleet. It was inconceivable that I was on the verge of being sucked out of it.

But Kat was coming in two days, and the only two options I could think of weren't even close to being options. If I called and told her not to come, she'd immediately suspect her father had somehow forced me to make the call. She'd confront him, he'd deny it, and she'd storm off to Jacksonville anyway. Whether I let her come or told her not to come, the result would be the same. We'd trigger her father's threat and my exile.

Daddy—that miserable son of a bitch—had us boxed.

That afternoon Concannon delivered some more ominous news. Earlier that morning a tropical depression had formed east of the northern Lesser Antilles. It was moving west-northwest and had become a tropical storm during the day. In the next twenty-four hours it was expected to become a hurricane, followed by a period of rapid intensification to 135 mph winds. It had been named Frieda and was headed directly for Florida. Even if it didn't make landfall, the storm track indicated that it would tear through our operating area off the Florida/Georgia coast on Monday or Tuesday. There was no way we would be attempting to land airplanes on *Saratoga* in that.

All the squadrons on the base got out their preprepared hurricane evacuation plans for the fly-away that would take us to the closest naval air station and out of harm's way. Our squadron would probably fly to NAS Pensacola, FL, if the storm stayed on its current track or, if it threatened to move farther inland, NAS Memphis, TN.

That night Doug and I continued listening to the storm warnings, and I told him about my new best friends—the senator from California and the undersecretary of the Navy.

He voiced his sympathy by suggesting I join the French Foreign Legion.

I voiced my thanks by suggesting he go fuck himself.

His one bright idea was to point out that the storm might buy me a little time.

I realized he might actually be right.

Kat knew a little about naval aviation even though she hadn't been a part of it for long, and she'd certainly know you had to get airplanes out of the teeth of a hurricane. I was guessing she'd buy the story that we couldn't meet in Jax, but I had to figure out a way to keep her from coming to either of our fly-away destinations—Pensacola or Memphis.

I filled a shaker with ice, Scotch, and Drambuie and did my best maraca impression while we considered the possibilities. After pouring the "Hot Starts" (Rob Roys to civilians) into a pair of tumblers, we retired to the patio and the crickets.

Doug sipped his drink. "How about the ship?"

There was only one ship in our lives. "*Saratoga?*"

"Why not?" he said. "Suppose for some reason you had to go out to the carrier instead of on the fly-away?"

"Great. But why?"

"There is no reason. Think bullshit . . . like a sailor came down with a rare tropical fever and you had to fly out the serum."

"They'd use a helicopter for that."

"Okay—how about they rescued the crew of a sinking fishing boat and the crew speaks nothing but Italian."

"What—an Italian fishing boat off the coast of Georgia?"

"Right. The fifteen-man crew's in bad shape. They're on the carrier and they need a translator to communicate between the Italians and the medics."

I answered him with a statement, not a question. "There's five thousand guys on that ship, and no one speaks Italian."

"Right."

"Ridiculous."

"You're not thinking bullshit."

True, I wasn't, but he was right about *Saratoga* being a possible solution.

"What if," I said, "because of the storm, all the squadrons in the air group had to completely revise their CQ schedules? One pilot from every squadron has to fly out to the ship to work it out with the carrier's air boss."

He stroked his chin. "Good," he admitted begrudgingly. "It's almost plausible."

"But more plausible than fifteen sick guineas on a flight deck."

"Agreed."

It was a little after ten—seven in California. I picked up the phone and caught Kat just as she was headed out to dinner with Sally.

"Hi, baby, it's me."

She chuckled. "Hi, 'me.'"

"I don't mean to worry you, but have you been following the weather reports?"

"Yes, and I'm worried sick that I may not be able to get in before that hurricane hits. I tried to get a flight out tonight but nothing's available."

Thank God, I thought. "It doesn't matter. Our weekend's been canceled anyway. The squadron will be on a fly-away tomorrow and I've been ordered out to the ship to redo the CQ schedule."

"Oh, Vinny," she said, sounding genuinely disappointed.

"I know, but the storm'll blow through and we'll see each other weekend after next, okay?"

"What choice is there?"

"None. I'm as disappointed as you are."

"Is it safe?" she asked.

"What?

"Flying out to the ship tomorrow?"

"No sweat," I said. "I'll be on the deck ahead of the storm."

"Be careful, darling." Her voice had gotten apprehensive. "I don't even want to think about something happening to you."

Now I was beginning to feel like a real shit for putting her through the lie. "I won't let it happen," I said. "I love you. Say hello to Sally, and I'll call you as soon as I'm back."

She blew a kiss. "Ciao, sailor."

I hung up the phone, now totally guilty and looked at Doug.

"You're a regular Laurence Olivier."

"I feel like a shit."

"As well you should—lying to the girl like that."

"You prick! It was your idea!"

"Don't confuse me with the facts."

"When was the last time I told you to fuck off?"

"About twenty minutes ago."

"I must be slipping."

CHAPTER NINETEEN

EARLY FRIDAY MORNING the weather reports were predicting that Frieda's eye would be fifty miles off the coast of Jacksonville by midnight. Every airplane on the base that couldn't safely be hangared was being manned for the flight to Pensacola. Our squadron had three aircraft that were grounded for mechanical reasons, but the rest would be off and westbound.

I passed the sick jets on my way up to the ready room to check the flight schedule, knowing there'd be eighteen pilots for thirteen airplanes. My name along with Doug's and eleven other pilots' were on the schedule. The five pilots not on the flight schedule would stay behind with the enlisted men.

I headed for Concannon's office hoping to catch him in a sympathetic mood. He was in his flight suit and had two small duffel bags on his desk in front of him ready to be stashed in his jet's empty ammo cans.

"Request, Skipper."

He was packing papers into his briefcase and said, "Very well," without looking up.

"I'd like to stay behind, sir."

That got his attention. He looked up and spoke evenly, "I sincerely hope I'm wrong about the reason."

"Yessir. I've called and canceled her visit."

He looked relieved. "Good. Then why stay behind?"

"I'd like to take the time to visit my family, Skipper."

"Nothing serious I hope."

"Nosir, but I haven't seen them since the Christmas holiday, and I figured all we'd be doing in Pensacola would be sitting around waiting for the hurricane to pass. It could be a good time to drop in on them."

"Okay, Vesta, with the Senate and the Pentagon on your ass, the least I can do is cut you some slack. Put in a set of papers for three days, and if we're not back here by then, I'll extend them."

"Thanks, Skipper, I appreciate it." I started to leave.

He stopped me with "Good luck, Lieutenant, and try to stay out of trouble. It'll be a new experience for you."

"Yessir."

Back in the ready room, I filled out a leave request and told Doug that I was headed for New York. He knew about the trouble my mother was causing and wished me luck. I needed it. I hadn't talked to her since our last confrontation about Genovese.

Jess and Jessie were boarding up the widows and moving anything that wasn't tied down into the house and garage. They'd been laying in supplies for the past two days, and I knew they could stay battened down for a week.

I had trouble booking a nonstop to New York because of the number of people trying to avoid the hurricane, but finally nailed a connector via Raleigh that would get me into La Guardia by six P.M. I called Stuff for a pickup and asked if we might have dinner with Angelo. "No problem," he said.

I packed my bag, told Jess and Jessie I was headed for New York, and left.

Stuff and Angelo were waiting when I walked out of the National Airlines terminal. They were both wearing neatly pressed slacks, open-necked sport shirts, and in spite of the unseasonable heat, jackets. I knew from experience that the only reason for the jackets was to conceal their .45 autos.

As the two men ambled toward me, I spotted Angelo's 1940 Ford "street car" at the curb. I suddenly felt as if I were in a seven-year time warp. He'd been driving the same inconspicuous old clunker for years. I'd heard him say more than once, "You get no attention if you draw no attention."

I dropped my suitcase, stretched out my arms, and the duo embraced me in a brawny vise. Of course I'd seen them just a week earlier in Florida, but I hadn't been back to New York since Christmas, and I was welcomed like the prodigal son. We climbed into the car—Angelo and Stuff in front, me in back—and as we pulled away from the curb, I glanced over my shoulder out of habit. A late-model Buick pulled out after us and I recognized the occupants—the Cavallo twins.

Matty and Dino were an identical pair of light-skinned, fair-haired Sicilian anomalies who looked deceptively like schoolteachers. They'd been in Angelo's crew for a decade and were among the deadliest killers in the city.

I flipped a thumb over my shoulder. "Expecting trouble?"

Angelo glanced in the rearview mirror. "Probably. Ever since Anastasia's been tryin' ta horn in on the Cuban casinos and Costello and Lansky said no."

"Christ," I said, "that's crazy. He's gotta know that Cuba belongs to Costello and Lansky. They'll never allow it."

"Exactly. But a few days ago they told him they'd give him a taste, and he believes it. Albert thinks he can muscle anybody. He believes no one's tough enough ta stand against him. He's wrong and I told him so."

"What'd he say?"

"That I was fulla shit. . . . But I still think they're settin' 'im up. Lettin' 'im relax before they make their move. Sooner or later this thing's gonna blow up in our faces."

Wonderful, I thought. I'd come to ask Angelo for a favor in the middle of a potential gang war.

We drove to a quiet restaurant on the West Side that Angelo had just purchased under his wife's maiden name. Lena's was decorated with red-checkered tablecloths, hanging Chianti bottles, and candles. With Mario Lanza coming from the sound system, it was the poster child for Italian trattorias.

He'd named it after his wife because the restaurant had been her idea. The couple had been married thirty-six years, loved each other dearly, but never stopped arguing about religion. Lena was a saintly woman, attending mass every Sunday, Rosary Society every Thursday, and observing all the customs and regulations of Catholicism—from Lenten fast to meatless Friday. Angelo observed nothing—the only rules he cared about were those he could enforce with his .45. He was an atheist married to a saint.

Lena of course insisted on taking over the restaurant kitchen, and although three cooks did all the work, the recipes were all hers, and the food was as good as anything you'd find between Palermo and Messina.

Father and son had not only identical frames—they also had identical appetites: They both ordered antipasto, linguine carbonara, breaded veal, salad, and a bottle of Barolo—and for dessert, spumoni, espresso, biscotti, and cigars. They ate for an hour and a half. I had witnessed this my whole life, but it never ceased to amaze me. I had a salad and the osso buco and was finished in twenty-five minutes.

After dinner, Angelo delicately sipped his espresso, then said, "So?"

I lit a Lucky and skipped a preamble, knowing it wouldn't help my case. He would still hate the reason I had come to see him.

"You remember the girl I had you keep an eye on while she was here?"

He nodded, glanced at Stuff, then back at me. His disapproval was obvious. "I take it ya didn't stay away from her."

I shook my head. "I didn't."

He pointed his cigar at me. "And I'm guessin' her father knows you didn't."

I nodded. "He does."

"And he made a move," he continued calmly.

I nodded. "He had the senator from California call the under secretary of the Navy, who called my skipper. He threatened to have me shipped to East Bumfuck if I didn't stop seeing his daughter."

"Christ! He can do that?"

"That and worse."

Stuff looked from his father to me but said nothing.

Angelo thoughtfully placed the tip of his cigar on an empty spumoni plate and rolled off the ash. "Interestin'. First he orders private muscle ta threaten you and then he can get federal juice to take you out of the picture. Like I warned ya, the guy's a big-time player with Mob and political connections."

"He's got me boxed, Angelo. Kat won't stay away no matter what I say. The hurricane bailed me out of this weekend, but she's sure to show up next week. When she does, I'll be toast."

"I'll ask ya again. . . . You sure you wanna go on with this? It's *pazzo*."

He was right. It was crazy and it made little sense to anyone but me, but I nodded and said, "I'm sure."

"Whaddaya want me to do?"

"Is there any way we can get to him—convince him to back off?"

Angelo's forehead wrinkled in thought a few seconds and he

shrugged. "I dunno. Like I said, our reach to the coast ain't so good, but maybe."

Stuff finally piped up. "We got a West Coast connection in Mickey Cohen through Lansky."

Mickey Cohen and Jack Dragna were bitter enemies who had been fighting for control of West Coast gambling for years. Dragna had tried to murder Cohen on five different occasions, but had failed every time. This, of course, contributed greatly to his Mickey Mouse reputation. I knew Stuff was thinking that since "Daddy" was both Dragna's lawyer and partner, perhaps Cohen could supply us with something we could threaten him with.

"No good," answered Angelo. "Mickey's about to do a stretch in Club Fed fer tax evasion, and I hear Dragna's dyin'. He won't make it to Christmas. That'll put Johnny Roselli in the driver's seat out there."

"Is that good or bad?" I asked.

Angelo shrugged. "I dunno how Roselli feels about Pennington. But he works fer Chicago and that's Accardo. Anastasia used to be pretty tight with him, so maybe we go that route. I'll make some calls, but one thing I know. We ain't gonna get shit done from here. We're gonna have to fly out to the coast and do this one-on-one. How much time ya got?"

"Until Monday."

"Christ," Angelo said, disgusted. "We always get six pounds of shit and a five-pound bag." He turned to Stuff. "Call and make round-trip reservations. Out tomorrow, back Sunday."

"How many?" asked Stuff.

"Three," said Angelo.

"No twins?"

Angelo shook his head. "Our problem's here, not in L.A. Out there we'll be guests in their house. Guests don't bring heat inta someone else's kitchen."

*　　*　　*

Since I'd only be in town overnight, I decided to bunk in with Stuff and not let my mother know I was there. I had enough on my plate already. His bachelor pad was a basement apartment on Thirty-seventh street off Tenth Avenue. It had once belonged to Benny Veal, a beloved, black member of our former street gang who'd been killed in a jewelry-store heist.

The others: Red O'Mara had died in Korea on Pork Chop Hill; Sidney Butcher had died in street violence; Boychick Delfina had dropped out of sight years ago; Bouncer Camilli had moved to Italy with his family; and Louie Antonio was working the borscht belt as a stand-up comic. The only one still in New York was Stuff.

We descended a short stairway, and Stuff opened the door and flipped on the lights. I couldn't help myself: "Outstanding, Mr. Maserelli!"

The apartment still had the pool table, player piano, and deer-horn chandelier, but the boxing bags, posters, and all the old furniture were gone. The new décor featured facing sofas, matching fabric recliners, area rugs, lamps, coffee and end tables. It had been repainted and had a new, fully equipped, modern kitchen.

"Get you anythin'?" he asked, calling over the counter that separated the kitchen from the living room.

"A beer's good." I sat in one of the recliners.

He popped two, came out, and handed me one. Sitting in the opposite recliner, he took a slug of beer, studied me for a moment. "Ya really gotta be hung up on that chick to go through this."

"She blindsided me, pal. I never saw it coming."

"Gotta be nice," he mused, then paused. "I hope she's worth it, Vinny."

CHAPTER TWENTY

W E LEFT FOR L.A. the following morning and arrived
a little after noon. From the airplane I could see the layer of
smog covering the city like a mustard blanket, and when we
got to the curb, I found myself gagging on exhaust gas.

Thankfully, our arrival had been preceded by calls from Anastasia to Accardo to Roselli, and a limo was ready and waiting to
deliver us to the Beverly Wilshire Hotel on Wilshire Boulevard.
My eighth-floor window looked straight up Rodeo Drive—Kat's
house was on Camden Drive, one block west and five blocks north,
and it was all I could do not to take the six-block stroll and pop
in. But I knew Daddy probably had the goddamn housekeeper on
his payroll, and I wasn't quite ready to explain to Kat what I was
doing in L.A.

I sighed just as Stuff stuck his head through my open door. "We're
about to call Roselli and set up the meet."

"The meet"—a few short weeks with Kat and I'd been propelled seven years back in time to my old life. I nodded and followed him across the hall.

Angelo was consulting a scrap of paper and dialing the phone. "Maserelli," he said, then paused to listen. "Okay. We'll be there." He hung up. "That was Roselli. La Scala at seven."

"A restaurant?" I asked, more than a little surprised.

"Why not?" Angelo shrugged. "Nobody in L.A. knows us, and we know nobody. You two've never been here, and if somebody from back East spots me, Roselli'll blow it off, sayin' it wuz a social thing with an old friend passin' through."

"I hope you're right," I said skeptically. "I'm either supposed to be in New York with my family or on an aircraft carrier off the coast of Georgia."

Angelo ignored me and checked his watch. "One o'clock—ya hungry?"

"Always," said Stuff.

"We had lunch on the plane," I pointed out.

Angelo said, "That was New York time. Now we're on California time."

"You're right," I answered, "God forbid we should miss a meal."

A half hour later, Angelo and Stuff tucked into overloaded pastrami sandwiches at Nat 'n Al's, and I kept them company with a celery soda. We burned up the rest of the afternoon strolling with throngs of tourists through the Beverly Hills shopping district.

Angelo was particularly fascinated as he looked into the elaborate window displays of Tiffany, Gucci, Cartier, and Saks Fifth Avenue among others. At one point he said, "They gotta be fuckin' kiddin'!" He was looking at a white silk shirt in a window with a price tag of ninety-five dollars. "You could buy ten shirts for that!"

He was right, but I laughed and said, "Most of the men who buy those shirts drive Ferraris, live in mansions, and spend winters in Aspen. The price means nothing."

"Christ. What the hell's the world comin' to? It's fuckin' indecent!"

That from a man who'd pulled the trigger on a half dozen hits.

We'd been wearing the clothes we'd traveled in all day and it was getting late, so we returned to the hotel. After we'd showered, shaved, and donned suits, I called the Jax house.

Jess answered and yelled out, "Hello!" I could hear the hurricane's fury howling in the background.

I yelled back, "How's it going down there, Jess?"

"We bein' lashed pretty good, Mistah Vinny," he yelled, "and a few trees went down, but so far the house ain't taken no hits."

"Screw the house, Jess. Are you and Jessie okay?"

"We're fine, 'cept we're both gettin' hoarse from havin' to yell everthin' to hear anythin'!"

I laughed. "Okay, Jess, it'll blow through by tomorrow, so hang loose and stay inside."

"Will do, Mistah Vinny. . . . Jessie wants to know can you bring us back a few pounds of Nathan's hot dogs."

I knew Jessie loved them, and we couldn't get them in Jacksonville. Unfortunately, I wasn't in New York but couldn't explain why, so I said, "I'll try, Jess . . . See you both on Monday," and hung up happy I'd gotten through with all the lines that had to be down.

La Scala was an upscale eatery not far from our hotel, but Roselli had sent a limo so we took it and arrived at seven on the dot. The maître d' led us immediately past tables of early diners to the rear of the restaurant, where we descended a flight of stairs to a wine cellar.

The room was small and softly lit with floor-to-ceiling wine racks that surrounded a beautifully worn wooden table that could seat twelve. A large chandelier hung overhead, and the stone floor was covered with lush burgundy carpeting. The private dining room had the feel of a comfortable den.

I recognized Johnny Roselli at the table from the numerous newspaper photos I'd seen through the years, but he was sitting with another man I didn't recognize. I realized from the private setting that Roselli was being more cautious than Angelo had anticipated.

Roselli and his associate rose courteously when we entered, and Roselli extended his hand. "Johnny Roselli," he said, "and this is Carlo Stanza."

John "Handsome Johnny" Roselli was fifty-two years old, had graying hair, leading-man good looks, and a movie-star tan. He was impeccably dressed in a finely cut Italian suit and was wearing horn-rim glasses that gave him the appearance of a powerhouse agent. He was a perfect fit for Hollywood. In another time he could have been Lew Wasserman.

Carlo was about twenty years younger than Roselli, with a thin, wiry body and black, curly hair that tumbled over a long, narrow face. He, too, might have been considered handsome if it weren't for his beady eyes and strangely thin lips.

"Angelo Maserelli," responded Angelo. "My son, Attillio, and our friend Vincent Vesta."

Roselli cocked an eyebrow as we all shook hands. "Gino's son?"

"You knew him?" I asked, a bit surprised. Roselli operated out of Chicago, Vegas, and Los Angeles—not New York.

"We met when Tony and I came to visit Albert."

That would be Accardo and Anastasia, I thought.

"Sit," said Roselli, waving his hand at the chairs opposite him. "What're you drinking?"

An open bottle of Barbaresco sat on the table next to a huge platter of antipasto.

Angelo pointed at the wine. "Wine's good."

Stuff and I nodded, indicating we'd have the same.

"Carlo—another bottle," instructed Roselli, and Carlo got up to remove a bottle from the hundreds that lined the walls.

"Some antipasto," said Roselli, passing the plate to Angelo. "We'll order after we finish our business, yes?"

Angelo nodded, took the plate, and passed it on, while Carlo filled our glasses. "I appreciate you seein' us on short notice," Angelo said.

"I've been told to help if I can," responded Roselli. "What is it you require?"

Angelo turned to me. "Vincenzo?"

I nodded and for the next half hour I gave two complete strangers chapter and verse of my meeting and love affair with Caitlin Pennington—and my problem with her father. At the end of the story I leaned back in my chair and waited for a response. I got the impression Carlo was unimpressed. Roselli, on the other hand, seemed amused.

He smiled. "A Romeo and Juliet thing. It's a bit out of my line."

"I understand," I said.

"We hoped there might be somethin' we could use ta back Pennington off," said Angelo.

"Like?" prompted Roselli.

Angelo leaned forward and folded his hands on the table. "We know Pennington's a big-time lawyer. High up in the political and social circuit. Lives the good life. But from what we found out, he's also in business with you—and most of it illegal. If it got out he was a part of that, he'd be disgraced and disbarred. Nobody'd touch him. We think it's his weak spot."

Roselli raised a wary eyebrow. "You want me to set up my partner?"

"Look, Johnny," said Angelo, "Dragna's on the way out. Cohen's goin' to jail. Someone's gotta take over this town, and there's gonna be a lotta contenders. We figure the guy with the most muscle behind 'im is gonna come out on top. That could be you. You already got Tony— now you could have Albert. That's Chicago and New York. No one could stand against ya."

Roselli glanced at Carlo, picked up his wineglass, and sipped. He stared at the three of us thoughtfully. "Okay, let's assume I can come up with something. What guarantees do I have you'll hold up your end?"

"Two things," said Angelo. "Anastasia's word to Accardo and the fact that we have no interest in anything on the West Coast. It's yours. And that includes Vegas. Anastasia's only interested in Cuba."

"I heard that," said Roselli. I could tell his interest was piqued. "I also hear Lansky ain't happy about it."

"He's not," admitted Angelo. "But that's no worry to you."

Roselli looked over Angelo's head at the wine bottles on the wall for a few moments. When he looked back down, he said, "It could be."

"Cuba?" asked Angelo, confused.

"Perhaps. Cuba just might be the answer to your problem."

"Forgive me here, Johnny, I ain't followin'."

"You wanted me to set up Pennington with a threat to expose him so that he'll let young Vesta off the hook."

"Right."

"It won't work. One, he's covered his tracks so deep there probably isn't anything that would stick, so, two—if there *was* something, he'd know the only two people who could've come up with it would be me and Dragna. Dragna's on his deathbed. That leaves me. Even if he didn't figure it out, our partnership's too profitable for me to fuck it up. But Cuba? That's a possibility."

"I still ain't followin'."

"Anastasia wants into Cuba, and the word is that the Commission promised to let him wet his beak."

Angelo nodded. I could see he was impressed. "You got pretty good sources alla way out here."

"Not me. Accardo. And I'd bet that if Anastasia promised him a piece of his Cuba action, Accardo would do anything Anastasia asks. In this case, he'd ask Accardo to tell me to have Pennington back off."

Stuff and I glanced at Angelo, waiting for his reaction. It was a helluva lot to ask for "a Romeo and Juliet thing" as Roselli had put it.

Angelo stroked his chin. "It might work. Anastasia loved Vinny's father and feels responsible fer him bein' killed. He thinks he owes the family." He looked at me and nodded. "I'll ask him."

"Good!" said Roselli, obviously proud of himself. "And tell your boss that Pennington doesn't have to know the reason he's being asked to back off. That'll be between us and Accardo."

Angelo finished his antipasto and I sipped my wine. I knew it was probably bullshit that Roselli couldn't come up with something to blackmail Pennington with. At least as far as he was concerned, Cuba had to seem like a far better idea. There was no doubt that Roselli would get a cut of Accardo's piece for negotiating the deal, and he didn't strike me as being so loyal to Pennington that he'd give a second thought to cutting him out of the action.

"We go back tomorrow," said Angelo. "I'll let ya know by Monday if it's a go with Albert. Then you talk to Pennington. We need to know where we stand before next weekend."

Roselli nodded. "Done. Now let's order." He picked up the intercom. "The gnocchi pesto here is excellent. It's Frank's favorite."

The casual reference to "Frank" meant Sinatra of course, but Roselli'd switched subjects so smoothly you would've thought the guy was running for mayor.

He was right. The gnocchi was excellent. And so were the other three courses and dessert that Angelo and Stuff put away under the astonished eyes of Johnny Roselli and Carlo Stanza. All in all, I figured we had a shot. A long one, since my situation depended upon Anastasia giving up a piece of Cuba—again, one hell of a price to pay for a "Romeo and Juliet thing."

After dinner we headed to our limo, which was double-parked across the street. Stuff and Angelo got into the car, and I was just about to follow them when I noticed a Rolls-Royce pulling up in front of the restaurant. Photographers materialized across the street, and flashbulbs began setting off a light show.

I paused, looked over the roof of our limo, and froze. The immediate object of the cameras was Victor Marino—tall, swarthy, and chisel-faced enough to belong on Rushmore. He was every inch the leading man. The two men behind him I recognized as Spig and Paulie—aka Frick and Frack—and the fourth man with them was a chairman-of-the-board type straight out of central casting. He was tall, distinguished, and had steel-gray hair and a trim, matching mustache. In his midfifties, he exuded an air of absolute confidence. This was undoubtedly Daddy—Marion Pennington.

The woman between Marino and Daddy was Kat.

Stuff and Angelo saw what was happening and got back out of the car.

"Victor Marino," Stuff said. The awe in his voice was unmistakable.

"That her?" asked Angelo.

"Yeah," I said, still semifrozen.

"Like I always said, ya got good taste."

Kat looked ravishing as she played to the cameras while holding the arms of both men. She was wearing a flowing white dress with a plunging neckline, and sling-back heels. The outfit a ringer for Marilyn Monroe's famous subway wardrobe in *The Seven Year Itch*—except Kat was flashing a matching suite of diamonds. Necklace, bracelet, and earrings.

The jewels were almost as dazzling as the woman.

Watching her, I realized why she was so confident, and Daddy so insistent that she become be a star. She was a natural. The three continued smiling for the cameras as Spig and Paulie gently eased the threesome through the crowd and into the restaurant.

What the hell was she doing with Marino? I thought. Hadn't she spoken to him after she talked to her father? Or had her father told her to say nothing to Marino for a short time as part of the deal? Did he think that once he had me boxed he would throw them back together? And if so, why hadn't she mentioned that part to me?

CHAPTER TWENTY-ONE

THE NEXT MORNING none of us felt like hanging around in the smog, so we caught the eight-o'clock flight out of L.A., and by early evening we were back in New York and on our way to see Anastasia.

The twins, Dino and Matty Cavallo, met us at Idlewild and we drove across the George Washington Bridge to Fort Lee, New Jersey, a leafy enclave overlooking the Upper West Side of New York. The G. W. Bridge stretched a mile or so across the Hudson and ended at the north end of town. Perched next to it high atop the Palisades was the Riviera nightclub, the Mob-owned showplace that was the first to book a skinny kid from just down the road in Hoboken, New Jersey, called Frank Sinatra.

When we arrived at Anastasia's estate, it was well after dark but the grounds were ablaze—the entire place was lit up like an amusement park. Two ornate iron gates and an imposing guardhouse protected the long drive leading to the capo's mission-style mansion. Two men who recognized Angelo waved us through. It was the first time I'd been to the home of the man who revered my father, and I knew Pop would be displeased by his mentor's ostentatious show of wealth.

Another pair of guards waited at the front entrance to the house and genially saluted Angelo, playfully slapping him on the back, and nodding perfunctory greetings to me. We left Stuff and the twins in the car, and the guards escorted us to Anastasia. He was waiting in an ornate den with high ceilings, oak paneling, wainscoting, Tiffany lamps, and Persian rugs.

A heavily built man, Anastasia still had the body of the enforcer he'd been in his youth. A pair of shark's eyes were set in his square, jowled face—brutish in its intensity—and a cigar was jutting from the corner of his mouth. Smoke drifted up directly past his eyes but didn't seem to have an effect. He was sitting at his desk wearing a smoking jacket and reading a newspaper, and I couldn't help but think the tableau would make a good *Saturday Evening Post* cover: "The killer at home."

A second after Anastasia registered our entrance, his face brightened and he bounded out of his chair. He threw his arms around Angelo.

"Ah, Angelo. How was your trip?"

"Good, I think, Don Alberto, good."

He turned to me. "And, Vincenzo—it's been a long time." He gave me a warm hug and kissed me on both cheeks. "So! How is the Navy man?"

"Fine, Don Alberto. I love the flying." Angelo had reminded me that there's no substitute for respect and little reason not to show it.

"You're still in those little jets, no?"

I smiled. "I am."

He nodded approvingly. "Your father would have been proud . . . I still miss him."

"So do I, Don Alberto."

"Something to drink?" he asked.

"Whatever you're having," I said genially.

"*Bene!* Angelo?"

"The same."

Anastasia snapped his fingers at a hovering servant. "Three Scotch and sodas!" he ordered, and waved us to a nearby couch and lounge chair.

"So," Anastasia asked, "success or no?"

"Maybe," said Angelo. "But it'll be expensive."

"Nothing's cheap," observed Anastasia. "What's he want?"

"He wants you to give Accardo a piece of your Cuban pie when you get it."

Anastasia yelped, "What?"

"That's what he said," Angelo replied quietly.

"He wants a slice of a pie I haven't even got yet?" Anastasia yelled. "That fuckin' Accardo!"

"Actually, it was Roselli who came up with it," explained Angelo.

"Roselli," Anastasia spit out, then, calming down, added, "It figures. When Dragna kicks off, he'll be number one if Accardo backs 'im." He let out a sardonic guffaw. "Gettin' Accardo a piece of my Cuba action'll guarantee it."

It was amazing how quickly these guys could put together plots, counterplots, and the motives behind them. In another world—with the right education—they'd be running the CIA.

"That's what I figure, too," agreed Angelo. "Whadda you wanna do?"

Anastasia looked at me as sorrowfully as his shark's eyes could manage. "Angelo told me this Pennington guy had ya boxed." He chuckled mirthlessly. "Roselli just threw me in there with ya."

"Don Alberto—," I began apologetically.

"No—no," he said, holding up his hand. "This is a debt of honor. I owe it to your father. *Bene!* I'll call Accardo tomorrow and tell 'im he has a deal."

"*Grazie*, Don Alberto" was all I could muster, totally flushed with relief.

"*Prego.* But lemme ask you a question. This girl—with an old man who put the arm on you in Jacksonville, tried to have you shipped to Siberia, and got you to ask me to give up a piece of my Cuba action—is she worth it?"

There it was again. The inevitable question, and I was beginning to think that maybe Doug, Angelo, Stuff, and Anastasia were right. Maybe it *was* crazy.

But the answer was always the same. "I love her."

Anastasia chuckled. "Everybody says love is blind and it never stops gettin' proved—she must be one helluva broad."

I smiled. "She is."

A servant returned with a tray of drinks, and we toasted each other with a chorus of *"Salute!"*

Anastasia chuckled again, but this time I could sense he was actually amused. He rattled the ice in his glass. "It will not be so bad. Cuba's a long way from Chicago. The only eyes they'll have down there watching the pie will be mine. The piece they'll get will have very little filling."

As always, these meetings amazed me. Already the scammers were being scammed.

We left Anastasia's and the five of us indulged in a huge celebratory dinner at Lena's. After a final round of grappa, Stuff and I returned to his apartment and immediately turned on the TV to check for news of the hurricane, which was now off the coast of South Carolina and moving out to sea. Jacksonville would be open tomorrow, and I could fly back to meet my returning squadron with a reasonably fair chance that the weight of the world had been hauled off my back.

If Accardo accepted Anastasia's deal at face value. *If* Roselli could convince Pennington that he had to back off because the big man in Chicago said so. *If* Pennington agreed. And *if* he kept his word.

It was a lot of ifs.

And there was one more: What if I was inexorably being drawn back into my old life? I had asked Anastasia for help and he'd given it to me. True, he felt that he owed it to my family. He'd said "a debt of honor." But what of the debt I owed him for his help? Wasn't that also a debt of honor? And what would I do if he ever came calling?

CHAPTER TWENTY-TWO

I SURVEYED THE hurricane damage to Jacksonville on my way home from the airport. Trees were down, store windows shattered, and rubble was everywhere, but the buildings, roads, and bridges hadn't sustained any major damage.

Our house—and the property—also looked to be in pretty good shape on my quick stop to change into a uniform. I checked in with Jess and Jessie and drove out to the air station. Our jets were just coming back in from Pensacola when I arrived. They roared in overhead in an echelon formation and executed a fan break with Blue Angel perfection.

The best, I thought. We were without question the best.

I found the four pilots who'd remained behind in the ready room, and fifteen minutes later we were joined by the fly-away group, minus Doug. A hydraulic leak had forced him to remain in Pensacola for repairs.

When Concannon spotted me, he headed over. "Your family pleased to see you, Mr. Vesta?"

"Yessir. Thank you."

"And have you reached a decision regarding your difficulty with our Senate and Navy department?"

"I believe the problem's resolved, sir."

"Good!" He smiled and slapped my arm. "Now that the hurricane's over and you're back in the fold, maybe we can all get back to doing our fucking jobs."

I got Angelo's call that evening while I was sampling Jessie's crawfish gumbo in the kitchen. I picked up the extension, sipped the broth, and learned I was officially off the hook.

Pennington had folded under pressure from Accardo.

I hung up, immediately called Kat, and told her she should be on a Friday-morning plane. I'd pick her up at the airport and we'd head to Sea Island. I only had to tell a small white lie about having just flown back from *Saratoga*.

Jessie overheard me, and when I hung up the phone, she chided, "My, my. Must've been somethin' to see that big old aircraft carrier cruisin' down Fifth Avenue."

I pecked her on the cheek. "A minor fib for a major reason."

She chuckled. "I 'spect Jesus kin live with that."

I was relaxed for the first time in over four days and decided to celebrate with a shakerful of "Steelies"—half gin, half vodka, and very little dry vermouth.

Doug walked in just then and said, "Yes, thank you, I will."

I poured the drinks straight up and we went out back where Jess was still cleaning up the yard. He had beached the Chris-Craft prior to the storm, but we'd lost half of our sixty-foot dock and debris was scattered all over the yard. He had cleared the patio though, so we sat while Doug told me about a trying weekend in Pensacola: too many pilots and not enough women to go around.

"And what about you, kemo sabe?" he asked. "The cavalry or the savages?"

139

"We got to Pennington. Kat and I are off the hook."

"No shit! That's great! How'd you do it?"

I told him, and he was impressed. He raised his glass in a toast. "I gotta hand it to you, pal. You boxed the boxer."

After a final day of FCLPs before Monday's CQ on *Saratoga*, I picked up Kat at the Jacksonville airport early Friday evening. She was wearing pale yellow slacks with a matching blouse and suede loafers—no jewelry. Her only makeup was a golden California tan. If anything, she looked more ravishing than when I'd seen her outside La Scala in her couture wardrobe and dazzling display of jewels.

She dropped her small carry-on bag as soon as she saw me at the gate and rushed into my arms squealing with joy.

I held her close and said, "Hi."

She nuzzled against my cheek. "Hi, sailor. It felt like I'd never get here."

I laughed and ruffled her hair. "You're here. Live with it."

"Oh, Vinny, I was so worried about the hurricane, and you flying out to the ship. I couldn't sleep until you called."

That cemented my guilt and ended any possibility of my telling her I'd seen her in L.A. with Marino.

It was another beautiful autumn evening as we drove up I-95 with the top down. I'd buried a bottle of Dom Pérignon in a plastic bag filled with ice, and she popped the cork at the Georgia border. By the time we got to the hotel we were both glowing and giggled like kids when we got the expected reaction from the desk clerk after I signed in as Vesta rather than Richards.

"We're trying to get on *The Ed Sullivan Show*," Kat explained. "We do a juggling act—us, two dogs, and a seal. We thought Richards was too common a name for TV. We changed it to Vesta—it has a far more lyrical ring to it, don't you think?"

The clerk smiled weakly and slammed his palm down on the bellhop's bell—slightly happier to see that this time we were both carrying luggage rather than paper bags. I had reserved our original suite and once again had to shoo out the bellhop before he went into his welcome spiel—so that we could go into our welcome romp.

We undressed each other slowly, savoring every second of anticipation, and after we feverishly kissed all of each other's significant body parts, I slid into her. All my life I'd heard that at some point sex with the same partner became boring. Maybe, but I sure as hell didn't see how it was possible.

What seemed like an eternity later we were lying on our backs, bathed in perspiration and practically breathless while we stared at the ceiling.

"Penny?" she asked.

I feigned shock. "That's all for my thoughts?"

She chuckled. "If they're not about me, that's all they may be worth."

"I was trying to see the future. Ours."

"I'll up the price. A million pennies."

"Kids," I said. "I was wondering about kids. Boys? Girls? Two? Three? You want kids?"

"I've never thought about it. I never had a reason to."

"And now?"

She rolled toward me and put her head on my chest. "Now anything's possible. I take it you want a big family."

Stroking her hair, I said, "Always the way with only children . . . After she had me, my mother couldn't have any more kids. I think only children are very unusual in our world."

"Miss not having brothers and sisters?"

"Maybe, but it was never really an issue. Stuff and the rest of my old street gang were as close as family. You?"

"The same. Never seemed to be an issue. When Mom died, I was off to boarding school and Vassar with summer vacations in Europe with classmates. Daddy was always there for me, and when I graduated, he flung me hell-bent into my career. There was never much time to speculate about a normal family life."

"Probably just as well—because there's nothing normal about family life in the Navy."

She took my hand and squeezed it. "We'll make it work. Whatever it takes."

"When was the last time I told you I loved you?"

"About ten minutes ago—when you were breathing exceptionally hard."

"Care for a repeat?"

"Always, but the gentleman should really buy the lady dinner first. She needs to regain her strength."

"Fish Shack?"

"Sold."

We drove over to Pier Village on St. Simons with the top down and the moon rising. The breeze had freshened and the fall air had a slight chill, but it didn't seem to matter.

"Chilly?" I asked as she snuggled under my arm.

"Uh-huh, but putting up the top would be sacrilegious."

"You know, Father D'Angelo would have given me three rosaries and a stations of the cross for an offense like that."

"Were you an altar boy?"

"All the Catholic kids in my neighborhood were altar boys—until they got old enough to figure out a way to ditch the job. There were very few teenaged kids wearing gowns."

She smiled. "I take it you're not still going to church?"

"Not since I was a kid."

"It's hard for me to imagine you as a kid."

"It's hard for me to remember being one."

We found an empty parking place near the lighthouse in Pier Village and made our way to the Fish Shack, a small restaurant at the end of the island's historic center. We'd made a note of the large wooden pompano hanging over the door during our first visit but had never made it back into town. Hell, we'd barely gotten out of bed.

A pretty blonde in a tank top and shorts met us at the door. Her name tag said Bunny.

I held up a pair of fingers. "Two."

"Table or bar?" she asked.

"Table," I answered, and she led us to a table on a raised platform that ran along the rear wall.

The place was once a warehouse and still had an open-beamed ceiling, visible air-conditioning ducts, and a forest of fishing gear hanging from the rafters. It was brightly lit, the tables and chairs were old oak, and the place settings consisted of straw place mats and paper napkins. Very basic, but the delightful aromas promised excellent dining.

Bunny handed us menus as we sat. "Kin Ah git y'all drinks?"

"Think you can manage a pair of margaritas?"

"We shu-ah can. Salt?"

I nodded. "Salt."

"Be raht back." She winked, spun on her heels, and was gone.

Kat smiled. "Cute."

"And perky." With a perfect name. "Doug would love her."

She laughed and opened her menu. "They've got oysters." She cocked an eyebrow.

"Think I need them?"

"For what I have in store for you, you might."

Feigning surprise, I said, "Frisky little devil, aren't you?"

"I continue to maintain that you bring out the best—and the worst—in me."

143

I bowed my head slightly. "Compliment accepted, but I think the oyster's reputation as a sex enhancer is a myth."

"What have we got to lose?"

"Point taken. Oysters to start. Next?"

"House salad, vinaigrette, sea bass, pecan pie, and you."

"Outstanding order. I'll make it two."

A waiter returned with our drinks and took our food order. I lifted my glass and held it out. "Us?"

"And the future," she responded.

We drank and I studied her in the harsh light. It was evident that lighting didn't matter. With or without makeup, day or night, fluorescents or candles, she was stunning. Her skin glowed and her eyes sparkled with happiness.

I said, "You know I was an altar boy when I was a kid, but I know almost nothing about you when you were a kid. Brownie? Campfire Girl? Girl Scout?"

"Please, I wasn't the joining type. But I did have a small group of friends in boarding school that had similar interests—drama society, debating club, and such."

"Sports?"

"Horseback riding, and at Vassar I took up tennis and golf—got pretty good, too. We sailed on the Hudson and occasionally went down to New York for the theater—Poughkeepsie is a pretty small town. And summers of course were always spent touring Europe."

"A spoiled little rich girl."

"I told you that in Mexico the first night we met. I've been very privileged and I know it. Does it bother you?"

"I wouldn't change a second of what made you who you are. I'll take the package and everything in it."

"Very gallant, sir. And I'll take the altar boy and everything he's become."

Dinner arrived and it was as expected. Excellent. I paid the bill, gave Bunny a large tip with a quick wink, and we drove back to The Cloister and a walk on the beach. In retrospect the oysters may have deserved their reputation.

CHAPTER TWENTY-THREE

UNWILLING TO LOSE one minute of our precious time in dreamland, we were up with Saturday's sunrise for an invigorating swim, and sex in the shower. After a light breakfast we dressed and headed back into town to pick up the makings of an early picnic lunch. The temperature was hovering in the mid to high seventies, and Pier Village was crowded with the usual bunch of weekend tourists milling about in shorts and T-shirts. Kat and I were similarly dressed, but Kat was wearing one of my white shirts with the tails tied above her navel and the three top buttons open.

I caught more than one head snapping around as we passed, but luckily traffic was light so there were no screeching tires.

The sign that caught my eye was DENNY'S DELI—DENNY BEVA-LAQUA, PROP. It was in the heart of Mallery Street and boasted "cold cuts a-plenty," so taking Denny at his word, we walked in and were met by an explosion of aromas. I immediately saw that the long glass showcase did indeed hold all the usual suspects—meats, cheeses, condiments, and salads.

"What's your pleasure, milady?" I asked.

"Ham on rye—Dijon and lettuce."

"Not very adventurous."

"You have a suggestion, Lieutenant?"

"I do." I turned to Denny. Denny was huge. He matched Angelo in girth and weight but was blond, blue-eyed, and taller. Probably a sophisticated northern-Italian type somehow transplanted to the Deep South.

"One-quarter pound each of prosciutto, mortadella, Genoa salami, and provolone. A half pint of the tomato and onion salad, and another of the roasted peppers. A loaf of Italian bread—halved and split down the middle."

Denny smiled. "Poifect hoagie—you gottit."

"Brooklyn?" I asked, startled.

"Canarsie—den after twenty-five years inna army and an extreme hate for the cold—here."

"The world continues to shrink," I replied. "You carry wine?"

"Onna back wall. We got red and white."

"A well-rounded selection," I said, and Kat and I walked to the back of the deli where we surveyed the possibilities and laughed.

"When in Rome," she chuckled.

"You pick."

"Hmmm." She perused the selections. "This—I think . . . a very promising red. It's quite expensive but we're splurging."

"It has a screw top."

"I noticed that. But it relieves the pressure of finding a corkscrew."

Denny finished packing our order; I paid him and loaded our goodies into a basket we borrowed from the hotel.

Kat had wanted to go riding, and although my equestrian talents left something to be desired (I explained that there weren't a helluva lot of riding academies in Hell's Kitchen and the only horses we saw had cops on them), I couldn't say no to her.

We drove back across the causeway and down to Jekyll Island, a short drive south of St. Simons, where we found a stable and rented two nice horses. That is, mine was nice: a docile gray mare with an understanding personality whose name was Dolly. Kat, however, selected a frisky gelding named Hank. He was coal black and at least two hands taller than my mare.

She handled Hank as if she'd been riding all her life, of course, but I hadn't, and for some reason my docile Dolly decided that she wanted to keep up with Kat's frisky Hank. So when Kat took off down the trail as if she had been shot out of a cannon, Dolly took off after him.

"Oh, shit!" I yelled, and desperately hung on for about a half mile. I bobbed and weaved in the saddle but couldn't duck being lashed by hanging Spanish moss. Kat finally pulled up under a majestic cypress and turned to watch me skid up beside her.

She was laughing her ass off.

I was breathing hard, but all in all was pretty proud of myself. "What made you think I wouldn't wind up in a full body cast?"

"Oh, I may not have known you long, sailor, but I know you well. There was no way you were going to let that nice little mare bounce you off her back."

"Thank you, my darling," I said sarcastically, "but I could have used a less hearty vote of confidence."

We tethered the horses, and an hour later I was sitting against the tree with her head in my lap. We'd finished our hoagies along with the wine and were enjoying a cigarette while looking across a quiet glade and out to sea.

Putting her hand on the back of my neck, she pulled herself up and kissed me. "Mmmm," she said. "On our last trip we made love under an oak. We wouldn't want this old cypress to be jealous, would we?"

*   *   *

148

On Sunday morning we again rose with the sun and realized that shower sex was becoming an addiction. I could think of a helluva lot worse habits. We'd decided to spend the morning fishing and drove over to the pier on St. Simons to charter a boat. There were few parking spaces in the area, so I dropped off Kat next to the charter dock and drove off to find a space. When I returned, I found that she'd already chartered a forty-four-foot boat for us and had paid for it.

Getting aboard, I asked, "How much was it?"

"What?" she asked blithely as the captain pulled out of the harbor and the mate began setting up tackle. The roar of the engines made us shout to be heard over them.

"The boat, of course!"

"What difference does it make?" she yelled back.

"All the difference. I'm an old-fashioned guy."

"You're very gallant and I love you, but you're being silly. Daddy's set up a very large trust fund that supplies me with more money than I can possibly spend, and you've paid for everything from the first moment we met."

"Naturally. I'm the guy—you're the girl."

A look of disbelief crossed her face. "You won't let me use my money . . . ever?"

"We'll talk about it. In the meantime, we're on my ticket."

She yelled, "You're being irrational, unreasonable, thickheaded, and stupid!"

I laughed and yelled back, "You're right. But I'm lovable!"

She laughed, too, playfully slapping me on the shoulder before turning her attention to the fishing gear—but I began to realize that we could have a problem down the road.

Three hours later we'd caught several redfish, sea trout, and a world-class pompano that Kat landed single-handedly. But since there was nothing we could do with the catch after we returned to the dock, we gave the fish to the captain and his mate. The catch would undoubtedly wind up in the kitchen of the Fish Shack that evening while the captain and his mate enjoyed a little extra grog money.

Back at the hotel we had lunch and a swim, and then, in what seemed minutes, suddenly found ourselves driving back to Jacksonville for Kat's six-o'clock flight.

She snuggled next to me with my arm around her shoulders. As we approached the airport, she joked that she was doing her patriotic duty by getting me home early—after two nights of debauchery she was finally going to let me get a good night's sleep before the next day's CQ.

I said, "Your country thanks you, kind lady. It's going to be a big week." And then I couldn't help myself. Even after our fabulous weekend together, I decided to touch on the subject that had been bothering me. "How about you? Anything new and exciting in your life?"

"Just the usual. The class I'm teaching plus auditions that I'm not interested in but go to anyway. It keeps my agent and Daddy happy." She laughed and snuggled closer. "When I told him we were engaged, he seemed to take it in stride, but he's hoping I'll be cast in a role that'll catch lightning in a bottle and make me forget about you. It won't happen, but since he's being nice to us, I'm being nice to him."

As casually as possible, I asked, "Is your father still trying to push you into seeing Marino?"

"Not really, why?"

Not really? I thought. Did that mean she *was* seeing him but her father *wasn't* pushing her? I pressed on, saying, "So you haven't seen him?"

She pulled out from under my arm. "Why the sudden interest in Marino?"

I retreated like the French army. "No reason. Just that you two were an item for a while."

"As I told you, darling," she responded evenly, "Victor Marino was a convenience. He meant, means, and will always mean nothing to me."

"Sorry I asked." But I wasn't sorry and it wasn't a satisfying answer. Why the hell was she still seeing him if he meant nothing to her?

"But if you must know," she continued, "I did see Vic last week. There was a fund-raiser at Zanuck's and Daddy asked me to be Vic's photo mate, so I humored him. Then Daddy, Vic, me, and my old friends Frick and Frack went to dinner at La Scala." She paused and fired one more shot across my bow. "And if you want to know something else, all I thought about that night was that goddamn hurricane and you in the middle of it!"

There it was—the truth, the whole truth, and nothing but. I was elated and blurted out, "Baby, I was wrong. But I am definitely not sorry I asked."

Ten minutes later we were once again saying good-bye next to a waiting plane. It was getting more familiar but not any easier.

"Next week," she said, holding me tightly.

"Five days," I said softly, hugging her back.

CHAPTER TWENTY-FOUR

THE SQUADRON ASSEMBLED in the ready room at 0700 on Monday morning—except for Kenny Willis, our LSO, who was already aboard *Saratoga* waiting to wave us in. Everyone was milling around and chatting excitedly when I arrived with Doug. We found Zaz waiting for us—but no Whitey—and Concannon was about to begin the briefing any minute.

I looked around and asked Zaz, "Where's Whitey?"

"Coming," he answered somewhat sheepishly.

"Coming! From where? He's late!"

"Umm, I think he's in the head."

I suddenly became concerned. "Is he okay?"

"I think so."

"You think? What's wrong?"

"Well, last night I took him out for Mexican food and I don't think the burritos and salsa agreed with him."

"Christ!" I mumbled, and shot out of the room.

I found Whitey in the head over a bowl chucking his guts out. "Whitey," I yelled. "Are you gonna be okay?"

He got up and wiped his mouth with a paper towel. "Yeah. Yeah, I think I'm gonna be okay, Vin. Must've been the salsa . . . never happened before."

He was the saddest, most apologetic-looking Nebraska farm boy on the map. His unruly red hair was plastered to his forehead and his eyes were wet and downcast—his entire six-foot frame slouched in embarrassment.

My heart went out to him. I'd seen it before. Nerves. Pure and simple. I said, "You've never been about to land a swept-wing jet on a carrier before."

"Yeah," he said miserably, "I didn't get much sleep last night."

I clapped him on the arm. "Of course you didn't! It's normal!"

He looked up. "It is?"

"Are you kidding? It happens all the time! The anticipation—the excitement—the worry that you'll fuck up! It's completely normal!"

He began to brighten. "Gee, Vin, I didn't know, I—"

"Of course you didn't know! You've never done it before. It happens a lot! It happened to me!"

A lie, but who gave a shit.

He brightened a bit more. "Really?"

"Absolutely! And to Doug! It happened to him!"

Another lie, but who was counting?

"Wow." A smile formed on his face. Then it dropped. "How come it didn't happen to Zaz?"

"He's Mexican!" I said as if that made all the sense in the world.

"Oh." He nodded in agreement.

"Now, wash your face and get your ass into the ready room. We're about to slam 'go-fast, belch-fires' onto moving runways!"

A minute later I walked in with a smiling Whitey. Everyone was seated and Concannon greeted us coolly. "Glad you could join us, gentlemen. With your permission I'll begin the briefing."

"Yessir," I mumbled as we hung our heads and sat.

Concannon announced that the first flight of eight planes would launch at 0745 and that *Saratoga* was steaming in our normal operating area off the Florida/Georgia coast. Unlike a week earlier when forty-foot seas turned the ocean into a naval nightmare, the water was flat as a pool table, the skies were clear, and a fresh wind was blowing.

The exercise was still only scheduled for a week because of the break in *Saratoga*'s schedule, and we wouldn't remain on the ship. Instead, every pilot in the air group would make eight carrier landings and receive eight catapult launches. The cat-shots would rocket us off the bow of the ship from 0 to 150 mph in under two seconds, and when we completed the exercise, we'd return to the Jax Air Station to repeat the process throughout the week.

The skipper again hammered home the message that CQ was not only a training exercise for the pilots but for the ship's crew as well. He reminded us that operating high-performance jets from an aircraft carrier was one of the most dangerous occupations in the world for all hands—an environment where simple miscues could be fatal.

We broke up into sections for last-minute briefings even though we'd gone over all of it countless times before. The Navy always figured one too many was better than one too few.

Concannon and Raney split off with Jake Raymond and wingman Pete Dane. Doug and Zaz were with Whitey and me. The four of us sat in a circle and I went through the drills, "Okay, Whitey and Zaz, listen up. Same as the FCLP drill—but this time, with the boat. Whitey, you're with me—Doug's got Zaz. We fly out in two two-plane sections and join up in echelon en route. We'll be following the skipper and Jake's sections. When we get to *Saratoga*, the skipper will lead us down the right side of the ship, wait eight to ten seconds, and break at eight hundred feet, four hundred knots. He'll pull about four g's onto the downwind and drop his hook. Everyone will follow. Once you're established downwind, it's gonna look a little different. . . . Doug?"

Doug continued, "Ashore you've had ground references to set up your distance abeam the runway. Out there, there *is* *no* nice long runway—only the ship, which will be well forward and to your left. Also, there won't be any roads or buildings to tell you when to start your turn into the ship at the one eighty. What you've got below you are waves, and every wave looks the same."

I picked up, "Line up dead-on behind the skipper and his sections. That should set you up pretty good. Establish your intervals, reduce speed, and ease down to six hundred feet on the way to the one eighty. That's where you'll hit difference number two. Ashore with a stationary runway, we turned in directly abeam. But this runway is a carrier and it's moving. If you turn directly abeam, you're going to wind up in too close with too little straightaway in the groove. Wait until the ship is about to disappear from the peripheral vision of your left eye before you start your turn." I nodded at Doug.

"Drop your gear and flaps and call, 'One eighty—gear and flaps down.' Roll into your twenty-five-to-thirty-degree bank, adjust your power, and begin the same three-hundred-to-four-hundred-foot rate of descent you had ashore. When you hit the ninety, same old, same old. You should be at five hundred feet."

I finished, "At the forty-five, you should be at three hundred fifty to three hundred seventy-five feet. You may pick up the ship's wake another forty-five degrees off to your left. Keep turning and overshoot the wake a bit so you can roll out on the centerline of the angle deck. Once in the groove, pick up the mirror—center the 'ball'—and call it. Start down the final—keep your scan going—speed—lineup—ball—and listen for Kenny to give you corrections. As you bore in, make smaller and smaller adjustments as you get nearer the ship. Wait for Kenny to give you the 'Cut' and hit the deck. Questions?"

Whitey and Zaz looked at each other, then back to me, and shook their heads.

Whitey beamed. "Let's do it!"

The butterflies were gone.

We strapped on our G suits, checked our survival gear, picked up our helmets, and rejoined Concannon.

He advised, "Don't make this drill any more exciting than it is by letting your heads drift up your asses. Look sharp out there, boys. God is watching."

We headed out to the flight line, and as we approached our aircraft, Doug asked, "Twenty a three wire, thirty a bolter, fifty a fubar?"

I nodded. "You're on."

This was the bet: A *three wire* meant your tailhook caught the third of the four wires that made up the carrier's arresting gear. It was a perfect *trap* and you were credited twenty bucks. A *bolter* was when your tailhook missed all four wires on the deck—you failed to trap and had to go around for another try. Embarrassing—and you were hit with a thirty-buck debit. A *fubar* was a wave-off that was your fault—not because of poor separation or a fouled deck. It meant your approach was so screwed up that your LSO had to make you go around before you even got to the deck because you were F-U-B-A-R—"fucked up beyond all recognition." Very embarrassing—and you were slammed for a fifty.

Our first eight FJ-3 Furies took off in four two-plane sections. Concannon with Raney on his wing. Jake Raymond with Pete Dane. Doug with Zaz, and I followed with Whitey. We headed out to sea, and fifteen minutes later the *Saratoga's* Air Traffic Control Center told us to set up a holding pattern at five thousand feet, twenty miles south-southeast of the ship. We'd be given our approach times shortly and would be called down as soon as the ship turned into the wind.

I looked down at the floating postage stamp that was actually a fifty-six-thousand-ton ship, over a thousand feet long. Manned by four thousand men and capable of accommodating eighty aircraft, it was one of the biggest and deadliest weapons ever invented by man. But no matter how big she was, to naval aviators she'd always looked like a postage stamp. And no matter how many times you landed on her deck, you'd always be thrilled and proud you could do it. By day it was merely a challenge—at night it was an ass-puckering son of a bitch that could put the fear of God into an atheist.

The radio crackled, "Harlequin flight, your approach time is zero five."

I checked my watch: 0802. In three more minutes Concannon would head down for the ship and lead us into the break. I glanced over at Whitey, flying tight on my right wing. He grinned and gave me a thumb's-up.

I smiled to myself. He was ready.

At exactly 0805 we started down and, exactly as briefed, leveled off at eight hundred feet, four hundred knots, aft and to the right of the ship. I saw the ship as we roared by and had mentally counted to ten when Concannon broke left. We followed and lined up downwind. Concannon called, "Gear down and locked," and started his approach. A minute later I heard him call, "Ball," indicating he had the mirror and was lined up on the carrier's angle deck. Raney and Doug followed and caught a wire without incident. Then I heard Zaz sing out, "Ball," and Kenny begin giving him corrections as he started down the groove. There weren't many, though, and fifteen seconds later I felt a shot of pride when Kenny gave him a "Cut" and he landed.

A few moments later I ran through my checklist one last time, called, "One eighty, gear down and locked," and started in. I was on speed and a little over 550 feet when I passed through the ninety. A touch high. I corrected my height and saw the carrier's wake as I continued through the forty-five I kept turning, passed over it, and lined up in the groove. Starting down, I felt my heartbeat begin its inevitable increase.

Kenny called, "A little high."

Shit, I thought. I hadn't corrected enough. I reduced power a bit, dropped my nose, watched the ball center, and added power.

For the next twenty-five seconds I glued the ball dead center, but as usual, everything seemed to pick up speed: cross-checks—airspeed—lineup—smaller and smaller corrections as the fantail loomed closer and closer. And then the deck rushed up and *wham*—there was the controlled crash that was a normal carrier landing, followed by *Uhhh*, as my shoulder harness kept me from flying through the windshield. I'd moved the throttle up to full power the second I hit the deck, but the airplane wasn't going anywhere. I'd caught the three wire.

Perfect! Put that in your mess kit and eat it, kemo sabe, I thought. I'm twenty bucks up, Douglas.

I throttled back and followed the instructions of the yellow-shirted sailor. I was then ushered to the bow of the ship by blue-shirted men—flight-deck crewmen—who finally handed me off to the green shirts—catapult people—who lashed my plane to the number two cat. It was an intricately choreographed ballet of men without toe shoes on a treacherous stage.

Once again time sped up: checklist—engine screaming up to full power—bracing for the shot—a salute to the catapult officer—and then the jolt and a suppressed scream as I rocketed to 150 mph in under two seconds.

Outstanding! I thought, and savoring a shot of adrenaline, I put my jet in a climbing left turn toward the downwind to repeat the process seven more times before heading back to base.

When the exercise was over, the final tally was Whitey with one bolter and Zaz with a wave-off; Doug and I both managed to pull off six perfect traps and no money exchanged hands. The rest of the squadron did equally well, but Concannon was furious that he'd had to take a wave-off, even though it wasn't his fault. The intervals had gotten too close and the deck was still fouled when he was closing in. Kenny Willis—our LSO—had been forced to order him to go around and the "Black Thing" was still swearing about it when we reconvened in the ready room.

The second flight of eight took off after we landed and did as well as we had. We repeated Monday's routine during the next four days, finishing our cycle on Thursday. All in all it had been a great exercise, and Concannon rewarded us with a long weekend by declaring "holiday routine" on Friday. I immediately began thinking about a long weekend with Kat and settled on surprising her with a four-star shocker.

As we were sitting down to dinner on Wednesday, Stuff called. It seemed that everything connected to my rotund friend was related to food. Coincidence? I wondered.

"Hi," he said, "it's me. Am I interuptin' anything?"

I chuckled. "Just dinner."

"It's eight thirty! You ain't eaten yet?"

Stuff was a "seven-one-seven" man. Breakfast at seven, lunch at one, dinner at seven. Missing a designated time slot was unthinkable. Going without dinner until eight thirty? Inhuman.

"It's been a long day," I said. "What's up?"

"Pop's birthday. It's this Saturday. We're figuring on throwing 'im a little surprise party at Lena's."

Shit, I thought, with everything that was going on, I'd forgotten Angelo's birthday. "Great idea. You gonna do gifts? I'll send one."

"Can't ya send you?" he asked, sounding disappointed.

"Well, no . . . I mean, I've got Kat coming in and—"

"So bring 'er! Dino, Matty, and Gus'll be there, plus my mom and yours. Everybody wants to meet 'er!"

"I dunno, Stuff." I felt torn. My heart really was set on a completely different trip.

"You being here'd mean a lot to Pop."

He was right, and after all Angelo'd done for me, it was the least I could do to show my thanks and respect. Kat and I'd still have a long weekend together, and I could surprise Angelo and see my mother. Why not? I thought.

"Vinny. Are you there?"

"Right. It's doable, Stuff. I'll fly in on Friday and have Kat meet me. I'll let you know where we'll be staying."

"What about with me?" he asked, sounding a bit hurt.

"No offense, big fella, but I don't think so."

"I thought you liked the place."

"I love it! But you want me to take a high-class broad to a cellar in Hell's Kitchen for a romantic weekend in New York?"

"When ya put it that way, maybe not. But I'll pick you guys up."

"Done. I'll call you tomorrow."

I immediately called Kat and enticed her with descriptions of a romantic three-day weekend in New York: I'd book us into the Essex House overlooking Central Park and we'd see a show, eat fabulous food, and attend a surprise party at Lena's—the best new Italian restaurant in the city.

She was thrilled. She loved the Big Apple and was looking forward to meeting my friends. She also wanted to know if I could get tickets to *West Side Story*. I assured her that Angelo Maserelli could get tickets to anything on planet Earth, and we hung up looking forward to a delightful three days. It would be the longest we'd ever spent together.

CHAPTER TWENTY-FIVE

K AT TOOK THE red-eye out of L.A. at midnight. With the three-hour time change, she'd arrive in New York at ten thirty Friday morning, and we'd have the whole day together. I took the first flight out of Jacksonville so I would arrive in time to meet her plane.

My flight landed a half hour ahead of hers, and Stuff was waiting for me at the gate. We took the short walk over to TWA's terminal, and I playfully cuffed him on the arm. "For Christ's sake, don't say something like 'You look even better than the last time I saw you.'"

"What am I, an idiot?" Stuff objected. "I'll just say, 'Ya look even better in *daylight* than the last time I saw ya!'"

I cuffed him a little harder. "Asshole."

Kat appeared looking as if she just stepped off the cover of autumn's *Vogue*—she was wearing a rust-colored ensemble of skirt, blouse, belted topcoat, and high-heel boots. I saw Stuff's jaw drop as we wrapped our arms around each other.

When we separated, she looked at my 260-pound friend and said, "And you must be Stuff." She extended her hand and introduced herself. "Kat."

Stuff hesitated a moment, took her hand. "Right." Then he smiled and quipped, "How'd ya guess?"

She laughed. "I'm clairvoyant."

After we picked up her luggage, the three of us piled into the front seat of Stuff's '57 Chevy Bel Air and headed for the Essex House. In their own way, both the car and the hotel would become classics.

"Does Angelo have a clue about what's going on?" I asked.

"Not even close. I told 'im me and mom'd have a birthday dinner at Lena's and maybe take in a flick later. When he sees you, he'll flip . . . By the way, there're two tickets ta *West Side Story* waitin' at the box office fer you tonight."

Kat shrieked, "Vinny, you did it!"

"Actually, Stuff's father did it," I corrected.

"Actually, *I* did it," said Stuff. "Usin' my father's name. We didn't want 'im to know you guys were in town."

Stuff took the Queensboro Bridge to Fifty-ninth Street and continued on to Central Park South, where the Essex House was located between Sixth and Seventh avenues.

Passing Sixth, we heard wailing police sirens behind us, then suddenly three police cars tore past us with their red bubble-gum lights flashing. They turned down Seventh Avenue, their tires screeching, and disappeared.

Stuff said, "Goddamn cops. They're prob'bly late for a coffee break."

He dropped us off in front of the hotel, a bellman took our bags, and we checked into a tenth-floor suite overlooking the park. Kat was tired after her night flight and wanted to catch a nap before lunch, so I tucked her in and called my mother.

When she answered, I said, "Hi, Mom—I'm in New—"

She cut me off immediately, sounding frantic. *"Gesù Cristo!* You heard?"

"Heard what? What's wrong?"

"They killed him!" she cried out.

"Who?" I shouted. "Who did they kill?"

"It's all over the radio and television," she wailed. "Albert! They shot Albert!"

Christ! I thought. Anastasia? Now what! "When?" I asked, reaching to turn on the TV.

"This morning, at a hotel," she said, sobbing.

"Okay, Mom. Try to settle down. Call Lena. I'm in New York. I'll call Angelo and then stop by as soon as I know what happened."

"First your father and now Albert! When will it stop?"

"It never stops, Mom. I'll be there later."

I hung up and called Angelo at his office. Naturally he wasn't there. With the hit on Anastasia there was no telling where he was or what would happen next. Another war? What? And here I was in the middle of it all again—what was I thinking?

I turned the TV to WPIX. A reporter with a mike was in front of the Park Sheraton in the midst of police cars, a crowd of oglers, and even more newscasters. From what I could gather, sometime around ten thirty A.M., Albert Anastasia, "the Lord High Executioner," aka the Mad Hatter, was gunned down in a barber chair by two unidentified assassins.

I redialed Angelo, and Matty Cavallo said Angelo was on his way. I said so was I and hung up. I left Kat a note saying I'd be back by one o'clock and grabbed a cab.

Angelo's office was on the corner of Twelfth Avenue and Fiftieth Street facing the midtown piers. After my father's murder, he had taken over both the office and the territory. If it walked, moved, or floated on the stretch of piers between Thirtieth and Fifty-seventh, it came under the jurisdiction of the longshoremen's union; Albert Anastasia had run the union, and Angelo was his delegate.

I entered the outer office through the Fiftieth Street door and found Gus Chello, Dino, Matty, and six other men waiting there. I didn't recognize any of the six but knew they had to be part of Angelo's crew.

"He here?" I asked one of the twins. I'd known them half my life and still couldn't tell them apart.

Familiar with the problem, Matty smiled. He flicked his thumb toward his chest and said, "Matty—I told him you were comin'."

"Thanks," I said.

"He ain't happy," Matty informed me. "Sit. He's on the phone."

I was about to take a seat when Stuff entered, scowling. "Now we know what all the sirens were about this mornin'," he said angrily.

"Unbelievable," I agreed.

Angelo opened the door, spotted me. "What the hell're you doin' here?"

"I came in to see my mom," I lied.

"Oh," he said, obviously agitated. He waved everyone into his office, adding, "But you should stay away from us while this is goin' down."

"What d'you figure?" I asked while everyone took seats and waited for orders.

"Genovese! Who else?" Angelo snapped. "He's already called a meetin' of the Commission! In an hour!" He pointed to the phone. "That was Profaci. That son of a bitch had to be in on it, and so did Lansky and Christ knows who else. They all had to know about this before it went down! I told Albert to stay the fuck away from Cuba! He wouldn't listen!"

"What're you going to do?" I asked.

"What the hell can we do? Start an all-out war?"

Dino agreed it was impossible. "With who? All of them?"

"Bastards!" screamed Angelo. "And we don't know shit yet, except that Genovese wouldn't act alone. He had allies. We gotta wait until after the meet to find out how many. In the meantime we stay here and lay low. Go back ta your hotel, Vinny. We'll let ya know what's happenin', but you stay out of it, *capisce*?"

"*Sì, capisco.* My girlfriend'll be happy I'm out of it, but my mother'll be pissed."

"I know," he said, shaking his head. "She'll never change."

My mother still lived in Hell's Kitchen in our old apartment. She'd refused to move out of the fourth-floor walk-up when my father was killed, and the apartment had been frozen in time. The only thing that had changed was the news on the radio.

The beautiful clandestine farm in Connecticut that my father had purchased in 1940 had been sold. With the proceeds she could have lived on Sutton Place for two lifetimes. No way. Hell's Kitchen was where her friends and memories were, and that was where she'd stay. My mother was a stubborn Sicilian widow and no one disputed her decision.

Because I'd refused to follow in my father's footsteps and we'd been estranged for so many years, every time I walked into my old home I knew who and what I'd be facing. I would rather have tangled with a bunch of MiGs over Moscow.

Although I'd spoken to her an hour earlier, I called again and said I was on my way. In that short time she'd become completely calm and sounded as distant as I'd come to expect over the years.

A cab brought me to the tenement on the corner of Thirty-sixth Street and Eleventh Avenue, and when I entered the building, I was greeted by the familiar aroma of garlic that was the lifeblood of its inhabitants. Climbing the four flights of stairs, I passed the usual sounds of crying babies, Italian opera, and an occasional argument in blistering Sicilian. Again it seemed that nothing had changed.

Although I'd tried to call weekly, I hadn't been home for ten months. And now Anastasia, my father's mentor and my mother's friend, had been killed. I wasn't expecting a particularly warm reception.

I knocked lightly on the door that opened into the kitchen and waited for her to open it.

She looked at me, nodded without emotion, and in her lilting Sicilian accent said, "So, the prodigal son returns."

The years had been good to her. She was still a strikingly handsome woman, but unfortunately her demeanor had been severely altered when my father was gunned down. The only indication of her earlier hysteria was the redness in her eyes, but I knew that she had to be seething inside.

"Hi, Mom." I moved to embrace her.

She returned my hug without fervor.

I noted that she was wearing a black dress. Not good. She was not "old school" and had ceased wearing black a month after my father was killed. But now she'd put on a mourning mantle for Anastasia.

Stepping back, she asked, "You spoke to Angelo?"

"I did."

"And . . . what does he think?"

"He's really not sure yet."

She eyed me suspiciously. "That's all he said?"

"Well, no, but—"

"What are you not telling me?" she demanded.

She was getting herself worked up again and I tried to stall. "Mom, it's too early, he—"

"Who does he think ordered it?" she asked coldly.

What the hell, I figured. She'd find out soon enough. She'd call Angelo. "He thinks it was Genovese."

I saw her face contort and fire flash in her eyes. "Again Genovese!" she yelled, and ripped her hand across the kitchen table, sending her coffee cup and saucer crashing to the floor.

I tried to calm her down. "Mom!"

"That *maiale* Genovese! First your father and now Albert!" The mere mention of the man responsible for my father's murder had caused her to erupt.

"Mom, please." I stepped toward her.

She lashed out, "And what will you do about it this time?"

I was taken aback. "Me?"

"Yes—you!" she screamed.

"Look, Mom, I know how you feel—"

"Do you?" she spat out, her voice rising. "Do you? You with your fancy uniform! You with your gold wings and medals! You who went off to kill for your country—but wouldn't kill for your own father!"

It was hopeless.

"Okay, Mom . . . I can't change how you feel about that . . . I'm sorry."

I saw the tears well up in her eyes. She sank into a chair and buried her face in her hands.

I shook my head. "I'll call you later, Mom."

CHAPTER TWENTY-SIX

I WENT BACK to the hotel and found Kat dressed and hungry. We decided on a late lunch in Central Park and strolled slowly through the crowds toward the Boathouse restaurant overlooking the lake. The cloudless day was warm, the leaves were turning, and there was a light breeze. New Yorkers were enjoying the last mild days of autumn before winter set in—most of them still oblivious of the brutal murder that had taken place a dozen blocks away.

There was no point in telling Kat about the scene with my mother, but on the way I told her Anastasia had been assassinated. She was shocked and immediately asked what effect it would have on me—on us—or on my friends. I said it would definitely throw organized crime into turmoil and would probably have a negative effect on my friends, but that I was well out it.

I was of course being overly optimistic. Anastasia had been the linchpin in my war to hold off Daddy's assault on us. But since there was no way to reveal this to her, I merely said we'd still be going to the theater and, as far as I knew, to Angelo's birthday party Saturday night.

At the Boathouse we sat on the deck and ordered a bottle of pinot grigio to go with fish platters. Swans swam by looking for a friendly handout, and we obliged with bread sticks. Watching the rowboats and a gondola drift by, I marveled at how easily the magical atmosphere could make you forget you were still in a violent city.

The message light was blinking when we got back to the hotel. It was Angelo, and I immediately returned his call.

"Vinny," I said. "I just got back."

"It's over," said Angelo. "It was over two fuckin' hours after the hit. We got word the Commission ruled that Costello was definitely out. The new capo of the Luciano family is gonna be Vito Genovese. And the first thing Genovese did after the rulin' was ta name a new head of *our* family. Anastasia's gonna be replaced by Carlo Gambino!"

Carlo Gambino was in Vito Genovese's pocket.

"Holy shit," I said. "Genovese is going for it all."

"Yeah," said Angelo, sounding disgusted. "And I don't see no way to stop him."

"That's it?" I said, amazed.

"That's it," he said, sounding resigned. "It's like I figured. Costello is convinced that it was Albert who tried to have him whacked, Lansky was pissed over his move on Cuba, and the rest of 'em found out he was 'makin' guys' for cash. They all okayed the hit."

"So now you're with Gambino?"

"Yeah. We'll see what happens."

"I'm sorry, Angelo."

"Yeah, me, too. Albert was a vicious son of a bitch but he was a good family man and he never treated me or your father with anythin' but respect."

"You talk to Elsa?"

Elsa was Anastasia's wife, whom he'd married in 1937 when she was nineteen. She'd always refused to believe the appalling stories about her husband, insisting he was a hardworking businessman who never drank and was usually home by nine P.M. The latter was actually true.

"Yeah. She wants a very private funeral. No long motorcade of limos, no giant wreaths."

"You think that'll happen?"

"She'll get what she wants. Albert's brother Tony's handlin' it and he says onny family. It's the end of an era, kid."

"Yeah, I guess it is."

"I'm havin' dinner at Lena's tomorrow with Stuff and Lena. It's my birthday. Can ya join us?"

"Love to, Angelo, but I gotta get back to Jax," I lied.

"Oh, okay, kid," he said, sounding disappointed.

"But thanks for everything, Angelo."

"No problem. See ya next time."

I hung up and called my mother's apartment. I wanted to apologize for upsetting her and tell her I'd pick her up for Angelo's birthday party. Lena answered however and said my mother was disconsolate and that she was taking her to the Maserellis' seaside home on the Jersey shore to comfort her. She explained that the murder had brought back the horror of my father's killing, and my mother had once again plunged into grief.

I wondered if, under the circumstances, the unspoken message was that she also didn't want to see me.

As Angelo had said, "She'll never change."

I added to myself, she can't.

That night I took Kat to "21" for dinner, where the topic of the hour was Anastasia's assassination. We sat at the oak bar and, after downing two exceptional straight-up martinis and devouring their renowned bouillabaisse, hurried to the Winter Garden Theater to take in *West Side Story*.

It was riveting, and I easily related to the street gangs, the conflicts, and especially the tragedy. Kat was captivated by the Romeo and Juliet update and noted that the war between the lovers' families was not unlike the one that had once existed between her father and me.

I hoped that she was right about "had *once* existed," but the day had left me more anxious than ever.

We had a nightcap at Joe Allen's and returned to the hotel, where we immediately crawled into bed. Kat snuggled up to me and put her head on my chest, but my mood must have been catching. "I've got a bad feeling, Vinny."

I tried to lighten things up. "About what? We've had a helluva night! Great show, great food, and conjugal bliss is minutes away."

"Not about tonight, Vinny. About today. I know you're not involved anymore, but it has to affect you. Your oldest friends are deeply involved. And what about your mother?"

"You're right. My friends are involved and my mother's definitely involved whether she needs to be or not. But on Sunday you'll go back to L.A., I'll go back to Jax, and this will all seem a universe away."

"You're sure?"

I wasn't, but said, "Absolutely. So why don't you put your mind to, um, other things?"

Kat and I both woke up in better moods and spent Saturday playing tourist. We ate at the Stage Deli, visited the Metropolitan Museum, rode the subway to Wall Street, and even took in the Fulton Fish Market. And at six thirty we met everyone at Lena's—sans Lena and my mother. Dino, Matty, Gus, Kat, and I sat at a large round table next to the back wall and watched Stuff lead Angelo in.

We all got up and yelled, "Surprise!" followed by "Happy Birthday" and "For He's a Jolly Good Fellow."

Angelo looked truly surprised—and especially delighted when he saw me. He hugged everyone enthusiastically, but when he got to Kat, he bowed dramatically and kissed her hand.

He turned to me. "How the hell do ya do it, Vinny?"

Kat said, "He didn't do it. I did. I chased him until he caught me."

Everyone laughed and Stuff cried out in a swashbuckling roar, "Wine for my men!"

A waiter appeared, filled all our glasses, and began taking orders. Stuff joked that for an appetizer he'd have the left side of the menu.

I wasn't sure it was a joke.

A few seconds later the hostess came over to tell Angelo that there was a call for a Miss Caitlin Pennington.

Angelo pointed to Kat. "Call for ya."

"Oh," Kat replied, obviously a bit surprised, and excused herself.

I tracked Kat to the hostess desk. Here? How? Everyone who could possibly know where she was, was already here.

The desk was next to the front door, and as Kat approached it, I saw two men in overcoats coming toward the entrance. Their collars were up and both wore hats—one black, the other gray—pulled low over their eyes. My antenna instinctively went up and I tapped Angelo on the wrist. He looked at me and I nodded toward the door.

He turned and immediately called to Stuff in a stage whisper, "Attillio! The door!"

Stuff looked toward it just as Kat picked up the phone and the two men outside the door drew their revolvers.

Angelo shouted, "Everybody down!" and drew his .45.

"Black hat" lunged at the door and threw it open—bursting into the room as everyone at our table scrambled to the floor. He opened fire. "Gray hat" rushed in behind him and raised his gun. Angelo was in the air and halfway to the floor when the lead assassin's shots hit the wall where Angelo had been only a moment earlier. Confusion instantly appeared on the killer's face, undoubtedly registering shock at how quickly his huge target had vanished.

The split second of confusion cost him his life. Angelo had made his dive for the floor firing, and his two .45-caliber rounds slammed into his target's chest. The impact sent him hurtling backward into the gray-hatted assassin before crashing through the door and out onto the sidewalk.

"Gray hat" was spun sideways and never got off a shot. Stuff, Gus, Dino, and Matty all fired at once, and the gray-hatted killer continued spinning until he flew though the door and landed on the sidewalk next to his partner. They'd almost cut him in half.

The other diners were still screaming when Angelo got up and rushed out of the restaurant. I jumped to my feet and ran over to Kat. Her face was ashen.

"Who was on the phone?" I yelled out.

She didn't seem to hear me. She just stared at the empty doorway in shock.

I grabbed her arms. "Kat! Who was on the phone?"

I still got no answer so I shook her gently. "Kat!" I yelled. "The phone! Who was it?"

That seemed to make her focus and she said, "No one . . . no one was on the phone."

It only took a moment for it to hit me. It was a ploy. One of the two killers had called, wanting Kat out of the line of fire. And there was only one person I could think of who would have issued that order.

Angelo appeared in the doorway and waved me outside. He'd removed the hats from the two bodies and pulled off their phony mustaches. "It's the two guys we saw in L.A."

I didn't even need to look at them. "Their names are Spig Whitten and Paulie Burkhardt," I said.

Angelo, realizing what had just gone down, responded knowingly, "This wasn't about me, kid. It was about you."

I knew Angelo was right. Daddy had probably used Anastasia's assassination as cover for a hit on me. Everyone would assume it was the beginning of a gang war and that Angelo was the target. I would have been a bystander killed by wayward bullets.

That clever, miserable son of a bitch. Now the question was, what the hell to tell Kat?

I needed some time to think so I said, "Angelo, don't tell anyone we knew these guys. Kat knows they worked for her father. I've gotta figure a way to tell her that her Daddy's a fucking psychopath."

When Detectives Santorum and Riley arrived, they questioned everyone in the restaurant. All the stories matched: Two men had burst in and started shooting at our table.

When they arrived at our table and recognized Angelo and Stuff Maserelli, their line of questioning immediately indicated they assumed exactly what Pennington wanted them to assume—that the shoot-out was the beginning of a gang war and that Angelo and his son were the first targets.

Angelo and Stuff of course both maintained they had no idea who the two shooters were, and Gus, Dino, and Matty, also known to the cops, maintained the same thing. In their case, it was true.

The other diners, obviously innocent bystanders, were perfunctorily questioned and let go, but my Navy ID and name raised their eyebrows. Detective Santorum wanted to know if I was any relation to Gino Vesta.

"He was my father," I said.

"Really," he said, intrigued. "He was shot some years back if I remember."

"You do. Seven years ago."

"And what's his Navy lieutenant son doing here in the middle of a shoot-out seven years later?"

"I'm stationed in Jacksonville. I came in for a birthday party."

"Oh, yeah? Whose?"

I pointed at Angelo. "His."

Santorum smiled slyly and held his hand out to Angelo. "Lemme see your ID."

Angelo opened his wallet and held out his driver's license. Santorum read the date of birth and dropped his smile. He turned back to me saying, "And I guess you have no idea who the two stiffs are?"

"Correct," I said.

Kat identified herself as an actress from L.A. and had the ID to prove it. She said she was my fiancée and that she'd flown in to meet me for the weekend. An airline ticket in her purse bore her story out. It never occurred to them to ask if *she* knew the shooters.

All in all, there wasn't much for the detectives to go on, so they left after the bodies were hauled off to the morgue. It was nine o'clock.

Stuff let out a deep sigh and said, "Christ— I'm hungry! Let's eat!"

Much later that night—after I left "do not disturb" messages on the door and phone—Kat and I fell into bed absolutely exhausted. We curled into each other's arms, and for the first time since we'd met, we didn't make love.

CHAPTER TWENTY-SEVEN

KAT AND I SLEPT until noon and had a room service brunch while watching the Sunday talk shows speculate about what was going to be the result of Anastasia's murder.

Not one of them had a clue.

It would be another twenty days before the world got its first inkling of the real repercussions. The first thing Don Vito Genovese did after taking power was call a massive meeting of La Cosa Nostra to declare himself *capo di tutti capi*—the boss of all bosses. It was held at the estate of Joe Barbera and was attended by all the heads of the major crime families across the nation.

When one of the attendees noticed New York State troopers taking down license-plate numbers in the parking lot of Barbera's home, the Mob leaders panicked and scattered into the adjoining woods. It was a fiasco. Among those arrested were Joe Bonanno, Profaci, Genovese, and Gambino. Newspapers all over America trumpeted the event, and J.

Edgar Hoover, after years of denying it, was finally forced to admit that there really was a Mafia.

But all of that would come almost three weeks later.

Kat was unusually quiet; something was obviously bothering her. Checkout time was at one, and we didn't have to leave for the airport until five, so I asked if she'd like to take the Circle Line cruise around Manhattan. She quickly agreed and we packed our bags and checked out.

We picked up the boat at the Forty-second Street pier and headed south down the Hudson River on yet another beautiful autumn day. There was salt in the air, a light chop on the Hudson, and as we motored by New York's skyscrapers, their windows reflected brilliant flashes of sunlight. Standing at the rail with my arm around her, I found myself grappling with the easiest way to tell Kat about her beloved daddy.

I was still struggling when the tour guide finished his brief history of Ellis Island. There were a few moments of silence, then I heard Kat take a deep breath. She said, "I know . . ."

I looked at her sharply. "Beg your pardon?"

She repeated, "I know who those two men were."

I managed a shocked "What?"

"The shooters were Spig Whitten and Paulie Burkhardt."

I was completely stunned. "You knew last night?"

She nodded slowly. "I got a clear look at them when they came through the door. Those two days they spent following me around the last time I was here—I saw them up close in the elevator, in the restaurant, and on the Chanel set. The mustaches were ridiculous."

Still dazed by the revelation, I muttered, "You realize your father sent them."

"Yes, and I also know how they knew we'd be at the restaurant . . . Last Thursday night I was with Daddy when he hosted a dinner party for Zanuck, the chief of police, and the mayor. Of course with Zanuck there, talk naturally turned to show business, and Zanuck said he was bidding for the film rights to *West Side Story*. And of course I bragged that I'd be seeing it this weekend in New York. He was very impressed, since tickets are hard to come by, and I told him my fiancé had some very powerful friends, and that after the play on Saturday we were hosting a surprise party for one of them at Lena's. Daddy obviously put together who 'the friend' was and sent Spig and Paulie to the restaurant . . . I guess I never realized the extent of his compulsion," she said, her voice catching. Tears began to well up and she looked away.

"He's a very determined man, Kat. We've got to face it."

She turned back to me and tears began to flow. "And now I suppose you or Angelo or *someone* will have to retaliate."

"I hadn't thought about that. I wanted to talk to you."

I watched her look out at the Manhattan skyline. She seemed to be searching for something. When she turned back, her voice was pleading, "He's my father, Vinny."

"Meaning?"

She started to sob. "Meaning I can't forgive him for what he's done, but he's still my father. He raised me alone from the time I was six! I can't forgive him, but I can't help loving him."

"I understand that, but—"

"And I love you, Vinny! I love you more than anyone or anything in the world. But you have to promise me, *promise* me you won't hurt him!" She came unglued and threw herself into my arms.

I was aghast. "Christ! Kat! You want me to do nothing? Not even find a way to make him listen to reason? He tried to kill me. Destroy *us*!"

She was still crying, her body shaking. "I know that! But something in his mind must have snapped for him to do this."

"This?" I protested. "It wasn't only this. There's a litany of what he's been doing since he had you kidnapped in Jax. And what you don't know is that three weeks ago he even tried to destroy my career."

She leaned back and looked at me. "What? When?"

"Right before the hurricane. He got your California senator to call the undersecretary of the Navy and threaten to have me shipped off to a rathole you'd never be able to get to—the same thing he threatened to do to Dave Stanfield. Angelo got one of your father's Mob cronies to lean on him and withdraw the threat."

She bit her lip, absorbing the new information. "So that's why he suddenly became so compliant and said he wouldn't try to stop me from seeing you."

"Exactly."

"My God, he's not rational. Don't you see that? He's sick!"

I couldn't believe she was still making excuses for him. "So what do you suggest I do?"

"Nothing. Promise me, Vinny. Let me talk to him."

"What the hell are you going to say? 'Please, Daddy, stop trying to kill my boyfriend. It upsets him?'"

She wiped away her tears with the back of her hand and once again became the coolly intelligent, sophisticated woman I'd first met in the San Diego train station.

"No, darling," she said. "I'm going to say that I'm willing to testify that it was his men who came into the restaurant and tried to kill you. The New York detectives took my statement saying I was standing right next to the door when they came in. Spig and Paulie have been seen with him all over L.A. There are pictures of all of us at restaurants, premieres, and fund-raisers, and I can prove they followed me in New York with Sally's testimony. He'll never let it happen—the accusation alone would cause a scandal that would destroy him. He'll back off and never try anything again."

I turned away from her and thought about it—slowly beginning to realize that it was a real possibility.

As the boat turned up the East River, I said, "Okay. We'll try it your way."

I called Angelo before I left town and told him what Kat wanted to do. He agreed it might work, reminding me that intimidating Pennington was our original idea before Roselli got us into the Cuba gambit.

I told him I thought he was right, but for the moment all we could do was hope.

When Kat returned to her home in Beverly Hills Sunday night, she called me in Jacksonville and said she found frantic messages from her father on her answering machine. He said he'd tried to reach her at the Essex House all morning after he'd heard the news about Anastasia and the hit at the restaurant. He'd been told there was a "do not disturb" message on the phone, and when he finally got through, he was told we'd already checked out. She said he sounded beside himself.

I reserved comment. The son of a bitch deserved an Oscar.

Kat said she was exhausted and didn't want to confront him at home. She wanted to do it when she was fresh and in his office—where he'd be surrounded by all the formal accoutrements of the legal system she was going to threaten him with. She told me she wasn't going to return his calls and, on the chance that he might come by her house, would be spending the night with Sally.

As much as he loved his daughter, I couldn't see Pennington wanting to face an attempted-murder charge over her. He was too enamored with money, power, and the good life.

And what the hell could I really do? I certainly wasn't going to whack him myself. I was determined to leave all that behind me. So maybe hers was the best option. Spig and Paulie were dead, and who really gave a shit. They were punks. And neither I nor any of my friends had been hurt.

CHAPTER TWENTY-EIGHT

O N MONDAY MORNING, Doug was still in bed with an overnight guest from the weekend follies when I came down to breakfast in my khaki uniform. Jessie was grumbling that Jess's snoring was louder than last night's party—which was louder than a revival meeting.

"Tween the two, y'all are tearin' up mah sleep time!" she said.

Jess said, "If it'll make yuh happy, I put a clothespin on mah nose!"

"That'd be good," she said. "And stuff a sock in yo mouth."

They were a cocoa-colored version of *The Honeymooners*. I chuckled to myself, poured a cup of coffee, and settled into the breakfast nook to read the Monday-morning paper.

The *Times-Union* reported the beginning of a gang war in New York in the aftermath of Albert Anastasia's murder. The story went on to say that Angelo Maserelli and his son Attillio had been attending a birthday party at a West Side restaurant when they were attacked. Neither one was hurt, but both assassins were killed by Maserelli, his son, and three associates. The would-be assassins were identified by their California driver's licenses as Stephen Whitten and Paul Burkhardt but were unknown to the Maserellis. The police were contacting the California authorities for further information regarding the assailants.

There was no mention of me, Kat, or anyone else at the party. As far as everyone was concerned, it was a Mob hit and everyone else at the scene was superfluous. I wondered, however, what would happen when the Beverly Hills police were contacted and their investigators revealed that Whitten and Burkhardt worked for Marion Pennington. *If* that was reported. Kat had said that the police chief was a close friend of Marion Pennington's, and the investigation could stay quiet awhile, perhaps weeks—when it might finally be alleged that Paulie and Spig were freelance bodyguards who worked for many of Hollywood's high-profile notables.

Doug finally came down and introduced a lovely young thing wearing a skirt, blouse, and sneakers. She had a ponytail and a shoulder bag crammed with books slung over her shoulder.

Books? On the weekend?

Doug was in his uniform and introduced her. "This is Sissy. Sissy, say hi to Vinny."

"Hi, Vinny!"

"Hi, Sissy," I replied. Perfect, I thought. Doug had a genius for picking up girls with cute names. And perky. Definitely perky.

"Sissy's a sophomore at U of F," Doug continued.

"That's in Gainesville," said Sissy.

"Is it?" I said, sounding amazed.

"She's a very serious student—a psych major," Doug reported. "She wants to be a psychologist."

"I can't wait," I said.

"Do you think you might need one?" she asked.

"No," I said, then looked at Doug, "but I can assure you, he will."

Doug cleared his throat and started easing her toward the door, saying, "Yes. Well, Sissy's got an early class and we have to get to the air station."

"Nice meeting you, Vinny," she called out over her shoulder.

"Likewise, I'm sure."

And they were off. A few seconds later I heard a car start and Doug returned.

"Christ, Doug! She looks sixteen!"

"She's twenty!"

"She was carrying books!"

"Sissy's very studious."

"Unbelievable."

"Ain't it?" He grinned.

I showed him the newspaper and watched his face as he scanned the article. He immediately got the picture. "This is bullshit! It was Frick and Frack! They came after *you*!"

"Yeah."

Doug was aghast. "Her ol' man put a *hit* out on you?"

"Apparently."

"Holy shit, Vinny, now what?"

"Kat knows it was him and she's going to confront him. She thinks if she threatens to expose him, he'll finally back off."

"Oh, man! What if he doesn't?"

"As usual, since all this began . . . I have no fuckin' idea."

All our pilots returned from the long weekend physically challenged but psychologically refreshed. Several of them had flown to Havana and reported a fabulous trip. They hadn't paid for anything—food, booze, rooms, or women.

To do a little gambling, all naval aviators had to do was show in the casino wearing their dress whites and gold wings. The chips were supplied by management. The pilots were magnets for the well-heeled widows and carefree daughters of the international set, and management was delighted to pick up a tab that helped fill the tables.

Whitey and Zaz agreed, "Those Cubans really know how to do things right."

I didn't mention that "those Cubans" were Meyer Lansky and Lucky Luciano.

We fell back into a normal routine now that CQ was over—flying two sorties a day, and waiting for word on whether we would be one of the first squadrons to get the new F-8 Crusader. The plane was to be the replacement for our aging FJ-3 Furies and was a truly supersonic air-superiority fighter capable of speeds up to one thousand miles per hour.

We were licking our chops.

Doug and I flew an aerial gunnery sortie that afternoon with Whitey and Zaz, which, like most of what we did in the air, involved a competition.

In aerial gunnery, we dived on a towed target sleeve and fired at it with our .50-caliber machine guns. Each aircraft carried ammunition marked with a different color. When the bullets went through the sleeve, they left a colored hole—thus allowing each pilot's hits to be counted. Hits counted for a buck apiece, and the more experienced pilots such as Doug and I enjoyed lightening the wallets of the cocky nuggets.

After the four of us had made multiple runs on the sleeve, we ran out of ammunition and returned to the base. We counted the holes, and as expected, Doug and I outscored the nuggets by over sixty hits. They grudgingly forked over their cash, and since it was five o'clock, we offered to buy them a round at the O club.

When we got home later that night, there was a message to return Kat's call—the call I knew had to be about her confrontation with Daddy.

When she picked up, I said, "Hi, baby. How'd it go?"

"Whole story or *Reader's Digest* condensed version?" she said in a strong, cocky voice.

"Your choice."

"A little of both then: I was determined to beard the lion in his den—set him on his heels and not even accept a glimmer of denial from the second I walked in."

"Sounds like a plan," I said, still doubting whether this had worked.

"Oh, it was. When he jumped up, throwing his arms around me and purring about his distress that his poor little baby had been involved in a Mafia hit, I calmly told him it wasn't the Mafia, it was Spig and Paulie."

"The 'setting on his heels' accomplished."

"It was the equivalent of an ice pick straight to the heart."

"Did he try to deny he sent them?"

"Only for a few moments when the shock made him incoherent, but then he broke down." Now suddenly her attitude changed. Kat's voice caught. "It was awful, Vinny. A man like that sobbing and pleading for forgiveness."

Christ, I thought. There it was. She was still feeling sorry for him.

"When I told him I'd expose him, he was petrified. At first he couldn't believe I'd do that to him, but then he realized I meant every word." There was anguish in her voice and she began to sob. "He swore he'd never do anything to keep us apart again."

"I'm sorry you had to go through that, darling. But at least now we know it's over."

"Yes, I know. I'm glad I did it. I love you, Vinny."

"You're the strongest woman I've ever met, Kat. For now, pour yourself a stiff drink and try to get some rest."

"I will—and I'll call you tomorrow."

She blew a kiss; I returned it and hung up—and made a second call to Angelo to tell him about my conversation with Kat. He was as relieved as I was and said he'd also just heard from Accardo, who'd been in Canada on a fishing trip over the weekend.

"He wanted ta know if the hit at Lena's last Saturday was the start of another war," said Angelo.

"What'd you tell him?"

"That it wasn't. That it's just what everybody figured. I told him that the two guys were tryin' to whack you, not me, and that they were sent by yer fiancée's old man. When he heard that, he went apeshit."

"Christ, what now?" I knew the Stardust deal was coming up, and Accardo wasn't about to let anything fuck it up.

"He's gonna have Roselli read 'im the riot act one last time. He lays off you or he gets laid out."

"You think it'll work?" In spite of the threats from Accardo and his daughter, I knew what a determined son of a bitch Pennington was.

"Yeah. From what I hear, Pennington wants the Vegas deal as much as Accardo. So he's over two barrels. One from yer fiancée, and a second one from Accardo and Roselli. If that don't do it, nothin' will."

"Okay, Angelo, let's hope this is the last of it."

"Your mouth ta God's ears. Ciao, kid."

CHAPTER TWENTY-NINE

AFTER A LONG WEEK of low-level air-to-ground missions—strafing and firing rockets at stationary ground targets, during which Doug and I relieved Whitey and Zaz of a bit more of their cash—I was more than ready for Kat's arrival. The last time I'd seen her was during a tearful airport farewell after a horrendous weekend in New York. Now I was looking forward to putting the nightmare behind us and to two joyous days in the sun. I picked her up at the Jacksonville airport late Friday afternoon and brought her back to the house without revealing the weekend surprise. Once again I knew she wouldn't have packed the wardrobe we'd need for where I was taking her, but I also knew there'd be no problem buying it when we arrived.

Jess and Jessie were thrilled to see her again after having been fed a steady diet of Willous, Joys, and Sissys by Doug.

"You're lookin' mighty fine to these ol' eyes, Miss Kat," said Jessie.

"Welcome indeed, Miss Kat," added Jess.

"Will y'all be stayin' for dinner?" asked Jessie.

"Tempt me," I said.

"Standin' rib roast, sweet taters, asparagus, and black-eyed peas," said Jessie, proudly flashing a wide grin.

"No dessert?" I asked.

"Rhubarb pie and ice cream—that suit you?"

Kat jumped in before I could answer. "It won't matter. It suits me just fine and I'm not letting him out of my sight."

"Will Mr. Doug be joinin' us?" asked Jess.

"I believe he will—him and his date," I said.

Jessie rolled her eyes. "I'll git out the Pablum."

Kat asked, "Do I take it Doug likes younger ladies?"

"They don't have to *be* young," I said. "They only have to *look* young. He's not a total pervert."

"Glad to hear it," said Kat.

"I can't wait for you to meet his latest acquisition."

"Oh?"

I made quotation marks with my fingers and said, "Sissy."

She cocked her eyebrow. "Sissy?"

"The one and only. And she's studying to be a psychologist."

"Perfect," Kat said. "He can be analyzed and tantalized at the same time."

Doug arrived at seven with Sissy fifteen minutes behind him and indeed looking younger than her twenty years. She had dressed for dinner in a short skirt, tight sweater, and heels. No stockings and a brain to match.

I made the introductions. "Kat, say hello to Sissy."

"Hello, Sissy," Kat replied.

"Kat?" said Sissy, appearing astounded. "As in *pussy?*"

Kat shot me a look. "No comment," I said.

"As in Caitlin," Kat offered.

"Oh. What kind of a name is that?"

"The kind that gets you called Kat."

Sissy's brow scrunched in confusion and Doug jumped in to save her. "Sissy's a sophomore at the University of Florida."

"I'm a 'Gator,'" said Sissy.

"A dream come true—," Kat started to say.

I cut off further commentary with "So! What're we drinking?"

Doug immediately chimed in, "Martini."

Kat said, "Two."

I said, "Three," and looked at Sissy.

"Do you have Blue Nun?"

"Is that a drink?" I asked.

"Uh-huh," Sissy replied. "It's all the rage at the U of F."

I turned to Kat and said, "That's in Gainesville."

"So I've heard," she responded.

"It's a sparkling wine," said Doug helpfully.

"Is it?" I said, acting astonished and turning back to Kat. "Doug's extraordinarily well versed on campus drinking habits."

"A dying talent," said Kat.

I turned back to Sissy. "I'm afraid our only nun is in a convent. Can I get you something else?"

"Do you have anything sparkling?"

"Only Dom Pérignon."

"I'll have that."

"Splendid," I said. "Hopefully it's on par with Blue Nun."

Dinner was a four-star success. The standing rib was succulent, the sweet potatoes and asparagus a wonderful complement, and the rhubarb pie peerless.

And the black-eyed peas sparked a lively dinner conversation since Sissy'd never heard of such things before. I told her they were regular green peas before they'd gotten beaten up in the canning process. That seemed to confuse her, so I didn't elaborate.

After dinner Doug took Sissy down to the dock for a moonlight ride in the Chris-Craft while Kat and I settled onto the patio with brandy snifters. The aroma of jasmine, a cricket symphony, and a harvest moon set the stage. We heard Doug kick off the engines and pull away with a deep-throated roar.

Kat chuckled. "How long do you give it?"

"Sissy? I'd make her a B. That would be three weeks. A C would be two—a D one. Max is an A—four weeks. There is no F because that's failing going in."

"Fascinating. And do you subscribe to this rating system?"

"No comment."

"Smart."

"You bet." I turned toward her. "Smart enough to ask what you'd say if I told you I'd rented an airplane?"

"Tired of the Navy's?"

"Hardly." I laughed.

"Then I'd ask, 'Why?' "

"I'm flying us to Havana."

"You're kidding!" Now Kat was laughing. I'd gotten the reaction I'd hoped for—her spirits were soaring.

"Nope. We were cheated out of going last week, and the guys who made the trip said it was fantastic, so I rented us a Twin Bonanza and booked a reservation at the Nacional."

Kat stood up, threw herself into my lap, and put her arms around me. "Oh, Vinny," she gushed. "What a wonderful surprise. Rum, rumbas, and La Floridita. You're an incorrigible romantic, sailor."

"Not until I met you, darling."

"But what makes you think I brought my passport?"

"I have a hunch you always carry it—plus, I saw it in your purse the first time we checked into The Cloister."

"You're a Peeping Tom?"

"No—a Peeping Vinny."

She swatted me. "I've heard the Nacional is a pretty formal place. I'll have to pick up a few little nothings for the casino."

"No problem. Havana is home to some of the finest shops on the planet, and I am sure they will be eager to cater to madam's every wish and desire."

"Oh!" she exclaimed. "Another shopping spree! Sea Island all over again."

"Not quite. Then it was Molly's Smock Shop. Now it will be Coco's salon."

"And with me being the new Chanel girl!"

"*Précis, mademoiselle.*"

"Do you suppose we'll see Hemingway?"

"He won't be able to avoid us."

"Dare we ask for an autograph?"

"We dare. But we're more likely to get a scowl."

She laughed. "It would be worth it just to be able to say you were scowled at by 'Papa.'"

I was amazed how a great dinner, a splash of alcohol, and the prospect of a romantic weekend could wipe out the horror of the prior Saturday night—it looked as if my plan was working.

The flight to Havana took a little over three hours. We took off at eight and flew down the east coast of Florida to Miami, followed the Keys to the Marquesas, and then over the Florida Straits to Havana. I gave Kat the controls on the way down and wasn't in the least surprised at the result. She handled the plane as if she were born in one.

Havana International Airport's customs and immigration venues were an absolute no-brainer. Fulgencio Batista y Zaldívar had no interest in turning away visitors from any country, but tourists from the United States were especially welcome. In the 1930s American mobsters had made the Cuban government a partner in their illegal smuggling operations, and by the late 1940s Batista was a partner in all the hotels and casinos—the Nacional being the most opulent.

Cuba was the home of sugarcane, rum, fine cigars, and Desi Arnaz, Lucille Ball's husband in real life as well as on the number one TV show *I Love Lucy*. Many of the quirky couple's fans flocked to the shark-shaped island off the Florida coast, and tourism became its lifeblood. It was an ideal haven for anyone who reveled in beaches, gambling, drinking, and prostitutes.

If you couldn't have a good time in Havana, you were dead.

The island's one problem was Fidel Castro Ruz. In 1956, he began bombing schools and cinemas. In 1957, his forces began burning sugar fields. In January 1958, *Time* would be reporting that the Batista government could not cope, but the fact was mainly ignored by the sun worshippers, gamblers, and thrill seekers, all of whom continued to flock to the island paradise—Kat and I among them.

We were slammed by eighty-five-degree heat and humidity when we threw our carry-on baggage into the back of a DeSoto taxi and headed into town. En route we passed Civic Square, which would become Plaza de la Revolución within two years, and the José Martí Memorial, which was still under construction. Central Havana was six miles north of the airport—from there Old Havana was a half mile to the east and the Nacional Hotel a half a mile farther north. Surrounded by gardens, the Nacional sat on a promontory next to the Malecón—a short walk from Santa María del Mar beach. We checked in, dropped off our luggage, and immediately went shopping for Kat's evening ward-robe, which, as predicted, was abundantly available. Within an hour she was outfitted, and for lunch we stopped by La Floridita, the famed watering hole of Hemingway. Although the place was crowded, we managed a table next to the bar and ordered a pair of the world-renowned daiquiris.

Before we could even ask the question, the waiter promptly identi-fied us as *norteamericanos* and said, "He's not here. He's fishing."

Kat looked surprised and foolishly said, "Hemingway?"

"No—Batista!" he said sarcastically. "Of course 'Papa.' It's the first question we get after the order."

"Sorry," she said.

"*De nada.* What are you eating?"

We both laughed and ordered the sautéed shrimp we had seen being flambéed at the next table. Our eyes swept over the British Regency bar, the drawings, paintings, and carved names on the walls, and finally Hemingway's favorite barstool and a bust of Hemingway made in his honor. The daiquiris were better than the shrimp, but we left satisfied that we'd paid homage to a mandatory landmark.

That evening we opted for dinner in the hotel, then made our way to the casino. Men in tuxedos and women in gowns mingled with slightly less formal but just as expensively dressed gamblers. Kat fit right in—she was wearing a bare-backed, open-shouldered cocktail dress in black crêpe by Luis Estevez, which caused jealous glances from the women and lingering stares from the men. I'd put on my dress whites because my civilian wardrobe was limited. Plus, I was well aware that the casino's owners told the dealers to be especially nice to military officers at the tables. We chose blackjack.

After out little "set-to" about money on our trip to St. Simons, we'd decided that she could spend money on herself but not on us. Clothes and gambling fell into the approved category. I knew I couldn't gamble on her level, and I didn't want to stifle her by insisting she gamble on mine, so I took a backseat. A little stupid but it preserved my honor.

Kat peeled off five one-hundred-dollar bills and asked for a stack of ten-dollar chips. I took my position behind her chair and swelled with pride as I watched the rest of the players ogle her—not the least of which was Ramon, our dealer. He was a handsome Latin with slicked-back hair, a narrow face, and a pencil-thin mustache. He was wearing a cutaway red jacket, and I speculated that well-heeled widows probably went to war over him.

Kat slid five chips into the card-shaped square in front of her while Ramon expertly shuffled a single deck—obviously putting on a show for the players and Kat in particular. He dealt with such dazzling speed that it looked as if the cards were literally flying out of the deck. He was showing a king, Kat was showing a jack. Kat stood pat, and after all the other players went bust, Ramon flipped over a nine for nineteen. Kat flipped over a queen for twenty.

The next half hour was full of the same. Kat lost only one in four hands and was starting to draw a crowd. On Ramon's final deal before he was relieved, he dealt her a natural twenty-one, which put her fifteen hundred dollars ahead. She dropped a black hundred-dollar chip into his jacket and we left the table to a round of applause.

"What do you think?" she asked.

"I couldn't pick it up, but the guy had to be feeding you."

"Of course, darling, I was smiling and licking my lips at him the whole time."

"Hussy. You could've gotten him fired."

"I doubt it. I've a feeling this isn't the first time he's seen to it that a lady won."

"You're right. And no doubt with the owner's permission. There's no better publicity than a big winner. Especially a beautiful big winner."

"With a handsome naval aviator."

"Are you flirting again?"

"Of course!"

We wandered over to the roulette table, where Kat gave back half the fifteen hundred dollars to a dealer who was in his seventies and a wheel that was not being manipulated, then moved to the craps table, where I bought a hundred dollars' worth of five-dollar chips. We drew a small crowd, and with Kat blowing on my dice, I made five passes in a row. But by the end of an hour no matter how hard they cheered and Kat blew, I dropped the hundred.

Kat didn't seem fazed in the least and quipped, "Unlucky in games—lucky in love."

"How then do you explain you?" I asked, taking her hand.

"I'm the exception."

"The dealer was cheating," I protested.

"It doesn't matter, I won."

"Point taken." I laughed. "Had enough?"

"Of gambling, yes. Of you, no."

We went up to our suite, I opened a bottle of Dom Pérignon for a nightcap, and we stepped out on the balcony to enjoy the view. The panorama of Havana's twinkling lights, the Malecón, and the Florida Straits was awesome. Fiery Latin music drifted up from below, punctuated by the sounds of rolling thunder from storms over the mountains. Lightning flashed, silhouetting the city, and filling the air with the faint scent of ozone.

Kat held out her glass. "To us?"

I touched her glass with mine and repeated, "To us," then took her hand and led her into the bedroom, where we slowly stripped each other standing up. Kat took my face in her hands and kissed me long and gently as if she were drawing my entire being into her. We lowered ourselves onto the bed, where she slid on top of me and deliberately kissed her way across my chest and down my body—exquisite agony.

CHAPTER THIRTY

O N SUNDAY MORNING the tolling Catedral bells boomed through our open windows joyously announcing the ten-o'clock mass. Squinting against the brilliance of the Caribbean sun, we blinked ourselves awake and had another of our refreshing showers. Shorts, cotton shirts, and sneakers held the heat at bay while we hit the sights: Old Havana, Plaza de Armas, La Catedral, and Parque Central.

Our last stop was a late lunch at La Bodeguita del Medio, the second watering hole made famous by Hemingway. We ordered *mojitos*, a black bean, rice, and steak combo, and took in the room. It was covered with four decades of graffiti, posters, and animal heads. The waiter took our order but failed to volunteer whether its most famous patron was present.

We were disappointed but didn't mention it.

By four o'clock we were back at the airport since Kat had an eight o'clock plane to L.A. from Jax. Technically the flying/drinking rule was eight hours from the bottle to the throttle, but I'd only taken a sip of the *mojito* and I didn't think that constituted drinking.

Reversing the prior day's flight plan, we cruised back up the Florida coast with clear skies and tailwinds. At the Jax passenger terminal I folded Kat into my arms and said, "Maybe we should buy an airline."

"I'll see if Howard wants to sell TWA."

"You know Howard?" I asked facetiously.

"No, but Daddy knows Bob Mahue—his most recent confidant."

"Have Daddy give Howard a lowball offer through Bob and I'll float a loan."

"What will you use for collateral?"

"My car."

"Brilliant! I'm marrying a financial genius!"

"The genius loves you."

She caressed my face and kissed me gently. "And I loved our weekend. I love all our weekends, sailor."

"Not getting tired of being a bicoastal Ping-Pong ball?"

"Mmmm," she murmured, pressing her body against mine. "Only of the days in between."

The PA system announced her flight and we savored a last, lingering kiss. Swiveling away toward the plane, she tossed her hair over her shoulder and said, "Next week, darling."

I nodded and she was gone. I was amazed by her stamina. Birds spent less time in the air. But in the short time that I'd known her I couldn't think of one challenge she'd backed away from.

A dozen cars were still parked around the fountain in front of the house when I returned from the airport. The house was ablaze with lights and I could hear music coming from the backyard speakers. High-pitched squeals of delight told me that the final curtain had not yet fallen on the weekend follies. It was after nine and Jess and Jessie would already have retired by now, but I'd gotten hungry so I decided to raid the refrigerator.

I walked down the central hallway and was about to enter the kitchen when I heard Doug swooping in with the Chris-Craft. I went out to the patio in time to see the speedboat inbound—towing a topless Sissy. Fifteen feet from the beach she expertly threw away the towline and smoothly glided ashore next to the dock. Doug circled back, pulled in, and tied up the boat.

I'd always thought that waterskiing at night was one of the stupider things we did, but that never stopped any of us. Living on the edge was part of a fighter pilot's MO.

As usual, a volleyball net had been rigged over the center of our well-lit pool, and a game was in progress. Whitey, Zaz, and three other pilots were in the middle of the action with half a dozen young lovelies I didn't recognize.

Whitey and Zaz, plus three topless girls, were facing three other pilots and three more topless girls on the other side of the net—five against six. There was considerable squealing and laughing, and the girl's topless bouncing made some interesting viewing. When we'd first established the weekend follies, we'd agreed that what was good enough for the French Riviera was good enough for us. There were no complaints.

Whitey spotted me and yelled out, "Vinny, come on in! We're one guy short!" He pointed at a girl on his team and added, "Darla needs a partner!"

Darla was a particularly well-endowed brunette who flashed a radiant smile, then an equally impressive Southern accent. "Hah theah."

I returned the smile. "Hah theah backatcha."

Whitey announced, "Darla Lou is a Gator cheerleader," as if it were a royal title.

"Really," I said. "I'm impressed."

"Are yew fond of cheerleaders?" she asked with a casual batting of her baby blues.

I smiled. "As a group, I can't say, but individually I confess my head has been turned on occasion."

"Oh?" she crooned, pleased. "Have yew been to any of ouah futbawl games?"

"No, but I'll put it on my must-do list—right after I grab a sandwich."

"Oh, do come on in, dahlin'," she said, bouncing on her toes. "It'll even up the sides."

I made a sweeping bow. "With you playing, darlin', they're already even."

She flashed her radiant smile again. "Whah thank yew, kind sir."

Doug walked up with Sissy, who looked lovely but did not look happy. He asked, "How was the trip?"

"Four stars. The only thing we missed was Hemingway's autograph."

"Somehow I think you'll live."

I said, "Hi, Sissy. What's new in psych world?"

Her face scrunched up. "I beg your pardon?"

"The world of psych. The heart of darkness. The analyst's domain."

Her face clouded. "Why do you do that?"

"That?" I asked.

"Yes, that. You're making fun of me again."

"*Moi?* Never."

"You see!"

I actually felt bad when I realized I was really hurting her feelings. "Sissy, I'm sorry if I hurt your feelings. I promise it won't happen again." I almost raised my fingers and said *Scout's honor*, but caught myself in time.

She wasn't sure if I was serious so she pouted and turned away, saying, "I'm going to rinse off."

"Be right up," Doug called after her.

She called over her shoulder, "Don't knock yourself out."

"She seems a little testy," I said.

"She is. I told her over dinner that she was beautiful, great company, witty, and fabulous in bed."

"And what part of that made her testy?"

"The part where I added that this would be our last weekend for a while."

"Did you explain the ABC rule?"

"I did and she took it personally."

"I can't imagine why."

He started off to the house, saying, "I'll go join her in the shower and assuage her wounded pride."

"A regular Lancelot." I laughed, followed him, and went into the kitchen to make a sandwich. I'd decided for the leftover roast beef but against the buxom cheerleader and had just opened the fridge when the phone rang. It was Angelo.

"Are ya sittin' down?" he asked.

"Why? What's up?"

"Your favorite asshole could be in very deep shit."

"Pennington? Why?"

"Roselli's contact in the Beverly Hills PD gave 'him a heads-up. She told Roselli that the NYPD requested info on Whitten and Burkhardt from the BHPD. The gal's assistant to Pete Dyne, the chief of detectives. Roselli's had her on his pad fer years, and a couple times a month he takes her out for dinner and a quick fuck. She told him they got a request from the NYPD fer information on Spig and Burkhardt. The request came in on Monday, and Dyne recognized the names as Pennington's two bodyguards. He knew the chief was a close friend of Pennington and showed him the request. He said Dyne predicted the chief would stonewall it and he did—it gave Dyne the opportunity he'd been looking for. He wants the chief's job. Uncovering a cover-up could go a long way to gettin' it for him. He's beginning an undercover investigation usin' his own formidable contacts without

clueing in the chief. If this guy ties Whitten an Burkhardt to
Pennington, it could be lights out—the NYPD cops are gonna wanna
know what a pair of Pennington's bodyguards from L.A. were doing in
New York tryin' to hit me."

"Does Accardo know?"

"I told 'im . . . and he went inta freakin' orbit!"

"Christ. You think they can actually nail Pennington?"

"Who knows? Probably not. But if Accardo thinks they can—it
won't matter. Vegas or no Vegas, Pennington's toast. Good news for
you, kid."

I wasn't so sure.

CHAPTER THIRTY-ONE

A BLACK '57 FORD FAIRLANE was parked in front of the house when Doug and I returned from the base the next evening. A red light on the dash identified it as the same car that had brought Detectives Dan McDermott and Jerome Paulson to the house when I'd reported Kat kidnapped two months ago.

Cops?

Jess seemed agitated when he met us at the door. "There's two police in the sunroom, Mistah Vinny."

"They say what they wanted?"

"No, suh . . . Jest that they wanted to see y'all."

"Both of us?" Doug asked.

"Yessuh. That's what they said."

I said, "Thanks, Jess," and we headed down the hallway.

The two detectives got to their feet when we entered.

"So, Lieutenant Vesta, we meet again," McDermott said amiably.

"Under more pleasant circumstances I hope?" I responded. "Can I get you something to drink?"

He ignored my first question and declined my second. Doug introduced himself and we all sat around the coffee table.

McDermott began by asking, "Do either of you know a girl named Sissy Cable?"

Doug glanced at me and said, "Sure. I've dated her the past few weeks—why?"

He turned to me and said, "And you Lieutenant Vesta?"

"She's been an acquaintance since she started dating Doug."

"What's this about?" asked Doug.

"She says she was raped," McDermott said flatly.

Shock crossed Doug's face and he cried out, "What?"

"That's ridiculous," I said.

McDermott turned to me. "By both of you."

Now it was my turn to be shocked. "Both?" I gasped.

"That's what she says," he said in the same flat, unemotional tone.

There were a few moments of stunned silence on our parts, then Paulson asked Doug, "Where were you last night?"

"I was here," Doug said, "and so was she."

He looked at me. "And you?"

"I came in around nine. I'd been in Havana for the weekend."

McDermott's eyebrow shot up. "Cuba?"

"Cuba. I was there with my fiancée."

"But you came back at nine," Paulson said, taking out a pocket-size notepad and jotting it down.

"Right," I said. "When was all this supposed to have happened?"

"According to Miss Cable, at about nine thirty, right after you got back, and also according to her, 'during one of your,'" he checked his notes, "'typically wild weekend parties.'"

McDermott asked Doug, "That right, Lieutenant? You have typically wild weekend parties?"

"We have parties. As far as I know there's no law against it."

"Miss Cable says they're topless."

"Same answer," said Doug.

McDermott took out a notebook identical to Paulson's and consulted it. "Miss Cable says she went up to Lieutenant McCaulley's bathroom to take a shower after you two were waterskiing." He looked up at Doug and again cocked his eyebrow. "At night?"

Doug sighed. "At night. She loved it."

"And while she was in the shower you climbed in and raped her."

"That's ridiculous! I'd been seeing her for three weeks! We had a helluva good time, and believe me, at *no* time did I have to force her to do anything!"

"But last night she said she wanted to end it and—"

"*She* wanted to end it?" Doug blurted out. "*I* wanted to end it!"

"So you two argued?" McDermott prompted.

"No, we didn't argue. I just said we should cool it for a while and she didn't like it."

"Was this before or after the shower?"

"Before."

"So you went into the shower *after* you told her you didn't want to see her anymore and you threw her a pop?" McDermott's eyebrow again shot up. I was beginning to think it was part of his interrogation technique. "What? One for the road?"

"It wasn't like that!" Doug was beginning to get hot.

"What'd you do after the shower?"

"I went back out to the party."

"What'd she do?"

"I assume she got dressed and went home like she always did."

"You didn't take her?"

"No! She had her own car. She lives in Gainesville."

"Oh, right," McDermott said. "University of Florida student. She said all the girls were from there last night."

"That's right," replied Doug. "They drove up for the weekend."

"Cozy. You see her leave the house?"

"No. I told you I went back out to the party."

McDermott turned to me. "And what about you, Lieutenant?"

"What about me?"

"Did you see her leave?"

"No. I was in bed."

"Was this before or after you raped her?"

I exploded, "I didn't rape her, goddammit! I didn't even touch her!"

"She says you stopped her in the upstairs hallway after your friend Doug went back to the party and you pulled her into your room."

"Bullshit!" I snapped.

"Okay—okay. If it's all bullshit, you won't mind comin' downtown to the lab so we can make some tests."

"What kind of tests?" asked Doug.

"You know. Blood, semen . . . When she reported the rape to the campus authorities, they took her to the hospital to be examined—they got a semen sample so there was definite evidence of intercourse."

"Of course there was for crissakes!" yelled Doug. "I told you, I was with her all weekend!"

"Well, you sure as hell won't see any semen from me," I said, "I wasn't anywhere near her."

"You could've been wearing a raincoat."

"I was wearing a pillow over my head to knock off the noise!"

"Fine. So you won't mind coming with us."

"Are you arresting us?" Doug asked.

"Not yet."

"Then you're fucking well right we mind," Doug replied. "I'm no Clarence Darrow, but I know enough to know that all you've got is the word of a pissed-off woman and nothing else."

"Well, actually we've got a little more than that. The other girls at the party said they saw Lieutenant Vesta return at about nine thirty, decline their invitation to join them in the pool, and then follow Doug here and Miss Cable into the house."

"I went in to have a sandwich!"

"Is that all you had?"

"Yes!"

"Okay—that's it!" snarled Doug. "We'll come in now and then sue your asses off for false arrest, or we'll come in after you convince a DA and a judge to give you a warrant and us time to get a lawyer."

"That attitude isn't going to help you," said McDermott.

"You're accusing me of rape. You expect a parade?"

"Okay," McDermott finally said, and he got up to leave, followed by Paulson. At the door, McDermott stopped and fired off a parting shot. "Just so you know—we could take you in tonight with what we've got, but we want to confer with NCIS before we proceed. They've been notified of the allegations, and we'll see them tomorrow—right after this hits the morning papers."

NCIS was the Navy Criminal Investigative Service. Since we were in the Navy, they theoretically had jurisdiction over us. But since the alleged crime took place in the city, the local police and DA would claim first call. It could be a pissing contest, but the Navy, wanting to be good neighbors, would undoubtedly cooperate fully with the locals. And if they suspected the allegations were true, they'd come down on us like an avalanche.

We stared at the empty doorway until we heard the front door close.

"Do you know the names of the other girls at the party?" I asked.

"Yeah," he said, "but mostly first names. This was a new bunch and I've been with Sissy for three weeks."

"How about Whitey and Zaz?"

"Maybe. They spent more time with them."

"I know one of them was a Gator cheerleader named Darla Lou. How many of those could there be?"

"You'd be surprised," Doug said.

"I'll call Whitey—you call Zaz and see if we can get some last names and phone numbers. We've gotta find out what she said and to whom she said it."

We got on the phones and found out that Whitey and Zaz—bless their black hearts—did indeed have a few names and phone numbers. They agreed to call the girls they knew best, and Whitey told me Darla Lou's last name was Lancer. He gave me her number—I immediately called and got her roommate. I left word. Finally Doug tried to reach Sissy, but there was no answer and no machine.

The minute Doug hung up the phone, it rang and he picked it up. He said, "Yessir, it is," and I watched as his jaw tightened. He glanced at me. "Yessir, he is," finally ending the call with "Yessir."

"The base?" I asked, knowing it had to be.

"NCIS. They want us in their office at oh eight hundred."

I went to the liquor caddie and poured three fingers of Scotch into a pair of tumblers and handed one to Doug.

I held mine out in a toast. "Another fine mess you've gotten us into, Ollie."

He touched my glass. "Un-fucking-believable!"

We drank and I said, "Hell hath no wrath . . ."

"Christ! All I did was tell her I wanted to cool it for a while!"

"Apparently she doesn't take rejection very well."

He nodded. "Damn ABC rule."

"Good guess, but why the hell would she throw *me* under the bus?"

"Probably because she finally figured out you've been needling her."

I shook my head with regret. "Blue Nun . . ."

He nodded. " 'Psych world' probably didn't help either."

I threw down the remains of my drink. "We've got a real problem, buddy."

"Tell me about it. When this hits Concannon, he's gonna go apeshit."

I nodded. "Exactly two seconds before he has us nailed to the yardarm."

"You gonna call Kat?"

I checked my watch. It was eight thirty—five thirty in L.A. "Yeah . . . She teaches on Monday and gets home at five."

"What're you gonna tell her?"

"The truth—that my dumb-ass room mate got me accused of rape!"

I dialed Kat, and from the moment she answered the phone, I could tell she was upset. "What's wrong?"

"It's Daddy, Vinny. He's had a heart attack."

"What? When?"

"Last Saturday. He wasn't feeling well so he called his internist, who examined him. The doctor thought he might have suffered a heart attack and rushed him to the UCLA medical center. They confirmed the diagnosis and admitted him for a battery of tests."

"How serious is it?" I asked, completely dumbfounded.

"He's home now and doing well, but they've said he has to drop everything and rest for at least a month."

"Makes sense."

"Of course it does! But he's insisting he has to fly up to Vegas next Thursday for The Stardust closing! He's been approved for a gaming license and will be named president. He says they can't postpone it, and if he's not there, the deal won't go through. I don't know what to do, Vinny. While we were cavorting in Havana, he could have died. I feel so damn guilty. I just know that everything that's happened with us the past few months must have something to do with what's happened to him! Do you think I was too harsh on him?"

"Nonsense, stop blaming yourself." Part of me was angry, but you also had to admire that kind of filial love, so I refrained from reminding her that the man she was so distraught about had tried to have me killed and was on the verge of becoming a front man for the Chicago mob.

I also refrained from telling her I'd been accused of rape. Under the circumstances it just didn't seem right—plus, Doug and I still had to meet with NCIS. I wouldn't tell her about the charges until after we'd talked to them and hope she wouldn't see or hear about the accusations before then.

CHAPTER THIRTY-TWO

TWO NAVAL OFFICERS ACCUSED OF RAPE was the headline on the first page of the *Times-Union*'s local section on Tuesday morning. The story was short on details but reported that LT Vincent Vesta and LT Douglas McCaulley were naval aviators from Fighter Squadron 176 based at the Jacksonville Naval Air Station. A University of Florida sophomore whose name was withheld had accused them of raping her on the prior Sunday night. Gainesville police were conferring with local authorities and NCIS to determine whether the two would be formally charged.

Doug and I had gotten up at seven, and Jess had brought in the paper while Jessie was making us breakfast. We read the story in the kitchen alcove, then passed the paper to Jess, who read it and shook his head in disbelief.

I told him to pass the paper to Jessie, who was at the center island sautéing onions and beating eggs. She stopped what she was doing, wiped her hands on her apron, and read the story in silence.

We watched her for a reaction, but there wasn't one. When she finished reading, she put down the paper and calmly poured the eggs into the skillet over the onions.

"Nonsense!" she said. " 'Ceptin' Ah'm sure not surprised. With all the carryin' on around here, sooner or later some-*body* was sure to git some-*one* wrapped around y'all's axels." She harrumphed. "But Ah don't believe none of it!"

"Thanks," said Doug, "I think."

Jessie salted the omelet. " 'God willin' and the river don't rise'— truth will win out."

"Anythin' we kin do to help?" asked Jess. "We been here all along."

"And from what you been watchin' all along," Jessie said reproachfully, "I don't 'spect you kin tell 'em anythin' they don't already know."

We got to the base and walked into the NCIS office with fifteen minutes to spare. The duty yeoman in the waiting room told us to have a seat and informed LCDR Andre Poulet that we'd arrived.

He kept us waiting until eight thirty, then opened his office door and waved us in. He was a perfect match for his name. With his long, narrow face and nose to match, a pencil mustache, slicked-back black hair parted in the middle, and a back that was ramrod straight, if he had been a foot taller, he would have looked like de Gaulle. As it was, he was a better match for Peter Lorre.

Wonderful, I thought, a martinet. How in the hell did these guys always wind up in some kind of law enforcement?

"My name is Lieutenant Commander Andre Poulet," he said in a clipped, icy voice, "and I'm the investigating officer assigned to your case."

The only flourish to his announcement was the way he drew out the second syllable of his name with a certain delight—*Poulet* became *Poulay*. A thin smile crossed his lips, then vanished as quickly as it appeared. The image in my head immediately changed from Peter

Lorre to Adolphe Menjou in *Paths of Glory* when he's about to hand Kirk Douglas his ass.

Poulet flipped the back of his hand at a pair of straight-back chairs in front of his desk. "Be seated, gentlemen."

We sat, confirming our suspicions that they were designed specifically for discomfort.

Poulet walked behind his desk at what seemed a deliberately unhurried pace and lowered himself into a captain's chair. The thin smile appeared once again, then disappeared instantly.

Folding his hands into his lap, he said, "So, what do you have to say for yourselves?"

We'd agreed that since Sissy had been Doug's mistake, he would answer any questions addressed to both of us. I just hoped he wouldn't blurt out, "It's all bullshit!"

Thankfully Doug responded with "It's a complete and utter fabrication. There's not a shred of truth to any of it."

"Really," said Poulet, picking up a file on his desk and glancing at it. "No truth to any of it? There was no topless party? Miss Cable wasn't there? You didn't argue with her?"

"No—I mean yes, there was a party, and she was there, but, no, I didn't argue with her."

"Did you have sexual relations with her?"

"Yes, but it was consensual. It wasn't rape."

"Then why do you suppose she would accuse you of rape?"

Please, I prayed, don't try to explain the ABC rule to him or we'll really be in the shitter.

"I have no idea except that she didn't take it well when I told her that we wouldn't be seeing each other for a while."

"So you did argue—"

"No!"

"But she was angry about it."

"No, but she wasn't happy."

"Were you angry about it?"

Doug said, "Why the hell would I be angry? I was the one who wanted to break it off."

Poulet again glanced at his file. "She says she was the one who wanted to break it off with you, and you were so angry that you followed her into the shower and raped her."

"That's bullshit!"

I cringed. Doug getting pissed, even if Poulet was an asshole, wasn't going to help. I was right.

"Mind your language, Lieutenant!" Poulet sternly admonished. "This is a formal inquiry by a senior officer!"

Doug hung his head in exasperation and Poulet turned to me. "And I suppose Miss Cable's statement that you also raped her is equally false."

"It is," I said.

He glanced down at the file. "You didn't pull her into your room?"

"I didn't even know she was in the building. I was in bed under a pillow."

"Did anyone see her walk past your room and leave?"

"I have no idea, Commander. I told the police and I'm telling you, I was in bed. I was exhausted from a weekend trip to Havana with my fiancée. There was a party going on. I put a pillow over my head and went to sleep. That's it."

Poulet looked back at Doug. "Do you have anything to add to your friend's story?"

"No—how could I? The girl was dressing in the bathroom when I went back to the party."

"So Lieutenant Vesta could have forced her into his room after you left."

Doug exploded again. "When pigs fly and whales walk! There is no fuc—" He caught himself. "There is just no way he could have done anything vaguely resembling that."

Poulet shook his head and closed the file. "Very well, gentlemen . . . Here's where we are. You deny the allegations but neither one of you can corroborate the other's story. There were no other witnesses to the events, but the allegations took place in your home during a wild topless party. Neither of you can refute that fact, and that doesn't help your denials. Therefore, I have no choice but to allow the local authorities to pursue the investigation and to bring charges if they see fit." Poulet dismissed us with a wave of his hand. "That will be all, gentlemen."

There it was. The Navy had decided that the better part of valor was to let the locals take the lead and appear to cooperate fully with whatever they decided. It was obvious they were covering their asses, but we also realized that the way the allegations went down, they had little choice. We could be pissed at that arrogant little shit Poulet, but not at the Navy.

As soon as we arrived at the hangar, we were informed that Concannon had taken himself off the flight schedule and was waiting in his office for us. Not good. Concannon never took himself off a flight schedule.

Doug knocked and Concannon waved us in, pointing to the metal straight-backs in front of his desk. He was seated behind it in a swivel chair with legs crossed and arms folded. He was wearing his flight suit and had the ever present cigar stub clenched in his teeth.

He looked at us without showing any emotion and quietly asked, "How'd it go?"

His demeanor completely surprised me. I wondered if it was the calm before the storm.

Doug said, "It didn't, Skipper."

"Civilian jurisdiction?"

We both nodded, and Doug said, "He threw us to the wolves."

Concannon shifted his cigar. "Poulet's a prick, but he probably didn't have a choice."

"Nosir," Doug agreed.

"I've already heard from CAG and the admiral. They're not happy. I told them I thought the charges were bullshit, but it didn't make them any happier."

"Thank you, sir," we said in unison.

He looked at me. "And you, Vesta, had best light a ten-foot candle to your dumb luck that they never heard about Pennington, the senator, or the secretary!"

I winced. "Yessir."

"What's your plan?"

I said, "They'll probably file charges so we'll have to get a lawyer."

"You know any?"

I glanced at Doug and he shook his head. "Nosir. Never needed one."

A knee pad was a sitting on Concannon's desk. He pulled a pen out of his flight suit, jotted something on the pad, and ripped off the sheet.

"Sean O'Hanlon. A Boston southie transplanted here. We grew up together. He ran from snow to sun a couple of years ago. He's impressive. A good guy and a fine lawyer."

I took the note. "Thanks, Skipper. We'll call him."

"Money a problem?"

There was no way of knowing, but if it got crazy, I knew Angelo and Stuff would have our backs. "I don't think so," I said.

"Take a couple of days off to line up a strategy with O'Hanlon and find out why the hell this girl's trying to crucify you."

"Skipper, we—"

"Enough thanks. Get the hell out of here and defend yourselves!"

We left the office and headed back home. Angelo and Stuff weren't the only friends who had our backs.

Before we left the hangar, Whitey stopped us and said he'd heard from Penny, the girl he was with at the party Sunday night.

"She lives with Sissy and Darla Lou in an off-campus house with another girl named Rose."

"Three of the six girls at the party live in the same house?" I asked.

"Right. When Sissy started dating Doug, she passed the word to her housemates. All of them except for Rose jumped aboard—salivating at the shot to snag a pilot."

"Does Penny know anything?" Doug asked hopefully.

"Not much. Penny drove home with Darla Lou that night. When they got there, Sissy was already home and Rose came in a few minutes later. Darla went up to her room and Penny went into the kitchen to make tea. Five minutes later she saw Sissy and Rose rush down the stairs and out of the house."

"That's it?" asked Doug, disappointed.

"No. The next morning they found out that Sissy and Rose went to the campus authorities and reported Sissy'd been raped."

"We know that," I said.

"They also found out that Sissy'd been home for two hours before she took off to see the campus cops. Then the local police and another pair from Jacksonville showed up to question Darla and Penny, but they told the detectives they hadn't seen anything at the party."

"It figures," said Doug. "There was nothing to see."

"Right. But the thing is, Penny said that when Darla first heard the news, she became very upset. She wouldn't tell Penny why, but she thinks Darla might have overheard something on Sunday night before Sissy and Rose rushed off to the authorities."

"But she didn't tell the cops that?"

"No."

"Did you get their address?" I asked.

He nodded and handed me a note. "I also found out that they usually hang out at a local watering hole called Monk's."

There was no way we could depend on getting callbacks from Sissy, Rose, or Darla, and they might not let us into the house if we knocked on their door.

We put Monk's on our schedule.

CHAPTER THIRTY-THREE

I CALLED KAT when we got home although I knew it was seven thirty A.M. in L.A. and she was still likely to be sleeping. Her housekeeper answered and I apologized for the early hour but asked her to wake Kat.

"Please, Millie. It's important."

About a minute or so passed and a groggy voice came on. "Hi, sailor."

"Hi, baby. Sorry I'm making you hit the deck so early, but I wanted you to hear it from me first."

"Hear what?" she asked, still sounding groggy.

"It's total bullshit, but I've been accused of rape."

There was silence on the phone for a few seconds, then she said, "I may still be half-asleep, but I thought you just said you'd been accused of rape."

"Unfortunately you heard right."

After another few seconds of silence she suddenly became alert. "My God, Vinny! What happened?"

"One of Doug's passing flames got pissed off at him. She accused him *and* me of raping her during a party Sunday night. You might remember her . . . Sissy."

"The Gator?"

"The same."

"And they believed her?" she asked, dumbfounded.

"So far, but we'll get a lawyer and question the other girls at the party. There has to be a pony somewhere in the middle of all this crap."

"Oh, Vinny, is there anything I can do?"

"No. Stay put for the moment and I'll let you know how it goes. So far they haven't filed formal charges. Maybe we'll catch a break."

"What's happening to us?" she asked sadly.

"We're having a bumpy ride for a piece. It'll change. How's your father?"

"The same. I tried to get his internist to talk some sense into him, but he's still determined to go to Vegas."

"Hang in there, baby. We'll figure all this out. I promise."

"I love you."

"That's the only thing making this bearable. I love you, too."

I hung up wondering what I was so positive about.

Commander Concannon's lawyer friend, O'Hanlon, returned our call at four that afternoon. He said he'd read the papers, and the sooner we got to his office the better. We changed into civvies and were there by four thirty.

"You are in one helluva world of hurt, my young friends" was the lawyer's greeting as we walked into his office past brightly colored, overstuffed furniture set on deep pile carpeting.

Sean O'Hanlon looked like the personification of the jovial English cartoon character John Bull. He had a rotund body and a round face topped by a monk's tonsure and red hair. I imagined he looked jolly even when he was angry.

He walked us to a pair of leather wing backs in front of a massive oak desk, and I noticed a Harvard Law School diploma on the wall. It was next to a signed photo of Senator John F. Kennedy.

As Concannon had said—impressive.

O'Hanlon shot out his hand and, firmly shaking ours, repeated his observation. "One helluva world of hurt, my friends."

"So it seems." I made the introductions. "Lieutenants Vincent Vesta and Douglas McCaulley."

O'Hanlon sat, leaned forward, and clasped his hands on the desk. "Give me the essence of the problem here—no embellishments, no opinions, just facts."

His severe tone belied his jovial appearance. I liked him. Straight to the point. No preamble—definitely no bullshit.

Doug described the Sunday-night party, the players, and the interviews with the Jacksonville detectives and NCIS.

When he finished, O'Hanlon asked, "What are your relationships with the other girls at the party?"

Doug replied, "They're new acquaintances for the most part. And as I said, I'd only been seeing Sissy for about a month."

The lawyer shifted his eyes to me. "And you?"

"With the exception of Sissy, it was the first time I'd seen any of them."

"What about the other officers? They know any of them?" he asked.

"A bit more encouraging," Doug answered. "We got a couple of names and phone numbers."

"Good. Follow up and see if they know anything."

I said, "We had planned on going to Gainesville when we left here."

He nodded at the plan. "In a case like this, the police depend on the victim, the physical evidence, and witness statements. Right now they're getting conflicting statements and they have no witnesses. But I'd bet the farm that they've already talked to the other girls at the party."

I said, "They have. The girls told them they didn't see anything."

"Which means the police initially concluded that they lacked enough probable cause to arrest you on the allegations alone."

Doug said, "That's good news, right?"

"For the moment," replied O'Hanlon. "But here's your problem. The local media have already made you cannon fodder. They don't care a fiddler's fart if you're guilty or innocent. They've got papers to sell and airtime to fill. And as long as it's news, the DA will feel the heat and he'll have to move forward. If he doesn't, he'll look like either a wimp or an incompetent lummox for backing off. Our only chance is to break the girl's story or get her to recant."

We shook our heads, knowing that was going to be next to impossible. If Sissy recanted, she could be charged with making a false police report. A felony. Why the hell would she do that?

"We'll see what we can find out," I said.

"Let me know," O'Hanlon responded. "The surest way out of this is to stop it before it starts. Once there's an indictment, there'll be no way to stop this train before it pulls up in front of a jury."

We took my Pontiac and hit the road to Gainesville at five thirty. After getting caught in some rush-hour traffic, we arrived two hours later and looked up Monk's address in a corner phone booth. I called Darla Lou and left a message on her answering machine asking her to meet us there.

Monk's was on University Avenue, and when we pulled into the parking lot, it was already filling up. The hangout was brightly lit and about what you would expect of a college-town beer joint: a long wooden bar, with a few pinball machines, shuffleboard tables, a dartboard, and a limited menu. Overhead fans whirled above center tables, and the wall opposite the bar was lined with booths. We took the last one in the rear and ordered a dinner of fried chicken, onion rings, and draft beer.

As the place filled up, Elvis Presley, Buddy Holly, and Jerry Lee Lewis dominated the jukebox at a megadecibel level with "Jailhouse Rock," "Peggy Sue," and "Great Balls of Fire." After our second beer, there was still no sign of Darla Lou, and the music was beginning to give me a headache. The noise level increased by the minute and the smoke rose with it. Dart players whooped at bull's-eyes, shuffleboard pucks clacked, and pinball machines rang out—combining with an ever-increasing cacophony of coed voices engaged in a mating dance.

Almost all of the revelers were drinking beer and appeared to be students. A lot of them looked underage, but no one seemed to be having any trouble getting served. The bartenders and waitresses looked as young as the customers.

A little after nine o'clock I finally spotted Darla Lou easing her way through the crowd. She fit right in among the collegiate crew and was dressed in a skirt and sweater that did nothing to hide her best assets. I noted a goodly number of admiring appraisals as she came toward us. I raised my hand in greeting and she acknowledged it with a smile, but looked nervous as she slipped into the booth beside me.

"Hah," she said, her accent as thick as I remembered. "Ah got your message."

"Thanks for coming, Darla, we appreciate it."

"Hi," said Doug. "What're you drinking?"

"Beer's fine."

Doug signaled a waitress and I offered her a Lucky. She accepted and Doug immediately lit a match and held it out to her. I put a cigarette in my own mouth, and Doug started to light one of his own.

"Oh, mah!" Darla said. "That's three! Aren't y'all superstitious?"

Doug blew out the match and laughed. "Darlin', there is no way our luck could get any worse."

"Are you superstitious?" I asked.

"A little, I guess. Black cats and ladders and such. Mah daddy won't step on a sidewalk crack or kill a ladybug. It must run in the family."

Three more beers came; we clinked glassed and sipped. I waited a few moments before saying, "I guess you know why we're here."

Darla nodded and stared at her beer.

"Is there anything you can tell us about that night, after you got back home?"

Darla shook her head sadly, "Sissy, Penny, Rose, and I've been together two years. Since we were freshmen. They're my friends."

Gently I said, "We know that, Darla, but we also know one of your friends is lying about what happened Sunday night. We think you know that, too."

Tears formed in her eyes and she took a handkerchief out of her purse. She wiped her eyes and turned to look at me. "You paid me a nice compliment and were a real gentleman that night, and we always had fun with those other boys." She looked at Doug. "Sissy really liked you! I don't understand it! I just can't imagine what's happenin'." Darla started sobbing.

Doug leaned forward and took Darla's hands in his. "Darla, I didn't rape your friend—and neither did Vinny. But right now, for whatever reasons, she's about to destroy our lives. You've got to help us."

Darla looked at him and nodded. "I expect you're right. It's just so hard."

I said, "Darla, please."

She looked at me and back to Doug. She slowly lifted her glass, sipped it, and put it back down. "When we got home Sunday night, Penny went into the kitchen and I went up to the bathroom. It's between Sissy's bedroom and mine. Then I heard Rose come into Sissy's bedroom and they began talking. I could only hear snatches of what Sissy was sayin'. Something about breakin' up with you . . . talkin' to someone else . . . and then Rose saying somethin' about you takin' advantage of Sissy . . . And then I heard Sissy say somethin' about your smart-ass friend." She glanced at me and back to Doug. "Then Sissy cried out, 'It would serve them both right.'

Rose said, 'You're dammed right it would!' And a few seconds later they left the house."

"You didn't hear her say I didn't rape her?" Doug sounded a bit disappointed.

"No . . . At first I thought the part about you taking advantage of her meant you *did* do it . . . but then I thought that neither Sissy nor Rose seemed the least bit upset! I couldn't imagine not bein' upset if somethin' like that happened."

"She wasn't upset because it never happened," said Doug.

"Then yesterday mornin' I found out that Sissy had been home for two hours before she left to go to the authorities. I wondered why she'd waited so long and why she wasn't upset. I thought that didn't make any sense, and then *I* got upset. I'm sorry, but that's all I know."

"Would you be willing to testify to what you heard?" asked Doug.

"Oh, Lord. I don't know if I could do that. I didn't tell the police what I just told you. They'd want to know why."

I said, "I understand, but—"

She interrupted, "And even if I did, Sissy and Rose would say neither one of them said any such thing!"

She had a point. It was a conversation only Darla overheard, and both of the girls would deny it ever happened. Darla's testimony would certainly cloud the issue in front of a jury, but our only real hope would be to somehow break Sissy and Rose's story before it got there.

I said, "You're probably right, Darla. But you and Penny live with those girls, so please, if you hear anything else, let us know."

She agreed that she would and left without finishing her beer.

CHAPTER THIRTY-FOUR

THE NEXT DAY, O'Hanlon's calendar called for him to be in court during the morning, so we made an appointment to see him after lunch. Neither Doug nor I thought we'd gotten much help on our trip to Gainesville, but then again neither of us was a lawyer.

Maybe O'Hanlon would see it differently.

Things didn't get any better when Angelo called right before we left. He said he had to talk to me and was on his way to Jacksonville. He wouldn't discuss what it was about on the phone—he just said he'd see me at six and hung up.

I knew that since Anastasia's assassination and Carlo Gambino's elevation to family capo, everyone in the family was under increased surveillance. Law enforcement was convinced another gang war was about to break out, and they'd stepped up their efforts to ferret out who was up, who was down, and who was doing what to whom.

To further throw all five families into paranoia, the rumor was that the cops were making extensive use of wiretaps. My guess was that was what had caused Angelo to suddenly shun the phone. But whatever his visit was about, I told Doug it sure as hell couldn't be good news.

We left to see O'Hanlon and were waiting in his office when he waddled in looking like an aging cherub and sounding like the wrath of God.

"Goddamned idiot judge ought to be stripped, flayed, and filleted!"

Amazing, I thought. His face looked completely jovial even while he was in the middle of a tirade.

"The senile son of a bitch would make better decisions if he ruled with a yardstick. We'll win on appeal, but we'll still have to go through the whole goddamn thing all over again!" He plopped himself into his desk chair and changed subjects as if they were on a toggle switch. "So what've you got for me, boys?"

"Well," I said, "we're not really sure. We went to Gainesville and saw one of the other girls at the party. She rooms with Sissy Cable."

He leaned forward impatiently. "And?"

"And," I said, "when they got back Sunday night, she overheard a conversation between Sissy and Rose—the fourth roommate, who wasn't at the party."

Doug added, "At that point Sissy had been home for two hours and still hadn't gone to the police."

"Darla," I explained, "the girl who heard the conversation, said that she heard Sissy say something about Doug's smart-ass friend—meaning me—and that 'it would serve them *both* right.'"

Doug said, "She also heard Sissy say something about talking to someone else."

"Who?" the lawyer asked.

"She didn't say," Doug answered.

O'Hanlon steepled his fingers together under his chin and nodded silently for several moments, finally saying, "So . . . she was home exhibiting no mental trauma for two hours before reporting she was raped, and then only after talking to her roommate."

"What do you think?" Doug asked.

"It's got a foul odor, but it's not proof she's lying."

"Shit," said Doug. "That's what we thought."

"It's not all bad. The attitude, the pattern, and the comments all seem off-kilter. We need to find out who she talked to besides this Rose girl and what she said to them."

"You want us to go back there?" I asked.

"No." He keyed the intercom. "Get me Nielssen on the phone." He turned back to us saying, "Sissy knows both of you. I've got a PI who I'll send down there for a couple of days. He's as inconspicuous as a Boy Scout at a jamboree. Looks like a milquetoast, thinks like a chess master."

"What can we do?" I asked.

"Pray."

When Doug and I arrived back at the house, Jessie told us that Angelo and Stuff were waiting in the sunroom. I checked my watch. It was only four o'clock.

We joined them. "You're early," I said.

"Had a shot at the noon flight and grabbed it," said Angelo.

"You skipped lunch?" I asked, amazed.

Angelo shook his head and Stuff said, "We brought sangwiches onna plane."

Doug said, "That must have thrilled the stewardesses."

Stuff said, "No—but we offered 'em a bite anyway."

"Drink?" I asked.

Angelo said, "Later," and opened a briefcase he'd brought. "I got

227

braced by the fuzz this mornin' about the hit at Lena's. It was Santorum and Riley—the same assholes who were there that night."

"They still think you were the target?"

"Yeah. But Gus Chello saw 'em pullin' up outside my office and gave me a heads-up." Angelo held up a small tape recorder. "I set it up before they came in." Chortling, he added, "What's good fer the goose . . ."

"You recorded them?" Now I was really amazed.

"Yeah. Listen."

He set the recorder on the coffee table, and his chubby thumb mashed the play button after the four of us took seats. After a few seconds of nothing, we heard a door open, steps getting closer, and without any other preamble, Santorum's gruff voice firing off a question.

"What d'you know about a lawyer named Marion Pennington?"

"Never heard of 'im," we heard Angelo reply without missing a beat.

"He's from Los Angeles," said Riley.

"I still never heard of 'im."

Santorum again: "We think he hired Burkhardt and Whitten to knock you off two weeks ago."

"I told ya then, I'll tell ya now. I never heard of them either."

We continued listening to the rapid-fire exchange between Angelo and Riley.

"How about Jack Dragna?"

"Yeah. I read he died in L.A."

"But you didn't know him?"

"No."

"So I suppose you didn't know Pennington was his lawyer?"

"You suppose right."

"How about Johnny Roselli? Ever hear of him?"

"I read about him in the papers."

"Tony Accardo?"

"The same. He's in the papers sometimes."

"You know, Angelo," Santorum spat out in a cynical voice, "for a guy who's now running the docks for Gambino, you don't seem to know shit."

"It's my curse."

"Try this one . . . Ever heard of Las Vegas?"

"Ya caught me."

"Good. How about The Desert Inn? Moe Dalitz? The Stardust? Jake 'the Barber' Factor?"

We heard Angelo sigh heavily. "Okay, Santorum, what the hell's this about? I know nothin' about any of this shit. L.A.? Vegas? We're in New York, fer christsakes!"

"True, Angelo, but the lawyer you don't know in Los Angeles is representing a syndicate that's buying The Stardust. The rumor is that Moe Dalitz put the deal together with Teamster money. Rumor also has it that said lawyer has a gaming license and is slated to be the syndicate's president."

"Very interestin', but what the hell does that have to do with me?"

Riley said, "One of the guests at your table was a Navy lieutenant. Vincent Vesta—son of Gino Vesta, your old boss. He was with Caitlin Pennington—daughter of Marion Pennington . . . the lawyer you don't know."

I glanced at Angelo. They'd made Kat and me. Angelo patted the air with his hand, and on the tape I heard him say, "I've known the kid all his life. I met his girlfriend that night. It was my birthday fer christsakes!"

Santorum sounded smug when he replied, "We just thought it was an interesting mix. Gino Vesta's son, Marion Pennington's daughter, and two hit men connected to her father who tried to whack *you*. We thought maybe you could shed some light on why."

"Where do you come up with this shit?"

"Actually it was the Beverly Hill's department. They finally answered our request for information regarding Burkhardt and Whitten. They were a two-man security service. Bodyguards. One of their clients was Pennington. High profile. Politically connected. We did some more checking and found out Pennington was their *main* client. Interesting, no?"

"You think it's so interestin', why the fuck don't you ask this guy Pennington?"

"Oh, we will, Angelo, we will."

"Good—now if there ain't anythin' else, I got a massage at two."

We heard Riley pipe up, "They can actually get to muscle through all that fat?"

"Nice," said Angelo. "Good manners come with the badge?"

"Good manners? With you? Gimme a break! Have a nice day, asshole."

We heard retreating footsteps and a door slam. Angelo punched off the machine. "Those two clowns still think it was me Burkhardt and Whitten tried ta whack. But now they connected 'em to Pennington. They know he's a big part of the Vegas deal with Dalitz and is gonna wind up president of The Stardust. They're still fishin', but if they keep sniffin' around, they're gonna find out that Pennington's involved with Roselli. And that'll lead them to Accardo."

Stuff said solemnly, "There's another bomb tickin', Vinny."

Angelo nodded. "The minute the cops put Pennington in bed with Roselli, they're gonna pick him up for questioning. Accardo can't let that happen. Pennington's a fuckin' civilian fer christsakes! He'll sing like Caruso!"

Doug said, "But if he talks, he also buries himself."

"Maybe. But not if he cuts a deal. He's a big-time lawyer. He knows the system and he's got friends in high places. Roselli and Accardo'll be scared shitless that he'll rat them out about being the Mob muscle behind The Stardust deal."

I finally said, "You're right. They won't let that happen."

"No," said Angelo, "they won't. They'll whack the dumb son of a bitch."

CHAPTER THIRTY-FIVE

O N THURSDAY AFTERNOON O'Hanlon called and said he wanted us to come in immediately. Nielssen, his PI, was on his way back from Gainesville with news.

Twenty-five minutes later we were in O'Hanlon's office when Nielssen strolled in wearing chinos and a tweed jacket over a plaid shirt. The PI was thirty-three but had a boyish Norwegian face and a fair complexion that made him look ten years younger. With a satchel of books thrown over his shoulder he would easily have passed as a graduate student.

O'Hanlon clapped him on the arm saying, "Fast work, Ed," and introduced us.

Doug and I shook his hand and sat in front of O'Hanlon's desk. Nielssen, however, remained standing and took out a small spiral notepad.

"Last night Sissy and Rose met a guy in a restaurant. Big guy—heavyset and tough looking. Reminded me of a bulldog.

There was no dinner and the guy didn't look local. During the meeting the guy slipped Sissy an envelope, and a few minutes later the girls left the restaurant grinning like gargoyles. I followed the guy to a Holiday Inn, and when he went to bed, I jimmied his car. The rental papers in the glove compartment were from the airport Avis and made out to Karl Kramer—California license, L.A. address."

"Can you run him down?" O'Hanlon asked.

"Sure. I've got an address and I can get a phone number."

"Excellent. At some point, locating this Kramer fellow might be key."

Nielssen nodded, flipped over a notebook page. "This morning I followed Sissy into the Washington Mutual Bank and stood behind her in line. She deposited four thousand seven hundred dollars. My guess is she got a five-thousand payoff from Kramer and kept three hundred for mad money."

"Kramer was from Los Angeles?" I asked.

"He was," answered Nielssen.

Doug jumped in. "And it sure as hell doesn't take a genius to connect the dots. It has to be your old friend Pennington again."

"But how the hell can we prove it?" I asked.

"At the moment," O'Hanlon said, "we can't. But if we go to trial, I can subpoena Sissy's bank records. She'll have a hell of a time explaining where she suddenly got almost five thousand dollars. I'll also subpoena Kramer. He'll have a worse time explaining what he was doing in Gainesville slipping an envelope to Sissy Cable the night before the deposit. And he can't deny it because we've got a witness in Nielssen."

"So we can't do anything now?" Doug asked, sounding decidedly disappointed.

"I think we can. That is, you two can."

"Name it," I said.

"Go back to Gainesville. Brace Miss Cable. Tell her we know she took a five-thousand-dollar bribe from a man named Kramer and that she deposited forty-seven hundred dollars in the Washington Mutual Bank. The accuracy of those two numbers alone ought to turn her into jelly. Tell her we had her followed. We've got a witness. Tell her that the longer she lets this go on, the harder it's going to be on her when you two are acquitted and she's indicted for filing a false police report. Finally, tell her it's a felony and she'll do time. If that doesn't scare her shitless, she's an iron maiden."

Doug said, "But if she confesses, won't she be indicted anyway?"

"Not necessarily," replied O'Hanlon with a sly smile. "I might be able to cut her a deal."

"You?" asked Doug.

"If she agrees to recant, I'll handle the case. Gratis. I'm pretty tight with the DA here, and I'll have him make a few calls to Gainesville. We'll say she was distraught after the breakup with you. She was drunk. On medication. Whatever. She's a nice girl from a nice family. She has no prior record. She's a college student whose life would be ruined by one mistake, et cetera, et cetera, et cetera . . ."

"Will it work?" I asked.

"If you do your job in Gainesville as well as Nielssen did his, we'll find out."

Doug and I figured the best way to brace Sissy would be in her house. And the best way to do that would be to first check into the Holiday Inn where Kramer had stayed. We'd give the number to Darla and have her call us when Sissy came home after classes. She'd let us into the house, and before Sissy knew what was happening, we'd confront her.

We checked into the motel at five P.M., and I left word on Darla's machine while Doug went to pick up sandwiches and coffee. It could be a long wait.

Doug got back with the food at five thirty, and the phone rang a few minutes later.

"Darla?" I said.

"Hah theah."

"Hi, Darla, I'm here with Doug. We need you to do something for us."

"Something?" she asked warily. "About Sissy?"

"Yes. Is she there?"

"Uh-huh," she responded hesitantly.

"Listen to me carefully, Darla. We have absolutely concrete proof that Sissy is lying. We can prove it. If we can't turn her around, she could be in very serious trouble. We need you to let us in the house to talk to her."

"Vinny, I . . ."

"She could go to jail, Darla. What she's doing is a felony."

"Oh my God."

"You can help her. Don't say anything. Just open the door and let us in. We'll do the rest."

"She could really go to jail?"

"She could."

"My God."

"Please, Darla."

"When would you—"

"We'll be there in fifteen minutes."

There was silence on the phone for several seconds, then she said, "All right."

It was dark when we pulled up in front of a tan Craftsman about a mile from the U of F campus. There were lights in both the first- and second-floor windows.

We walked up the front steps onto the covered porch and were about to ring the bell when the door sprang open. Darla must have been watching for us.

She waved us in and pointed to the stairway. "She's in her room," she whispered. "First door on the right."

"Is she alone?" Doug asked.

Darla nodded. "Rose just went out and Penny's in the kitchen. I told her what was happening."

I said, "Thanks, Darla," and Doug led us up the stairs.

Sissy was sitting at her desk using a highlighter to mark passages in a textbook. She had her back to us but I could see she was wearing a pleated skirt and sweater. Her hair was in a ponytail held by a hairclip—a smiling Gator.

Even from this angle she looked sixteen. I couldn't help it. I actually began to feel sorry for her.

Doug quietly called out, "Sissy . . ."

Her head popped up and she spun around so quickly that her ponytail whipped around and hit her across the cheek. Disbelief spread across her face, and her lips began to quiver. Her wild-eyed glances danced back and forth between us as she frantically struggled for words.

She finally jumped up and blurted out, "H-how did you get in here? You can't be here!"

"We're here to help you, Sissy," Doug said.

"No!" she screamed. "No! I don't want to talk to you."

"You have to, Sissy, for your sake."

"No! I'm calling the police!" She reached for the phone and picked it up.

"Are you sure you want to do that?" Doug asked. "We know you took a five-thousand-dollar bribe from Karl Kramer on Wednesday night."

Sissy gasped and froze. O'Hanlon was right. We had shocked the shit out of her.

"H-how . . . h-how . . . ," she stammered. She stared at the phone for a few seconds, then put it down with a shaking hand.

Doug said, "We had you followed."

"No, I don't believe you. You're trying to trick me!"

"It's no trick, Sissy. If it were, how would we know you deposited four thousand seven hundred dollars in the Washington Mutual Bank?"

She sucked in a sudden breath and her hand shot up and covered her mouth.

"Thursday morning," Doug continued, "at ten fifteen."

That did it. She began to shake and tears flooded her eyes as she sank into the chair burying her face in her hands.

"Nooo." "Nooo . . ."

Doug walked over to her and put a hand on her shoulder. "I think we know why, Sissy. But we want to know how. How it happened. How you met Kramer—where—what he said. Do that and we'll help you."

She looked up and wiped her eyes with her sleeve. She was smart enough to realize it was over. You could see her come to the conclusion and make the decision to be honest.

"The night of the party," she began, "after you broke up with me, I was very angry—hurt. I thought you'd been using me." She glanced at me. "And he'd been making fun of me again. I rushed out of the house crying and tripped. I fell down pretty hard and hit my head. I was dazed, and then suddenly Mr. Kramer was there helping me up."

"He'd been watching the house?" I asked.

She nodded. "That's what he said. He asked me why I was crying and I just shook my head because I was still dazed from the fall and had no reason to tell my troubles to a stranger. But then he said he understood why I came out of the house crying. He said a lot of girls did. He said you were two very bad people and had reputations for mistreating girls."

"And you believed that?" cried Doug. "When the hell did you ever see or hear of us mistreating even *one* girl?"

237

"I was angry! And I was hurt!" she cried out. "At that moment I hated you." She pointed at me. "*And* him!"

"Okay . . . I get it," said Doug. "What then?"

"He said he was there because he was a private investigator working for another girl's family. They wanted to see if he could catch you doing something they could put you in jail for."

"Like rape?" Doug asked.

She shook her head. "Not right then. What he said was that you'd beaten up some other girls but they were afraid to testify because he"—she again pointed at me—"was in the Mafia."

"Christ." I threw up my hands in frustration.

"Then he asked me again what had happened to me, and I told him about us and that night."

"Did you say we raped you?"

She shook her head. "No. But he said you might as well have. He said you raped my mind and told me that I should stop you from hurting any more girls."

"And then he offered you money to say we'd raped you," said Doug.

She nodded. "He gave me a thousand dollars and said if he read in the papers that I'd gone to the police and accused you of rape, he'd come to Gainesville and give me four thousand more."

Doug shook his head sorrowfully. "Sissy, for God's sake, we had a good time together."

"Yes! And then you suddenly ended it!" She sobbed and cried out, "I wanted to get back at you!"

"Okay, but now it's over. We're going to help you." Doug hunkered down in front of her. "Here's what we're going to do."

It took another ten minutes to convince her that she had to admit her story was a lie. We told her that Sean O'Hanlon would represent her without charge and would do everything in his power to see that she didn't go to jail.

Darla and Penny came in and told her they'd been pretty sure the accusations weren't true, but they were glad she was going to admit she had lied and offered their support from then on. Rose showed up and was shocked that Sissy had recanted, then was sorry for her part in it. None of it might have happened if she hadn't egged Sissy on.

I called O'Hanlon at home, told him where we were and what had happened. I put him on the phone with Sissy, and she repeated what she'd told us. She'd taken a bribe from Kramer to say she'd been raped and would tell the police her original story was a lie.

When I took back the phone, O'Hanlon was confident enough to say he'd get it into the morning *Times-Union*. He didn't want to waste a minute in squashing the accusation and restoring our reputations.

Before we checked out of the motel, I called Kat and gave her the good news.

She was delighted but amazed. "Why did she do that?" she asked.

Once more I was faced with the dilemma of how to tell Kat the truth—that we'd caught Sissy accepting a bribe that had undoubtedly been arranged by Kat's father and that he had been, was, and would probably continue to be a goddamn psychopath. But there was no way I was going to tell her the story over the phone. Sooner or later we'd have to deal with him, but for now it could wait.

"I'll tell you the whole story when you get here."

"Oh, Vinny, I've been crazed thinking about it. Are you all right?"

"With this off our backs, the only way I could be better would be if you were here."

"I will be, tomorrow. I'm catching the first plane out."

"Great." Then, even though I hated the son of a bitch, I felt obligated to ask, "How's your father?"

"Still determined to fly to Las Vegas tonight, and I'm very worried."

"I'm sure he'll be all right." Secretly, I hoped he would drop dead.

"I hope so—it's just that he's so determined."

Tell me about it, I thought. "Stop worrying, Kat. Just be on that airplane tomorrow. Same flight?"

"Same flight."

"I'll be there. Same place."

We hung up. I paid the motel bill, Doug got the car, and we headed back to Jacksonville.

CHAPTER THIRTY-SIX

O N FRIDAY MORNING Jess came running in with the *Times-Union*, waving it over his head like a winning lottery ticket. He had already opened it to the second section. Jessie was stirring pancake batter at the center island, and Doug and I were at the breakfast table.

"It's in here!" he called out jubilantly. "The story's in here!"

He handed the paper to Doug, and I got up to read over his shoulder. A few seconds later I was joined by Jessie, craning her neck over Doug's other shoulder.

The headline in the local section of the paper was not nearly as large as it had been on the prior Tuesday. It read GATOR STUDENT REPORTEDLY RECANTS! It went on to say that her attorney, Sean O'Hanlon, had called to report that he'd spoken to the girl, but wanted her name to remain anonymous. He also said he was going to defend her and maintained, "She was a very disturbed young lady who was blinded by rejection, alcohol, and medication—confused enough to think that something happened that never did."

It sounded suspiciously as if he was already setting up his case for outright dismissal, or a temporary-insanity plea. He'd already started trying his case in the press.

Jessie said, "My, my, my . . . praise the Lord! I 'spect he got into that li'l' gal's conscience and tweaked it a bit."

"True, Jessie," Doug said, looking over his shoulder and smiling, "but this time we gave him a bit of help."

Jess asked, "That mean this bidness is really over?"

"It is," I said.

"Praise the Lord!" cried Jess.

"I already did that," said Jessie.

Jess growled, "I ain't deaf! Twice never did hurt."

Doug and I were just about to leave the house for base when the phone rang. It was Angelo. He said he had to see me before the day was out and that he and Stuff would be on the afternoon plane out of La Guardia. Once again he refused to give me a hint regarding what it was about and hung up saying they didn't want to be picked up—they'd rent a car at the airport and would be at the house by six.

I hung up and said, "Figure on two more for dinner, Jessie—with a pair of world-class appetites."

Doug asked, "What's up?"

"Angelo's on his way. Twice in three days. It can't be anything good, kemo sabe."

When Doug and I entered the squadron ready room that morning, we were greeted like conquering heroes. We actually received a round of applause, followed by a lot of backslapping. Whitey and Zaz were especially ebullient since they were the ones who had, in their words, "cracked the case."

Zaz said, "Where would you to be without us, *mes amis*?"

Doug said, "French? I thought you were Mexican."

Zaz proudly thumbed his chest. "Ensign Pedro Zazueta is a sophisticated man of the world."

Whitey interjected, "Of burritos and salsa!"

"What?" Zaz shot back. "A Nebraska hick is making fun of a cultured *mejicano?*"

Whitey looked indignant. "*I'm* the one who came up with Darla Lou! The key name!"

Zaz pressed on, "But I'm the one who came up with her phone number!"

I held up my hand. "You're both veritable Sherlocks. But you'd be better off playing Nick and Nora Charles. That way you can argue about who wears the dress."

Concannon arrived in his flight suit chewing on his unlit cigar. He greeted us enthusiastically, "Ah! My two favorite fuckups."

Doug raised a finger. "*Alleged* fuckups."

"May I point out that there would have been no allegations if there had been no fucking?"

"Who would want to live in that world?" asked Doug, aghast.

"Point taken. Now get your asses in flight gear. In case you haven't noticed, this is a fighter squadron, not a home for oversexed delinquents."

He flashed a smile, tapped Doug on the arm, and left, saying, "See you on the flight line. Instrument-card checks. You're with me. Vesta's with Willis. Gear up at eleven hundred."

Instrument checks were exercises flown with the pilot being checked flying his jet under a canvas hood, which was deployed under the canopy. They were a pain in the ass, but mandatory for keeping you out of "a crash and burn" on a dark and stormy night. The hood prevented the pilot from seeing anything outside his cockpit. The check pilot flew in a safety plane behind him, allowing him to radio "break it off" if the "blind" pilot got into a dangerous situation.

This particular hop was a round-robin. I took off under the hood from Jax with Willis following and performed some basic air work—

steep turns and stalls—en route to NAS Sanford, south of Jax. We arrived at twenty thousand feet, performed a jet penetration down to two thousand feet, and picked up a GCA (radar ground-controlled approach) to a touch-and-go. We then proceeded to Cecil Field, also south of Jax, at low altitude, where I shot an ADF (automatic direction finder) approach to another touch-and-go. We wound up the check ride by flying back to Jax for another jet penetration and a nonprecision radar approach to a final landing. Total time round-trip: an hour and ten minutes. Even though check rides were a pain in the ass, it was still flying. And a pain in the ass in the air was a hell of a lot better than the pain in the ass I was having on the ground.

I was in the ready room playing acey-deucey with Doug when LT Bill Raney stuck his head in and informed me that I had a call in the duty office. I took a last roll and came up with the name of the game— an ace and a deuce. I moved my men three spaces, took the extra roll, and came up with two sixes—all but assuring victory. We played by backgammon rules, which allowed me to double our existing bet by placing a die with the 2 facing up. I did it. Doug now had a choice—he could concede or continue at his peril.

He frowned, "Lucky prick."

I smiled and singsonged, "Testy, testy," leaving him to consider his unpleasant options while I went to pick up the call.

"Lieutenant Vesta," I said.

"It's me."

She sounded agitated. "Kat?"

"I can't get there this weekend, Vinny. It's my father. He's had another heart attack."

I immediately had mixed emotions but covered them, saying, "Kat, I'm . . . I'm sorry. When did . . ."

"This morning. He flew to Las Vegas last night and . . . And now this. I told him not to go! I knew how upset he'd been. I begged him!"

I flared. "Kat—don't blame yourself! You told me last Monday that he was a very determined man. If he wanted to go, no one could have stopped him."

"I know . . . I know . . . Dr. Sergeant, his internist, flew up with him last night and we spoke a few minutes ago. Sergeant called a specialist from the university medical center and he's on his way to the hotel. Oh, Vinny, I'm petrified. Two attacks in one week! Sergeant wants me fly up to Vegas right away. I'm leaving as soon as I hang up."

"Okay, baby, do what you have to do and call me when you get there. I'll stay home tonight and wait for your call."

"Thanks, sailor. I'm sorry."

"Nothing to be sorry about. Fly safe and take care of yourself."

"I will. I love you."

I said, "Me, too," but hung up wondering whether Daddy's heart attacks were legit. They'd once again kept Kat away from me, and based on his track record, I wouldn't put anything past him.

Doug and I got home a half hour before the Maserellis arrived, and Jessie told me she'd had Jess set up the grill for steaks, roasted corn, and yams. I made myself a martini and put in a call to Kat at The Desert Inn.

When she picked up, I said, "It's me. Are you okay?"

"Just worried sick." She sounded it. "I just talked to Sergeant and I think he's an idiot."

"Why?"

"He doesn't seem all that concerned! I mean he said all Daddy needs is rest and a lack of stress. But damn it, he collapsed over breakfast today, and tomorrow he'll be named president of The Stardust!"

"What did the specialist say?"

"That he agreed with Sergeant that there didn't seem to be any immediate danger."

"Then I think you should just relax and—"

"I can't, Vinny! I've got to talk him out of this insanity."

It took all of my willpower to refrain from pointing out that insanity was a perfectly normal state for someone who was insane.

Instead I said, "Okay, darlin', do what you think is right."

"I will. Will you be at home later?"

"All night—waiting to hear from you."

"Thank you, darling. I'll call right after I see Daddy."

We hung up. I shook my head and made myself another martini. She was still calling him Daddy for chrissakes.

Angelo and Stuff arrived with their suits and game faces on. After we exchanged greetings and hugs, they removed their jackets and loosened their ties, and I poured them a pair of three-finger single malts before we all settled into the sunroom.

"What I got to tell ya," Angelo said, "should make you very happy, but it could also ruin your weddin' plans."

I thought about that a second and realized the only thing that might harbor both those possibilities would undoubtedly involve Kat's father.

"Pennington," I said.

"The fishin's over. He's on the hook. The Beverly Hills cops tied him inta Roselli. Roselli got the tip from his contact in BHPD that they're gonna pick up Pennington for questionin' as soon as he gets back from Vegas."

Stuff added the obvious, "And you know Accardo's gonna figure there's no way Pennington is gonna take a fall for him, Roselli, or the Dalitz syndicate."

"It's like I told ya Wednesday," said Angelo, "Accardo and Roselli got no choice. They'll whack 'im. As soon as the deal closes, they won't need 'im anymore. They might make it look like an accident, but make no mistake, if Pennington winds up dead, it'll be because they killed 'im. Once they got The Stardust title in a legit syndicate, they'll come up with a new president who's either got or can get a gamin' license."

"I still don't get how this affects our plans."

"Think about it. After all that's gone down between you and her old man, who d'ya think your girlfriend's gonna suspect had somethin' ta do with it if her father gets knocked off?"

"No, Angelo, I told her I wouldn't touch him. I meant it and she believed me. And I still haven't told her about that bastard setting me up for a rape charge!"

"Vincenzo," he pleaded. "Think! She knows Roselli, Accardo, and Dalitz set up The Stardust deal. So she's gotta believe they'd want Pennington alive so he can take over and run it. In her mind she's gonna think, why would *they* wanna kill 'im?"

I thought about it and realized he could be right. When Kat and I were on the Circle Line cruise, the day after the attempted hit at Lena's, she had been sure I'd want to retaliate. She'd begged me not to have her father targeted and said that in spite of all that had happened, she still loved and wanted to protect him.

I sighed and relented. "You're right. In her mind, she would think Roselli, Accardo, and Dalitz would have no reason to kill her father."

Angelo nodded. "And the onny other person she knows who'd have a reason has gotta be you."

"Christ, Angelo, what the hell can I do?"

"Get yer ass out to Vegas, get 'em both inna room, and lay it out."

Completely frustrated, I blurted out, "The closing's tomorrow!"

"Then ya better jump in one of those shit-hot little flamethrowers ya fly and get out there tonight. The minute Pennington signs those papers, he's a dead man, and you, my friend, are fucked."

CHAPTER THIRTY-SEVEN

I KNEW CONCANNON would already have left his office by six thirty, so I called his home. He hadn't arrived yet. I asked his wife to have him call me as soon as he got in and tell him it was extremely important.

Angelo was right, the only way I was going to get to Las Vegas before The Stardust closing the following morning was via a U.S. Navy jet.

It wasn't unusual for pilots to occasionally check out squadron aircraft for cross-country flights on weekends, but normally the requests were made well in advance of the flight. The official military purpose of these flights was training, which they were, but the secondary purpose was a quick visit to family and friends via a landing at a Navy or Air Force base close to the pilot's hometown. It was one of the perks of a low-paying, often dangerous profession that made everybody happy.

I watched as Angelo and Stuff tucked into Jess's grilled steaks, corn, and yams, but I'd lost my appetite trying to figure out how I could convince my commanding officer that I needed a Navy jet for an emergency night flight to Las Vegas.

Christ, a request couldn't sound any more ridiculous than that.

Doug said, "Your best bet is to steal one."

"Thanks for the advice, counselor. It'll get me ten years in Leavenworth for trying to save the ass of a maniac—who's trying to bury mine."

"Look at the upside. There's no way your future father-in-law can get to you in Club Fed."

Concannon called at seven. "So? What's extremely important?" he asked, already sounding annoyed.

"Skipper, the only way I can ask this is to do it straight out—I need to check out a jet for an emergency flight to Las Vegas."

Concannon only hesitated a second. "Why? Your casino burn down?"

"Nosir. My fiancée's father's there. He's had a heart attack."

"He lose his ranch in a poker game?"

"Nosir. He—"

"You're going to perform open-heart surgery on him."

"Nosir, I—"

"Vesta, have you gone completely batshit?"

"Nosir."

"Then what the hell are you babbling about?"

"My fiancée's father."

"The one you say had a heart attack."

"Yessir. I think his life's in danger."

"Have you been drinking, Vesta? If he had a heart attack, of course his life is in danger. But what the hell can *you* do about it?"

"Skipper, I swear it really is an emergency."

"It's seven o'clock on Friday night!"

"I know that, Skipper. So you have to know it's *gotta* be an emergency."

"If you're handing me a bucket of bullshit so you can spend the weekend with your girlfriend, you're gonna wish you joined the fucking Army!"

"It's not, Skipper, I swear."

He said nothing for a few seconds, then blurted out, "Christ!" after another few seconds of silence he said, "All right, Vesta, I'll call the squadron duty officer and backdate a cross-country request to Nellis Air Force Base in case you crash and burn. But I won't process it. You've got one day. You get your ass back here before midnight tomorrow and the cross-country request will disappear as if you'd never left. I don't want CAG to think I've lost my fucking mind."

"Thanks, Skipper."

"Don't thank me," he growled. "Just get that jet back here before midnight tomorrow or you can stay in Las Vegas until you rot or get picked up for desertion!"

"Yessir. You have my word."

"One day, Vesta! By midnight tomorrow night your ass is back here safe and sound with that airplane in the same condition or I'll personally crucify you!"

He ended the conversation by slamming down the phone. I had twenty-four hours. If everything went well, it should be all I'd need, but it didn't leave a heartbeat for unforeseen fuckups.

I hung up, redialed The Desert Inn, and asked for Kat's room. She was out and I said I'd call back. I certainly couldn't leave a message saying her father was in danger. What kind? When? From whom? Plus, I didn't want to give her time to build a "Jack's story" about why I was suddenly flying to Las Vegas.

I also didn't tell Jess or Jessie my plans. If Kat called back, I didn't want them telling her that I'd packed a bag and left without saying where I was going. I asked Doug to drive Angelo and Stuff back to the airport, stuffed a shirt, slacks, sport coat, and shaving kit into a pair of small duffels, and left for the base.

*   *   *

I filed a flight plan for a fuel stop at NAS Olathe, outside of Kansas City, and took off at eight thirty P.M. It was an 850-mile leg and would take me almost two and a half hours. I'd pick up an hour with the time change, and figuring an hour on the ground to fuel, refile, and take off, I'd be on my way again at eleven P.M., CST.

The second leg, from Olathe to Las Vegas, was 990 miles and would take over two and a half hours. But I'd be picking up an additional two hours with two more time changes. If all went well, I would be landing at Nellis Air Force Base outside Las Vegas, Nevada, at twelve thirty A.M., PST, with fatigue in my muscles and fumes in my tanks.

Leveling off at forty thousand feet, I settled back into the ejection seat of the swept-wing Fury and watched the glittering lights of Tallahassee slip under my wing as I jetted west.

It was my second cross-country trip in as many months, but this time I was in the cockpit. I could be headed toward hell, but up here I was in heaven.

After landing at NAS Olathe, and while the line crew was refueling my jet, I went into Flight Operations to file my second flight plan and call Kat. It was eleven P.M. local—nine P.M. in Las Vegas. Again there was no answer in her suite, so I figured she was probably still out to dinner with her father. I hadn't changed my mind about telling her I was on my way, so I left another message saying I'd call back.

I'd had time to think about how much I'd tell Kat when I saw her. Certainly I'd have to tell her about Angelo's prediction that her father was a dead man the minute he signed The Stardust sale papers, but what about the rest? Should I tell her that the rape accusation was set up by him as well?

She'd said that she thought it was our affair that had caused him to become demented—demented enough to order me assassinated. And he'd had his first heart attack when she confronted and threatened to expose him. If I told her about his latest plot and she confronted him again, would he have another attack? Could it kill him? Would she blame us again?

It was a tangled mess that didn't seem to have a real answer, so I decided to only tell her about the threat, get them both the hell out of Vegas, and worry about the next step down the line.

At twelve forty-five I landed at Nellis Air Force Base and taxied to the transient parking ramp. I retrieved the duffels I'd jammed into my jet's ammo cans and told the line crew to top off the tanks. After checking in with the duty officer and closing my flight plan, I told him that I'd be leaving the next day and asked him to call me a taxi. The Base Ops bathroom doubled as a changing room, and I removed the rumpled shirt, slacks, and sport coat I'd stuffed into the duffels.

After changing, I checked the mirror and my watch: one fifteen A.M.—four fifteen in Jacksonville. Less than twenty hours to stop a murder, fly back across the country, and avoid incurring the awesome wrath of Kelly "the Black Thing" Concannon.

CHAPTER THIRTY-EIGHT

NELLIS AIR FORCE BASE was a mere eight miles from downtown Las Vegas, and the cab arrived fifteen minutes later. When I asked for The Desert Inn, the driver was surprised I hadn't asked for The Dunes.

"Why?" I asked.

"Because all the flyboys comin' in here for the weekend are stayin' there. It's because of their new show. They booked in *Minsky's Follies*."

"Bare tits and all?"

"Ya got that right. It's the first time there's been nude broads on the Strip. But everybody says pretty soon all the showgirls'll be bare-assed."

"Progress in the making," I observed. "The town crowded?"

"Jammed. Steve 'n' Eydie are playin' the showroom at the DI where you're stayin'. And Rickles, Buddy Hackett, Shecky Greene, Louis Prima, and Keely Smith got all the lounges jumpin'. It's amazin'. The town's growin' so fast I hear people say they're even gonna build two more hotels."

When we arrived at The Desert Inn, I gave the cabbie a five-dollar tip, thanked him for the latest update, and walked into the casino—a spectacular gambler's paradise three stories high and dripping with chandeliers. As I headed for the house phones adjacent to the check-in desk, I heard the unmistakable roar of happy gamblers coming from a craps table surrounded by players and onlookers.

I chuckled—the check-in desks in all Vegas hotels were adjacent to the casino because the owners wanted you to be tempted from the moment you arrived. Apparently, the DI's was no exception. I was just about to pick up the phone and ask for Kat's room when I heard another roar coming from a nearby craps table and glanced over.

The man shooting the dice—and whom everyone was boisterously cheering on—was unmistakably Jimmy Hoffa. I'd seen his scowling face in newspapers for years. He was apparently on a roll and was enjoying the urging and accolades of a crowd of well-wishers. Three men in dark suits were standing directly alongside him at his end of the table, but a pair of bulky security guards were making sure the onlookers didn't get anywhere near the quartet.

I strolled over and stood behind the crowd next to a cocktail waitress, listening to the shouts of "Go, Jimmy," "Attaboy, Jimmy," "Keep it goin', Jimmy," and "Break the bank, Jimmy."

I immediately recognized two of the men standing next to Hoffa— Johnny Roselli and Tony Accardo—but I didn't know the third. I turned to the cocktail waitress and said, "Exciting, isn't it? That's Jimmy Hoffa!"

"It sure is. He's had the dice for ten minutes." The waitress nodded toward the end of the table. "The boss must be having a fit."

"The boss?"

"Moe Dalitz. That's him standing next to Hoffa."

"He owns the casino?" I asked naïvely.

"Yep." She leaned in conspiratorially. "And that's Tony Accardo—

'the Big Tuna'—standing next to Johnny Roselli. Now, he's handsome, isn't he?"

"He most certainly is," I said agreeably, and walked back to the house phones.

When Kat answered, I said, "Hi, darlin', it's me."

"Vinny," she said groggily. "I tried to call you back earlier and I got your second message—but no phone number. Where are you?"

"Downstairs."

"Downstairs where?"

"In the lobby."

"Here? How . . .?" she cried out.

"It's a long story, which I'll tell you as soon as you tell me what room you're in."

"Six twenty-two." She sounded ecstatic. "And it's a suite, sailor!"

"Only the best for the best. See you in two minutes."

I rushed to the elevators and punched 6. When I reached her floor and walked into the hallway, I saw the door to 622 fly open. A second later Kat stepped into the doorway wearing nothing but a pair of heels.

I dropped my bag and we hurtled into each other's arms.

"Please tell me I'm not still in bed and dreaming."

"It's no dream. I'm here."

She kissed me hungrily, then leaned back. "Make love to me darling—right now—so I can believe it."

I laughed. " 'The truth will set you free.' John eight: thirty-two."

I took her hand, swept up my duffels, and led her into the bedroom. There was plenty of time to tell her why I'd come and no reason to wreck a beautiful moment. I'd flown almost two thousand miles to save the ass of a man I hated and felt I deserved a reward before delivering a death threat.

"Why didn't you tell me you were coming?"

"Later. We'll have plenty of time to talk. Right now concentrate on your request—which, as you can see, I'm clearly prepared to grant."

She chuckled and felt the bulge in my pants. "A perfect time to quote Mae West, but I feel like doing—not talking."

Vegas was a repeat of Havana, which was a repeat of The Cloisters, Point Loma, La Jolla, and all the first nights we'd spent together since we'd met. Passionate, tender, needy, joyous, and all the adjectives that describe transcendent copulation.

We devoured each other ravenously until we both got leg cramps during an especially explosive session. We yelped, bent forward, grabbed our toes, and pulled them back with cries of *Ooo! Oh! Ah!* and *Damn!*—interspersed with gales of laughter.

When the charley horses finally subsided, I lit a pair of Luckys and handed her one.

She said, "Thank you, Paul."

"You remember *Now, Voyager?*"

"Uh-huh . . ." She took a deep drag, blew it out. "You're my second surprise of the evening. Vic showed up earlier while I was having dinner with Daddy tonight."

I felt a jab of jealousy. "Marino? In town for Steve and Eydie?"

"Hardly. It was a setup choreographed by Daddy."

I shook my head. "Amazing. He remains relentless." For the moment I stopped short of telling how relentless.

"This time the bait was an offer by Zanuck, who asked Vic to deliver it."

"What kind?"

"A part in a film."

"Another setup by Daddy?"

"That's what I thought—an excuse to get me together with Vic . . . So I called Darryl at home before I went to bed, telling him how 'excited' I was and expecting him to ask me what the hell I was talking about."

"He didn't?"

"*Au contraire.* He said he'd seen my Chanel commercial and was bowled over. The studio's about to begin preproduction on Irwin Shaw's *The Young Lions*. It's scheduled to shoot in Germany, and there's a part he said he was about to offer Hope Lange, but that I, quote, was perfect for, unquote."

"What d'you think?"

"Well, everyone knows he's been searching for a replacement for Gene Tierney for years. She's over, and he thinks I'm it. I'm flattered but not interested—of course I told him I'd think about it in order to end the discussion without a harangue."

"What'd you tell Daddy and Marino?"

"The same thing for the same reason. I didn't want to get into it and get Daddy all excited."

"And they accepted it?"

"Eventually—except Vic kept ranting on and on about how this was the Irwin Shaw blockbuster with Eddy Dmytryk directing. He predicted it would be huge, the break I've been working for my whole adult life!"

I hated to admit it but said, "He's right you know."

"Vinny, it's what I *was* working for my whole adult life. But not anymore. Not since you, darling." She rolled on top of me and planted a lingering kiss on my lips. "So now that I've given you my news, what's yours? Why didn't you tell me you were coming?"

I sighed. "Would you mind if I made us a nightcap first?"

"Do you think we'll need one?"

"It's possible. What about a touch of the bubbly?" I got out of bed.

"Why not?" She laughed. "I'm celebrating the return of my hero—back from the clutches of a lying little coed bitch. There are some splits in the minibar."

I took two robes out of the bathroom, handed her one, and set out to liberate the champagne. I popped open two splits and poured them into flutes, thinking about how to begin. As always when it concerned her father, there was no easy way.

Kat came out of the bedroom and I handed her a flute.

"Cheers," I said, and we touched glasses. I drank mine down in one gulp and immediately poured a refill.

"Wow," she remarked, "did I make you that thirsty?"

"It's been a long day."

"Now will you tell me why you wouldn't tell me you were coming?"

"Yes." I led her to the couch.

She sat and faced me, pulling her legs up to her chest and resting her chin on her knees. I sat close to her and threw an arm over the back of the sofa.

I began, "Last night around dinnertime Angelo and Stuff Maserelli made an emergency trip to Jacksonville . . . Do you remember the two NYPD detectives who questioned us that night at Lena's?"

"Of course I remember them. There's nothing about that night I'll ever forget."

I nodded, took a long drag on my cigarette. "They braced Angelo and told him they'd been talking to the BHPD about Burkhardt and Whitten. They found out the two ran a security service and that they worked almost exclusively for your father. That sent their cop's antenna sailing through the roof. They also checked their notes and realized that you and I were in the restaurant that night. It was all too coincidental, so they began an investigation." I paused, inhaled another drag on the Lucky, and slowly let it out. "The bottom line is—they've been trying to tie your father into what they think was a failed Mob hit on Angelo."

Kat's hand came up to her mouth and she murmured, "Oh my God."

"It gets worse. They continued checking your father and tied him into Johnny Roselli—and that means Tony Accardo. They found out he'd applied for a gaming license and that he's representing a syndicate buying The Stardust. Moe Dalitz—who's got a very shady background, and who owns this hotel—put together the syndicate. They can't prove it, but NYPD and BHPD suspect Tony Accardo and Johnny Roselli are supplying the money through Jimmy Hoffa's Teamsters' pension fund.

The bottom line is, once your father is named president, his syndicate will be the front, but Accardo, Roselli, and the Chicago Mob will be the real owners of The Stardust."

"And Daddy knows that," she said, seemingly resigned.

"Undoubtedly. BHPD knows all the players and thinks they might have a case. They're going to bring your father in for questioning as soon as he returns to L.A. But right now your father doesn't have a clue about what's been going on."

"Will the police be able to prove Accardo and Roselli are involved?" she asked.

"I don't think so. They're too well covered. Investigators have been trying to tie the Mob into Vegas for years, but nothing's stuck."

Kat leaned toward me and took my hand, a look of anguish on her face. "Vinny, I hate what Daddy's doing! And I still think his heart problem isn't his only sickness. But surely he can handle some questioning. He's spent half his life dealing with questions—in and out of a courtroom."

"It's not the questioning that's the problem—it's that he's about to *be* questioned."

Kat's face grew puzzled. "I'm not following."

"Angelo believes that Accardo and Roselli won't let your father be brought in by the BHPD."

"Can they prevent it?"

"They can," I said. "They'll kill him."

Her eyes widened and her jaw sagged. It was obvious she realized her father's associates could and would commit murder.

"We think it'll go down after he signs the papers putting The Stardust into the syndicate's hands."

"We've got to stop him." Her voice started to rise. "We've got to tell Daddy what's happened and stop him!"

"Exactly."

"We'll call him right now!" she cried out, and started to get up.

I stopped her. "Kat, there's no point in waking him up now."

"We've got to warn him!" she insisted.

"It's two thirty in the morning."

"I know, but——"

"He needs his rest. Let him sleep for now. When does the closing take place?"

"Noon at The Stardust. A few speeches, some photos with the stars, and lunch. But I'm meeting Daddy and Dr. Sergeant for breakfast at eight o'clock."

"Good. We'll tell him then. Maybe he'll even be happy to see me when he hears what I have to say."

She finally relented and settled back onto the couch. "Actually he was glad to hear that'd you'd been cleared of that rape charge when I told him about it."

I'll bet, I thought. He was the bastard who'd set me up, but under the present circumstances I still felt that I shouldn't go there—yet.

CHAPTER THIRTY-NINE

KAT AND I LEFT the suite to meet Pennington a few minutes before eight. Her lithe body was encased in skintight, black cigarette pants and a white blouse. She was wearing tinted glasses, and her heels accented her gait, causing her long auburn ponytail to bounce from shoulder to shoulder. As we made our way to the coffee shop, she kept drawing appreciative as well as inquisitive glances from curious onlookers, many of them probably thinking she was a movie star. This was Las Vegas—it was the weekend—and Steve Lawrence and Eydie Gormé were headlining in the showroom.

The hostess at the coffee shop gave Kat an admiring smile, then dropped it when she saw me. By contrast, my rumpled sport coat, shirt, and slacks left a lot to be desired. She showed us to a quiet table against the wall and we ordered coffee.

I was feeling a little edgy about finally meeting the man who was my bitter enemy, so I lit a Lucky. How would I react if he reached out to shake my hand? I'd discussed it with Kat, and she said I should respond like the officer and gentleman I'd taken an oath to be. Terrific. This for a guy who'd try to machine-gun me in my parachute.

My thoughts were interrupted by Kat. "There's Dr. Sergeant." She nodded toward a man who'd stopped at the hostess desk and was surveying the tables. He had a tall, wispy body topped by a scrawny neck, a long face, and graying hair that looked permanently disheveled. He was wearing a suit but it didn't help. He looked like a scarecrow. Kat had earlier said she didn't like him and never had. I understood why.

He spotted Kat at our table and walked over to join us. "Good morning, Kat," he said, briefly admiring her low-cut blouse and tight jeans. "Lovely, as always." He then looked at me inquisitively.

Kat said, "This is Lieutenant Vincent Vesta, my fiancé. Dr. Mark Sergeant, my daddy's internist."

I put out my hand. "Nice to meet you."

"Dr. Sergeant is here keeping an eye on Daddy's condition," Kat explained as if she approved and I'd never heard of him.

Sergeant smiled. "Which, I'm sure, is going to be perfectly fine if we can convince him to obey a few simple rules."

A waitress appeared and took Sergeant's coffee order, but we all decided to wait for Pennington before ordering breakfast.

"When did you arrive, Lieutenant?"

"Late last night," I said.

"From?"

"Jacksonville."

"Oh? Plane—train—car?"

"Navy jet. I'm a pilot."

Sergeant cocked an eyebrow. "They let you borrow their aircraft?"

"They do occasionally. It's called a training flight."

Sergeant glanced at Kat and smiled. "Dare I ask—training for what?"

She returned his smile and wryly tossed her head to the side. "Anything for my country."

When the waitress returned, I saw Kat glance at her watch. It was eight twenty and she was obviously concerned.

"Daddy's almost never late." Kat turned to Sergeant. "Have you spoken to him this morning?"

Knowing he was supposedly in Vegas as her father's medical guardian, Sergeant nervously said, "Well, no . . . I called him earlier, but there was no answer."

"How long ago?" Kat asked, visibly anxious.

"At about seven thirty."

"That was over forty-five minutes ago!"

Sergeant immediately became defensive. "I know, but I—"

Kat jumped to her feet and threw down her napkin. "God!" she cried, and rushed to the hostess station. "Call security! Have them meet me at suite 808 with a passkey. It's an emergency!"

Sergeant and I caught up with her at the elevator, and we took it to the eighth floor. We arrived before hotel security and alternately leaned on the buzzer and pounded the door until the guard arrived.

As he came down the hall, Kat yelled out, "I'm Caitlin Pennington." She indicated Sergeant. "This is my father's doctor and this is his suite. He has a heart condition and we think he may have had an attack. Please open the door."

The intensity of her plea brought immediate consent. "Yes, ma'm," the guard said, and thrust the key into the lock. Kat flew through the door ahead of us and called out, "Daddy?"

She rushed into the bedroom and then toward the bathroom with us on her heels. She stopped in the doorway and froze—blocking it.

She screamed and, before I knew why, slumped toward the floor, crying out, "My God, Vinny—he's had another heart attack!" She sobbed, "Another heart attack," and I caught her just as she fainted, slowly lowering her to the floor.

Sergeant stepped past us and cried out, "My God! Penn!"

I looked into the bathroom and saw Pennington lying facedown in the tub. There was pink water drifting around his head and little doubt he was dead. Christ! I thought. They'd done it! They whacked the bastard and made it look as if he'd slipped or had another heart attack and fell into the tub!

Sergeant seemed to be in shock. His eyes were glazed and he was trembling. "This can't be," he murmured, "it can't be," backing out of the bathroom in a daze.

I turned to the security guard. "You'd better notify your office. Mr. Pennington's in the tub. He's dead."

The security guard immediately went to the phone in the living room. I lifted Kat onto the bed.

"Get me a cold towel," I said to a glassy-eyed Sergeant.

He just stared at me as if he didn't understand a word of English.

"Now!" I yelled. "A cold towel! And then call the house doctor unless you've got a sedative with you—she may need one."

"Yes, yes," he mumbled, his face drained of color, "of course." After the security guard was finished, he slowly picked up the phone.

Kat finally began to come around. Her eyes blinked open, but when she saw me and registered where she was and what she'd seen, she broke down crying again. She threw her arms around me and sobbed uncontrollably.

Five minutes later the house doctor showed up with a syringe and gave Kat a sedative. I continued to hold her, and after a few moments her sobs slowly subsided. But her eyes were red, her cheeks pale, and her makeup, along with her persona, were gone. Even her distinctive accent seemed dulled.

I let her talk with the doctor for a while and walked back into the bathroom to take another look at the dead man who'd been my unseen enemy for so long. I noticed a smear of blood on the wall above the tub where he was lying facedown in the water. It looked as if he might have been getting in when he pitched into the wall, breaking the skin on his forehead before sliding down into the tub. It was next to the toilet, and his robe was draped across the seat where he'd obviously left it before getting into his bath. Something caught my eye on the floor behind the toilet. I bent over to get a closer look at it and saw it was a dental bridge. Leaning even closer, I noticed dried red stains on the false teeth. Blood?

I heard some unfamiliar voices coming from the living room and quickly walked back out. Three men had arrived. A middle-aged man in a dark suit and hat greeted me saying, "Detective David Rosen, LVPD." He indicated a second man in similar attire. "My partner, Detective Paul Pangaro." Pointing to the man in uniform, he added, "And Captain Sonny Chechefsky, head of DI Security."

The cops? I thought. Already? Why? The security man had reported a heart attack—not foul play. I shook Rosen's hand. "Vincent Vesta, Lieutenant, USN. The deceased is my fiancée's father."

"I understand you discovered the body."

"I did, along with hotel security, my fiancée, and her father's doctor."

"At what time was that?"

"About eight thirty. Perhaps a bit after."

Rosen nodded and looked at the rest of us. "And I assume no one has disturbed anything since then?"

We shook our heads.

"The medical examiner's on his way." Rosen pointed toward the bathroom door. "In there?"

I nodded, and he walked briskly toward the door, followed by Pangaro.

"LVPD?" I asked Chechefsky.

He nodded. "When I was told who had died in the hotel, I called Mr. Dalitz. I knew Mr. Pennington was a friend and they were both involved in The Stardust deal. He told me to notify LVPD."

Interesting, I thought. If Angelo's suspicions were correct regarding a hit on Pennington, and Dalitz had told security to call LVPD, it seemed obvious that Dalitz knew nothing about the hit. Either that or he was covering all his bases. It might seem suspicious if he didn't call the police as a matter of course when his partner died in his bathtub on the morning he was to sign The Stardust deal. Dalitz was well connected and would also have to know that the local police knew Accardo and Roselli were in The Desert Inn and were tracking them. The cops couldn't prove a thing, but damn sure suspected they were in town because of The Stardust sale.

The only thing confusing me was that now Pennington obviously *wouldn't* be signing the papers at The Stardust closing.

I was still trying to figure this out when a man strode into the room as if he owned it and announced, "Justin Colbert—medical examiner. Where is Detective Rosen?"

Colbert looked suspiciously like LCDR Andre Poulet, the asshole who was in charge of NCIS Jacksonville. Colbert was a little over five feet tall, had a long nose, and a pinched face. His black suit and black wing-tipped shoes made him look like a funeral director.

Why not? I thought. Death was his business.

Detectives Rosen and Pangaro reentered the living room and nodded at him. The body language of the two men said that no love was lost between them.

"Well," Colbert sniffed, addressing Rosen as if he were annoyed just to be there doing his job, "what do we have?"

Rosen's eyes narrowed. "Why don't you go in there and answer your own question for us?"

Colbert absorbed the jab, popped his chin forward, and reluctantly sauntered toward the bathroom to begin his preliminary examination. Two other men, apparently his assistants, appeared in the doorway and followed him.

Rosen turned to Pangaro. "Someday they're gonna autopsy that little shit on his own table and be astounded by the cause of death."

"Which will be?" asked Pangaro.

"My shoe up his ass."

I chuckled. Rosen noticed and smiled. "Navy?"

I nodded. "Pilot. Stationed at NAS Jacksonville."

"My father was Navy before he became a cop," he said. "Signalman on a destroyer. Where're you from?"

"New York. Hell's Kitchen. You?"

"Chicago. South Side."

"What brought you here?" I asked.

"The weather. My old man lived through the last days of Capone, then died of pneumonia walking a beat." Rosen took out a Camel and offered me one, which I took, and he lit. He lit his own, exhaled. "How much do you know about the deceased?"

"He's my fiancée's father."

"You said that. You know anything about his involvement in Vegas?"

I started to get uncomfortable. "I know he was about to become the president of The Stardust."

"Actually, the president of a syndicate headed by Moe Dalitz. And rumor has it that the Chicago Mob is backing him with Teamster pension-fund cash."

"Oh?" I said noncommittally.

"Tony Accardo and Johnny Roselli," continued Rosen, shaking his head in disgust. "I've known their names since I was a kid. Accardo took over after Capone, and Roselli's his man on the coast. We know who and what they are. We can't prove anything, but we keep an eye on them when we hear they're in town. Ever hear of them?"

"I don't think so, why?"

"Because we think your future father-in-law was in bed with them."

Colbert reappeared and interrupted us without apology. He reported that preliminarily, he would put the time of death somewhere between ten and eleven the prior evening.

Rosen asked, "You notice if he had any teeth missing?" He'd apparently seen the dental bridge behind the toilet, too.

Colbert responded gruffly, "I won't complete my examination until we get to the morgue."

"Would you mind checking now?" asked Rosen with a forced smile. "It's important."

Colbert heaved a deep sigh and returned to the bathroom. A minute or so later he returned, looking irritated.

"He appears to have had a bridge, but it's not in his mouth. There's an abrasion inside his cheek next to the spot where it was fitted. Why do you ask?"

Rosen led the ME back into the bathroom and I heard him say, "Because we think that could be it."

Kat said she wanted to leave the scene, and Rosen asked me to bring her and Sergeant to Chechefsky's office until they finished their investigation.

Meanwhile, the bruise inside Pennington's mouth and the dental bridge behind the toilet were suspicious enough for Rosen to call in a forensics team.

CHAPTER FORTY

K AT STILL HADN'T put on any makeup, but in her
jeans and heels, she continued to turn heads as we left the
elevator and headed for Chechefsky's office. And Sergeant
continued to look as if he were about to have a seizure. He was
snow white, his hands were trembling, and he was sweating profusely
in spite of the air-conditioned casino. When we got to the office, he
lowered himself into a chair and began mopping his brow.

I asked, "Are you all right?"

"Yes . . . I mean, no," he stammered. "Could I have a glass of
water?"

"Sure." I went to the cooler to fetch one.

Kat apparently felt sorry for the distressed man and said, "It's been a
shock to all of us, Doctor."

Sergeant mumbled something under his breath and I returned with
the water. He gulped it down and said, "Lieutenant, may I see you
privately for a moment?"

"Sure." I glanced at Kat. I called out to Chechefsky, "He's feeling nauseous—I'll take him outside a minute."

Chechefsky nodded and I walked Sergeant out to the pool area, which was already crowded with sun worshippers in bikinis sipping Bloody Marys.

He stopped me in the shade of a palm and said, "I don't know what to do. It's . . . it's not what you all think!"

"What we all think?"

"Yes! You, Kat, the security people. The police!"

"About what? What isn't what we think?"

"The heart attack! He didn't have one! He couldn't have! His heart was as strong as an athlete's." He wrung his hands together. "He lied about it. We both did."

I thought I might know but asked, "Why?"

"You . . . you were the reason. He wanted to keep Kat away from you this weekend. He thought you were about to be indicted for rape and was hoping she'd be stunned by the news. He even had Victor Marino come to town. Penn wanted him here to comfort Kat when she got the bad news that you'd been arrested."

"Christ," I said, blown away by the latest revelation. "His twisted mind will never cease to amaze me."

"Perhaps . . . but there was nothing wrong with his heart."

I began to realize that what Sergeant was saying meant something more sinister might have happened in Pennington's suite's bathroom. I knew it had to be murder but I wanted to nail it down. "There's no chance he could have had a heart attack even though you thought he had a healthy ticker?"

"There's always a chance—something we missed—an anomaly—but it's one in a million and I don't think it could have happened."

"Neither do I."

"And I'm sure the autopsy will prove us right," responded Sergeant nervously.

Now I had two questions: Should I tell Kat about her father's lie? And what really happened in the bathroom? There was a million-to-one shot that he could have slipped and fallen into the tub, a *two*-million-to-one shot if you counted the reason he was in town and who his business partners were.

But I was still confused. Why the hell would they want Pennington dead when The Stardust deal was only hours away? I still thought Angelo's scenario made the most sense: Let Pennington sign the papers, put the syndicate in control of the casino, and whack him after the fact. Killing him before he became president just didn't add up.

I got Sergeant's promise to let me handle Kat and to remain silent for the moment about what we knew.

Rosen and Pangaro were waiting for us when we got back to Chechefsky's office. On the way we saw the white-uniformed "meat wagon" personnel arrive and roll a gurney toward the elevators. They drew the normal stares from guests, and I watched as several people stopped hotel employees to ask what was going on. At that point I'm sure none of them knew.

Sergeant quickly gulped down another three cups of water at the cooler before slumping into a chair. He looked exhausted.

I sat beside Kat and held her hand.

Rosen asked, "Miss Pennington, you said you returned from dinner with your father about ten o'clock."

"Yes," she replied, "or a bit thereafter."

"We think your father died between ten and eleven, so presumably you were the last person to see him alive."

"Yes, except for Dr. Sergeant. Daddy said he was going to call him as soon as I left."

Sergeant's head snapped up. "W-what? What's that?" he stammered.

"Did Mr. Pennington call you after dinner last night?"

"No . . . No, he didn't. But I saw him before he left with his daughter."

"Did you examine him at that time?" Rosen asked.

"W-what . . .?"

I knew Sergeant probably hadn't, but I also knew he wouldn't want to look incompetent. I listened to him lie, "Yes. He seemed stable."

"Thank you, Doctor." Turning back to Kat and me, Rosen said, "I'd like all of you to remain in town for the weekend. I'm sure you planned to do that anyway, so it won't be an inconvenience. There are a few things I'd like to clear up."

"I have to fly back to Jacksonville this afternoon," I said.

"Ah, Lieutenant Vesta . . . I'll be happy to call your commanding officer and request permission for you to remain until Monday."

I choked. As much as I would have liked to stay with Kat, and in spite of Marino's being in town, that was the last thing I wanted. I could just imagine Concannon's reaction when he was told I was being held in an inquiry into the death of my fiancée's father. After everything that'd happened in the past four months it wouldn't take a U.S. senator to have me shipped into oblivion—Concannon would gladly bury me himself.

I said, "Thank you, sir, but I flew here in a squadron jet, and that fighter has to be on the flight line in Jacksonville by midnight tonight. I gave my word on it. So unless I'm being held . . ."

Rosen held up a hand. "Of course not, Lieutenant. It was merely a request—as it was for everyone. I certainly know where you are if I need to reach you."

Kat spoke up. "What kind of things?"

Rosen said, "I beg your pardon?"

"The things you need to clear up? What are they?"

"Ah," he answered, easily waving off the question. "Merely routine, nothing you—"

"Detective," Kat said evenly, "I've read enough novels and seen enough films to know that 'merely routine' is anything but."

Rosen smiled and in a completely friendly way said, "Then you also know enough to surmise I can't say anything more during an ongoing investigation."

Kat let go of my hand. She was slowly coming out of her shock, and I could tell she was taken aback at the word *investigation*. It was probably the first time she was putting together what I'd told her earlier about a possible hit on her father and his death. "Investigation?" she asked. "Investigation of what?"

He tilted his head forward in a small bow and left, saying, "As I said, 'routine.' I'm sure you'll be hearing from me shortly as soon as a few small points are resolved."

Kat grabbed my wrist and nervously asked, "Do you have any idea what he's talking about?"

"Maybe . . . I'm not sure."

"What does that mean, Vinny?"

I glanced around the room at Chechefsky, his deputy, and Sergeant. I said, "Not here," and called out to the others, "We'll be in Miss Pennington's suite."

We remained silent until we were back in the suite and seated in the living room. Once again I decided on candor—immediate and direct.

"An hour ago Dr. Sergeant informed me that your father's heart was perfectly normal."

As she absorbed the information, I watched her face—at first confused, but then comprehending. "Normal," she said in a quiet, emotionless voice.

"Normal," I repeated. "He doesn't believe your father could have possibly had a heart attack."

"But they told me he'd already had two." The emotion started coming back into her voice.

"I know. It was a lie—both times."

"But why?" she cried out.

"Based upon what's happened in the past, it shouldn't be too hard for you to understand. He faked the attacks to keep you away from me. He didn't want you in Jacksonville this weekend."

"That's absurd!"

"It's no more absurd than anything else he's done to keep us apart. Sergeant was in on it with your father from the beginning. He'll corroborate what I'm telling you."

"How could keeping me away from you for one weekend possibly make him think it would be permanent? It doesn't make sense. He knew how I felt about you!"

"Yes, but he thought the news that I'd be indicted for rape might change your mind."

"How could he possibly know that would happen?"

"Because he hired a private detective, had him find Sissy and give her a five-thousand-dollar bribe if she'd accuse Doug and me of raping her."

Kat's eyes squeezed together in anguish and she shook her head. "My God. My God."

"And they came damn close to making it stick. I knew your father hated me, but I had no idea he'd keep trying to destroy me after the disaster in New York."

Kat wrapped her arms around her shoulders and rocked back and forth. "Daddy," she moaned, "oh, Daddy . . ."

I reached out to take her in my arms, but she held me off. She wiped her eyes as she recovered from the initial shock and seemed to focus. "But if he didn't have a heart attack and fall into the tub . . . what did happen?"

"Those are the 'small points' Rosen is trying to clear up. Although not for the same reason. He still doesn't know that it probably wasn't a heart attack that caused your father to fall into the tub. But if we don't tell him, an autopsy will. He's suspicious because of something else."

"What?"

"Your father's dental bridge was found behind the toilet. Apparently it got knocked out before he went into the tub."

"He thinks Daddy was murdered."

"It's possible."

"Accardo and Roselli," she said. "Just as you predicted."

"Maybe. But it doesn't add up. Why would they want him dead *before* he signed The Stardust deal? As Angelo said, after, yes, but why before?"

I heaved a sigh of frustration, then closed my eyes and pinched my nose in an attempt to figure it out. Seconds later, when I looked up, Kat had an intense, accusatory look in her eyes. "What?" I asked.

"If Accardo and Roselli didn't want Daddy dead, who did? Who else could it be, Vinny?" Her voice started to rise. "Who else!"

She was on the verge of becoming hysterical. I suppose I should have expected it. I tried to take her hand. "Kat, please—"

She pulled it away violently. "No! Who else, Vinny? Tell me!" She was starting to rant.

"Kat," I pleaded.

"Angelo!" she cried out. "Angelo knew everything Daddy did to you! You told him! He was there when Daddy tried to have you killed in Lena's. He knew who Daddy was connected to! He's like a second father to you! Angelo would have wanted him dead from the beginning! And now he's killed him!"

"Kat, for christsakes! Angelo's in New York!"

"You're not!" she screamed.

"What?" I screamed back, dumbfounded.

"You suddenly show up in Las Vegas! You get here and tell me there's a plot to kill my father. You say Accardo and Roselli are behind it! Why? To cover up his real killer!"

"You think *I* killed him?"

"Did you?"

"God*dammit*, Kat! Of course not! I didn't get here until after one in the morning!"

She went completely hysterical and started pounding on my chest. "So you say! How do I know that? You said you were calling from the lobby at one forty-five but you could have gotten here before ten!"

I grabbed her by both arms and shook her. "For God's sake, Kat— my flight plan was canceled the moment I landed at Nellis Air Force Base! The time stamped on it will be twelve forty-five this morning— not ten o'clock last night."

She broke down sobbing and babbled, "You could have bribed someone to change the records . . . You and your people are good at that."

"Kat, you don't believe that."

She collapsed into my arms and buried her face against my chest. "No . . . no . . . I don't." She was limp, completely exhausted, and silently crying.

I held her tight, caressed her hair. "It's okay, baby. It's okay . . ."

"Vinny . . . I feel drained . . . drained, numb, and so tired."

"We had a long night, and a horrific morning. The sedative is starting to do its job. Why don't you try to get a little sleep? I'll wake you and we'll have lunch before I have to leave."

She nodded and allowed me to take her into the bedroom. She lowered herself on the bed and I pulled a light blanket over her. She closed her eyes and I kissed her cheek. She was in terrible shape, and in a little over four hours I'd have to leave.

It wasn't much time to figure out what the hell had happened and why.

CHAPTER FORTY-ONE

FTER I PUT KAT to bed I called Chechefsky and said I wanted to talk to Rosen if the detective was still in the hotel. Chechefsky said he was still questioning some guests and he would give him the message. I hung up thinking, "Questioning some guests?" What guests? He'd already questioned Kat, Sergeant, and me. Whom else would he want to question?

And then it hit me. Accardo and Roselli.

Of course Rosen would want to question them. He'd told me earlier he knew they were in town and suspected them of being the shadows behind the syndicate. And of course Accardo and Roselli knew they'd be suspects for the exact same reason. They were well aware of the rumors about them—*that's* why they killed Pennington *before* the signing—exactly because it made absolutely no *sense* for them to do it then! They needed to keep Pennington from testifying in Los Angeles, but killing him after he signed the deal and became even more high-profile would automatically make them suspects.

Killing Pennington before he signed the deal logically eliminated them.

Those clever, conniving bastards.

Impatient to talk to Rosen, I turned on the TV. Predictably, the reporters were all over the story as soon as they'd heard the news. They'd flocked to the DI wanting information and details.

A reporter from KLAS had set up under the massive hotel sign advertising STEVE AND EYDIE and was reading from a notebook: "Preliminary indications are that Marion Pennington, the man who was about to assume the presidency of The Stardust today, died suddenly of a heart attack in his suite sometime last night . . . Moe Dalitz, who owns The Desert Inn and was a partner in The Stardust acquisition, issued a statement saying, 'Marion Pennington was a great man, and his death was a terrible tragedy.' He offered his condolences to the family and said the syndicate Mr. Pennington was leading would postpone The Stardust closing until further notice . . . Jake Factor, who is the current owner of The Stardust, also made a statement repeating the mantra that Marion Pennington was a great man and his death was a terrible tragedy. He was very disappointed that the sale did not go through as planned and hoped the syndicate would be able to regroup . . . Our sources tell us that . . ." The phone rang and I flipped off the TV. It was Rosen. I put a Do Not Disturb sign on the door and went down to Chechefsky's office.

When Rosen appeared, I asked if I could talk to him privately and I led him out to the same spot by the pool where Sergeant and I had talked earlier.

"Pennington didn't have a heart attack," I said. "His doctor said his heart was fine."

Rosen didn't react. He merely said, "Interesting."

"You don't think it's important?"

"It may be very important, Lieutenant. Thank you."

"That's it? It *may* be important? Don't you get it? Considering who his business partners are, it means there's a very good chance Pennington was taken out!"

"I already have my own suspicions in that area for other reasons."

"The dental bridge," I said.

"Ah, of course. You were there. Enough for an inquiry, but without other evidence as to how it got there, I'm afraid the investigation will dead-end."

"But the autopsy will show he didn't have a heart attack."

"Perhaps, but he could have slipped."

"That's bullshit."

"Of course it is, and even if we both know it, it's not proof."

"So Accardo and Roselli'll skate?"

He shrugged. "I questioned them."

"Let me guess—they're covered deeper than the Pacific Trench."

"At the moment, yes. They have alibis. But I must confess I fail to see a motive for them to kill Pennington before The Stardust sale if they are in fact the shadows behind the syndicate."

"I think that's precisely the reason they did it then—to eliminate themselves as suspects."

"You have a reason for this theory?"

"Yes," I said, knowing I could be taking a step off a very high cliff. "Pennington was about to be brought in for questioning by the Beverly Hills police about an attempted murder in New York two weeks ago."

This time Rosen did react. His eyes grew larger. "And how, pray tell, do you know that?"

"It's a very long story, Detective. But you can corroborate the information with the Beverly Hills police."

"I'll do that. But I suppose you realize I can now hold you as a material witness."

"A possible material witness. You said yourself that Accardo and

Roselli have alibis. If you can't develop a case against them, who are you going to charge—and when?"

"I have no idea where this is going, Lieutenant . . . but as I said earlier, I know where to find you if it comes to that." He put out his hand. "You're free to go."

"Thank you." I shook his hand, then hurried back up to Kat's suite.

It would be years before I found out how Pennington's dental bridge wound up behind the toilet, and by then Handsome Johnny Roselli would be dead.

At a drunken dinner in New York with Angelo Maserelli, Roselli proudly informed Angelo that he'd personally taken care of the Pennington problem himself. He said he'd carried off a perfect hit and made it look like an accident. He'd gone to Pennington's suite and lured him into the bathroom saying he'd dropped his glasses behind the toilet and couldn't see without them. When Pennington leaned over to look for them, Roselli got behind him, grabbed his ankles, and jerked his feet out from under him. His head hit the toilet on the way down and knocked him out. Roselli stripped him, stood him up facing the wall in back of the tub, then shoved him into it—the skin breaking on his forehead before he slid into the tub facedown and drowned.

What Roselli never knew was that when Pennington's head hit the toilet, it jarred the dental bridge out of his mouth. Roselli never saw it and it remained a mystery—eventually becoming a nonissue in an investigation that went nowhere.

A month after Roselli had dinner with Angelo, and just days before he was to testify before the Warren Commission in its investigation of John F. Kennedy's assassination, his body was found floating in a fifty-five-gallon oil drum in Miami's Dumfoundling Bay. He had been garroted—his legs had been sawed off and then squashed into the drum with the rest of his body.

*   *   *

I figured I'd need about the same six hours, including a fuel stop, to get back to Jacksonville by midnight as I took getting to Las Vegas. But I'd lose three hours with the time change, so I'd need a total of nine hours from wheels-up to touchdown. That meant takeoff from Nellis had to be no later than three P.M. Because of the conversations with Sergeant, Kat, and Rosen, I was already an hour behind.

The only break I'd get would be tailwinds on the way back.

Kat was awake and on the phone when I got back to the suite a little after two o'clock. The sleep had helped. Even the redness in her eyes was gone. She was still wearing her jeans, heels, and blouse, and she'd reapplied her makeup. I even caught a whiff of perfume. Strange, I thought, I loved that scent but had never asked her what it was.

I saw no reason to tell her about my conversation with Rosen and my new theory. There would be plenty of time for that later. In the meantime my suspicions had little chance of ever reaching a courtroom, and they wouldn't bring back her father.

I let my eyes roam over her and smiled appreciatively. "The sleep helped," I said.

"I feel better . . . Still a little numb, but a bit better."

I hugged her. "I've got to get moving."

"I called for a hotel limo to take us to Nellis."

"We can say good-bye here. You don't have to . . ."

"I want to see you off. Come on."

She took my hand and led me out. The limo was waiting out front and we slid into the backseat.

"When do you think you'll be leaving?" I asked.

"Tonight."

"You spoke to Rosen?"

"I will. But there's no reason for him to keep me, and less for me to stay. I'll make funeral arrangements from L.A. The charter company that brought me here is picking me up at six."

"Is Sergeant staying?"

"Yes. He's still shaken, but I think he wants to take advantage of an all-expense-paid weekend with his wife."

When we pulled up in front of Nellis's Base Operations, I was reminded of the very first time we'd said good-bye to each other, at Miramar's Flight Ops.

"Seem familiar?" I asked.

She nodded. "Miramar—a lifetime ago."

"Two lifetimes."

She smiled wistfully. "I loved them both."

"Agreed, but I'm looking forward to a brighter future—and seeing you there." I leaned over to kiss her good-bye, but she held me back.

"Why don't you go in and change. I've never seen you flying your jet. I want to watch you take off."

"Really?" I said, pleased. "Good." I pecked her on the cheek. "I'll be right back."

I took my duffels into Ops, filed a flight plan, and once again changed in the men's room. Ten minutes later I came out in my flight suit and saw Kat standing next to a decorative three-rail fence overlooking the flight line. The top rail was chest high, and Kat had her arms folded over it with her chin resting on them.

A twenty-knot wind had come up and she'd let out her ponytail. Her auburn hair whipped in the breeze, and I was again reminded of our first good-bye when she'd dashed away in Victor Marino's pink Cadillac. Strange, I thought—a lot of "firsts" were suddenly flooding back.

I said, "Impressive isn't it?"

The late-afternoon autumn sun was casting long shadows over rows of the silver, swept-wing jets—Air Force F-86s and my lone FJ-3 sitting close by.

I proudly pointed to it. "My Fury is almost identical to those Sabers. The difference is the tailhook. It lets me land that baby on the world's largest postage stamp."

She turned to me and smiled knowingly. "You love it, don't you?"

"Flying—the Navy . . . ? Sure. They're my life—my home."

"I know. But you once told me that if it came to a choice between me and the Navy, the Navy would be in trouble."

I chuckled at the memory. "Sea Island. I remember. Is the Navy in trouble?"

"Do you still feel the same way?"

"If you're asking if I still love you as much, and do I still want you to be Mrs. Vesta, the answer is yes."

"You'd really give up the Navy for me?"

"Are you asking me to?"

"No, I could never do that."

I took her hand and kissed it. "But you gave up your career for me."

"Yes, and you just said you'd do the same for me if I asked."

My antenna went up. "We're discussing this for a reason?"

She nodded. "Yes, I know I'm still drained and exhausted. And maybe my thinking is a bit jumbled, but . . ."

"But?" I asked, beginning to get a bad feeling.

She looked out at the jets and back to me. "I need some time to recover from what's happened, Vinny. Next weekend . . ." She was obviously struggling for words. "Next weekend I won't be coming to Jacksonville."

"Oh?" The bad feeling arrived full-blown.

"We need time to think . . . To regroup . . . My God, Vinny, an hour ago I was accusing you of murdering my father."

I ignored the observation. "How much time?"

"I'm not sure. Actually, I'm thinking of going back to work for a while."

"Acting?"

She nodded. "Zanuck's offer . . ."

I was stunned. "You're thinking of taking it?"

She nodded slowly. "It's an A production with an A director." She paused. "It's scheduled to shoot in Germany."

Christ, I thought, she was leaving the country. "Is all this because you still think we're responsible for what happened to your father?"

"I don't know, Vinny. All I know is that I feel so damn guilty. If I realized how mentally sick he was, maybe I could have done things differently. And I keep thinking that none of it would have happened if we'd never met."

"Of course not! But we did meet and we fell in love. That hasn't changed."

"No. But it caused you to think about giving up the career you love, and me to give up what I've worked for my entire adult life. What if one day we find out it was a mistake? What if it's true that when you ask someone to give up something they love, they may one day hate you for it?"

"And you think you may hate me for not giving you a chance to become a star?"

"No—I just want us to step back and take a breath to be sure. I married Dave Stanfield after a whirlwind romance in spite of my father's objections. And now after another whirlwind romance I'm about to do the same thing again in spite of his death!"

"Christ, Kat! You're comparing us to that?"

"Vinny—look at the facts! We've had a whirlwind romance—we're planning to marry over the holidays—and then you're going overseas! How can I not?"

I paused and searched for an answer. There wasn't one. She was right. The circumstances were eerily alike. I felt a sadness I'd never experienced. "All right, Kat. We'll try it your way."

She put her hand on my face. "I just need some time. We're not over—we're just coming up for air." She suddenly brightened and became more animated. "I'll be shooting in Germany when you put into all those ports on the Mediterranean! Villefranche, Naples,

Taormina! I can fly in. We can have gloriously romantic reunions and then . . . and then . . . who knows."

I took a deep breath and nodded. "You have a date." I kissed the hand she was holding against my face, then held her as tight as I'd ever held anyone.

"Take care, sailor. I love you."

"And I love you, Kat."

I turned and walked out to my plane. She watched me stow the duffels and climb up to the cockpit. I paused before climbing in and took a last look at her. I waved and she blew me a kiss.

Ten minutes later I hurtled down the runway and took off. I sucked up the gear and flaps and immediately began a steep 360-degree turn. I keyed my mike in the turn and said, "Nellis Tower, this is Navy 5333 requesting a low-level pass."

"Navy 5333, Nellis Tower. Permission granted. Be advised there are some tall jackrabbits at the end of the runway. Try not to clip their ears—they're friendlies."

I smiled and transmitted, "Roger that, Tower."

I completed the circling turn and lined up on the spot from which I'd just taken off. Fire-walling the engine, I screamed down the runway centerline ten feet off the concrete. Kat was still standing at the fence in front of Base Ops, and I saw her wave as I shot by. I rocked my wings in answer, then pulled up into a sixty-degree climb. At one thousand feet I said a final good-bye with three victory rolls and headed east.

By the time I leveled off at forty-one thousand feet, the sky had darkened and I began to see the lights of small towns winking on. My instrument panel glowed red in the cocoon of the cockpit, and the roar of the jet engine was muffled by my helmet. I could taste cool oxygen flowing through my mask and heard the hollow hiss of my breathing. Glancing up at the canopy of stars, and in spite of the emptiness in the pit of my stomach, a warm glow of contentment spread over me. This was where I belonged.

My mind drifted back to what she'd said: "I'll be shooting in Germany when you put into all those ports on the Mediterranean! Villefranche, Naples, Taormina! I can fly in. We'll have gloriously romantic reunions and then . . . and then . . . who knows."

I smiled and thought, the lady was right—who knows indeed.

ACKNOWLEDGMENTS

As always, my continued thanks to Fred Altman, my intrepid business manager, Ed Victor, my matchless agent, and Karen Rinaldi, the amazingly gifted publisher at Bloomsbury USA.

Once more I was blessed by the exceptional talents of my editor, Lara Webb Carrigan, who led me through the pitfalls of a second novel while blithely dealing with the trials of a second pregnancy. To my editor at Bloomsbury, Lindsay Sagnette, my heartfelt gratitude for the insight and understanding that added much to the final version.

Finally, thanks to the inimitable Internet whose Web sites brought forward those dates and places that time had fogged in my memory, and to Jerry Capeci, Gus Russo, Selwyn Raab, William Roemer, Jr., and all the authors before me who have so eloquently written of the Chicago Outfit and the New York Mob.

E. Duke Vincent, a native of New York and Bloom-field, New Jersey, graduated from Seton Hall University in February 1954. He was designated a Naval Aviator in 1955 and was selected to fly with the U.S. Navy Flight Demonstration Team, or the Blue Angels, for the 1960–61 seasons. He flew the F9F-8P Cougar from which the team was filmed for the NBC television series *The Blue Angels*, launching his interest in television. He resigned his commission in 1963 and went on to a successful career as a TV writer and producer. In 1977 he joined Aaron Spelling at Spelling Television, where he became executive producer and vice chairman. His credits include the series *Beverly Hills 90210*, *Melrose Place*, *Dynasty*, *Charmed*, and *7th Heaven*, as well as TV movies including the Emmy Award–winning *Day One* and *And the Band Played On*.

A NOTE ON THE TYPE

Linotype Garamond Three is based on seventeenth-century copies of Claude Garamond's types, cut by Jean Jannon. This version was designed for American Type Founders in 1917 by Morris Fuller Benton and Thomas Maitland Cleland, and adapted for mechanical composition by Linotype in 1936.